VIOLET RIBBONS

A STORY OF LOVE

Veronica Sirkis Dunning
with
Iberia Cornelia Dunning

This book is a work of fiction. Names, characters, places, and incidents are products of the authors' imagination or are used fictitiously. Any resemblance to actual events, or locales, or persons, living or dead, is entirely coincidental.

Night Latch
Enterprises LLC

For Athena

Acknowledgements

Our warmest appreciation is extended to Donald T. Dunning whose diligent and skillful work granted us the opportunity to write this novel. We also thank Karen, Britta, and Danika Welsch for their marvelous feedback around many campfires. Our recognition would not be complete if we did not express a warm thank you to Francine Phillips and Gail Bones who not only enhanced our technical expression but encouraged us to write. We thank Sara Howard and Rebecca Bryson for expressing enthusiasm toward the story. Our deepest gratitude is given to the editorial contributions of Mar van der Burg, Anna Lee Rothenberg, and Juliet Rothenberg. Of utmost importance are those who impacted our understanding of bull riding and horsemanship, Michael Smith, Katie Shipley, the Paniola, and my dear friend and champion of horses, Holly Bean.

CHAPTER ONE

THE ADVENTURE BEGINS

Dad's voice pierced the silence, "It's never too late to turn back, Annie." Dense fog covered the road and I stared at pines cloaked in violet blue mist, encased by ominous darkness from the forest. The only sound was the hum of the car's engine.

"I'm fine," I lied trying to calm anxiety that swelled in my body. The nausea in my knotted stomach snarled, but I didn't want Dad to cut off my escape. "We're almost there. I promise I won't let you down."

"*Promise* isn't a word to take lightly. Don't be afraid to call. I'll come get you in an instant."

I nodded. Dad and I turned off the highway onto a dirt road that ended in a dusty parking area among towering trees. He killed the engine of his Maserati. We sat listening to the breeze in the aspens and smelling the aroma of pines. Then he opened his door, walked around to open mine, and I slowly stepped out.

Dad saw my hesitation. He patiently held the door watching me take that step as I wondered why I decided to spend my summer alone in this unfamiliar place.

We headed down a path toward the main building. A carved wooden sign hung off the porch rafters by heavy chains. It read *Welcome to Trotter Blue Ranch.*

We walked up the steps. Dad pulled back the wooden screen door. The door was painted ranch red and creaked on its hinges. The paint was faded and rough. It matched the rustic atmosphere of the ranch.

Inside, we found another wooden sign. It read OFFICE →. Dad took my arm and steered me in that direction. He knocked on the closed door. A scruffy old man's voice said, "Come on in." Dad turned the iron door handle and let me pass through first. Behind a large, worn, antique desk was a wrinkled, leathery skinned man. Sprigs of curly gray hair stuck out from underneath his old, dirty, black cowboy hat. "Howdy. I'm Trotter Blue James III. What can I do fer yuh all?"

I took a step forward and held out my hand. He took my extended hand. His hand was callused and amazingly strong for such a slight, old frame. Shaking hands I said, "Hello, I'm Anna Lisa Lona Clay and this is my father Mansfield Vokome Clay." No doubt the cotillion classes Mother forced upon me helped with that smooth introduction.

"Ah, Miss Anna Lisa from Bel Air," Trotter Blue said as he examined my hand. "Yep, comin' here to transform a soft horn with manicured paws into a country gal. Welcome, welcome. Sit yoreselves down," he said pointing to two overstuffed chairs draped in Navajo blankets. The weavings didn't match but the colors complimented one another. They gave the dark little office a bright touch.

"Yesiree Miss Clay, yure my favorite type. There ain't nothin' better than watchin' the city critters become honest-to-good, hard workin', God fearin', country modified top waddies." He hesitated like he had nothing more to say.

Then, he continued just as slowly, "Yore ma, I believe her name is …uh… some type of cloth, feed sack…" His bright eyes looked around the corners of the office, like the answer was in the air. "Hold yore horses now," he said scratching his bristly chin. "I'll get my think tank workin'. Oh yeah, *Velvet*, there yuh have it, Mrs. Velvet Clay. Anyhoo, she called three times this mornin' tellin' me I'm to send yuh home anytime. Said she'd fly out personally to get yuh." Trotter Blue stared deep into my eyes. It was almost impossible to hold his gaze, "Yuh ain't no trouble maker are yuh, Missy?"

My face flushed and my mouth dropped open. He must have seen my shock because he looked away like he was ashamed to ask such a brazen question. Then, he cocked his head, bushy hair, and hat to address Dad, "Mr. Clay I ain't meanin' no disrespect but yore wife sounded like yore kidlet's a bundle of trouble."

Dad said, "Anna Lisa is a fine young lady. I give you my word you'll find her to be of no trouble."

Trotter Blue looked at Dad and said, "That's settled then. I'm glad yuh left Mrs. Velvet back on the homestead because she ain't gonna like our way of life. Sounds like a star gazer to me.

"Yore daughter here, however, well she's hungry to listen and learn. She's ready fer adventure. I can see the spirit in her eyes.

3

"I bought a hoss one time with the same spirited eyes. Don't mind my sayin' that filly grew into the loveliest, brave creature yuh ever saw, Mariah of the West. Broke my heart when time came to sell her." He dropped his head and looked at his folded crusty hands.

I interrupted his solemn state, "Why'd you sell her, sir?"

The old cowboy donned a little smile, "Aw, it ain't all bad, Curious One. Yuh see she went to a grand top hand. The finest chopper yuh ever seen - wild, wooly, and full of fleas. He's livin' the Cowboy Code like it was carved in his heart. This young man's got sand. He's honest, helpful, clean mouthed, hard workin', respectful of the women, and he treats me with courteousness. Yuh ain't never seen one like him. No doubt, he rides fer the brand. And around here that's what we need. Well anyhoo, yuh ain't come here to listen to an old man jabber. Yuh come to work. Miss Anna Lisa yuh start by waitin' tables."

I said with surprise, "But sir..." Trotter Blue raised his rough hand above his messy desk. I stopped talking.

"I know yore application says yuh want to work with the hosses. But to work with them yuh'll need a bale or two of experience and yore California hide will get crispy fried in this mountain air. Yure indoors fer most part, servin' breakfast and supper. Dinner's poolside. Yuh get a day off fer a fair week's work and one evenin'. I got a nice crew of sage hens waitin' tables."

I looked at Dad who was following the old man's conversation, even the part about *sage hens*. I was lost. I had no clue what Trotter Blue meant. He continued, "Yuh'll fit right in and become friends. The gals' bunk house is down past this buildin'. Get yore trunk and settle in. Yure startin' tonight. More than likely we're havin' the cook's delicious son-of-a-gun stew."

"Son-of-gun stew?" I asked quizzically.

"Yep. Ain't never had none? It's a delicious mixin' of all types of beef. Everythin' except the hair, hooves, and holler. If we're lucky the cook will whip up some sinkers. Be sure to set out the axle grease."

"I beg your pardon, sir," I interjected. "What accompanies this stew?"

Trotter Blue and Dad laughed. I elbowed Dad.

"Ooowee, she's green from the city pasture. My darlin' sinkers are what soft horns call biscuits. Axle grease is what yuh call butter. There ain't nothin' like fresh butter on a warm, plump biscuit."

"Ahhh, I see," I said sheepishly.

Trotter continued, "Oh yeah, be nice to the bean master. He can be mighty mean while he's tyin' on the feed bag fer a guest round-up. He's called Sam. Not Sammy. Not Samuel. Plain old Sam. He's the best cook yuh can find. Stay out of his kitchen and use yore nice polite *yes sir, no sir, thank yuh sir*. Now, get." He flung his arms up shooing us away.

Dad politely thanked Trotter Blue, wished him a nice day, and directed me out of the little office.

I turned abruptly toward Dad, "Why'd you laugh like you know what a darn sinker is?"

"Annie, that's a long story. Trotter Blue seems like an honest country man. He's long in the tooth. You'll be in good hands."

"What? Why'd you look at his teeth? He seems like a loony, old quack to me. I didn't understand half the stuff he said."

"Honey, he's the one they call the Big Auger. It might not have hurt you to have watched a few western movies before you dreamt up this plan. Just relax and enjoy it. You'll catch on to the dialect before you know," Dad smiled and put his arm reassuringly around me.

We walked to the car and unloaded my Louis Vuitton suitcase. Always a true gentleman, Dad carried my bag. I only had to carry my purse and stainless steel canteen.

Approaching a weathered structure on the far side of the main building, Dad said, "This can't be the women's bunk house. It's a tool shack or tack house. Let's walk down the path."

"Dad, this has to be the bunk house. There aren't other buildings on this side of the office."

Dad said, "Let's go back for directions."

"Why don't we take a look first?" I whispered.

Entering the door, Dad looked for a light switch. A single 100 watt bulb hung from the ceiling. Dad pulled on a dangling chain. Light illuminated a narrow entry. Several small rooms extended from the hall. We peered into each one. This was the bunk house all right.

I took the first room because it had a window and was the lightest. The room had two bunk beds squeezed into a nine by nine foot area. The upper bunk next to the window wasn't taken so I chose it.

Dad asked me, "Are you o.k. Anna Lisa?"

"Yes. Why?" I replied.

"I've seen housing like this but it's a far cry from the five star resorts you're used to. Look at it, Annie. The inside plywood is the outside plywood. There's no insulation or drywall. The wind will whip right through this shack. Look at that bunk. It's something from the Civil War."

"It's fine Dad. This is all part of my adventure."

He whispered, "If your mother saw where I'm letting you live this summer, she'd throw a royal fit."

I chuckled.

Seeing his *precious* daughter in those quarters flustered Dad and he didn't stop, "Really, Annie, migrant workers in the canyons build better shelters than this."

"It's fine. Look, there's a bathroom with a shower. And there are towels and soap bars with specks of dirt. I bet they're left over from guests. They'll exfoliate!" I said optimistically, "Don't worry, Dad."

He sighed. "I'm relieved you don't have to use an outhouse with a crescent moon whittled in the door. Annie, if used bars of soap, and old, crispy, gray towels don't frazzle you, you're more of a trooper than I thought, and different from your mother. You're more like me," he said with pride.

"I'll let you settle in and meet the other workers."

"Thanks, Dad. I love you."

"I love you too. I'll miss you on the drive back. Have fun, learn lots, and don't fall in love with a cowboy."

"Me? Fall in love with a cowboy? Really, Dad." I gave him a hug. Then he left me to organize the room as best I could. I silently hoped there weren't rats.

~ ~ ~

Thank goodness, the linens were clean. I pulled a moth eaten navy wool blanket over graying sheets. I stuffed a limp pillow into the old pillowcase and held it against my face. It scratched my cheeks so I pulled a silk robe from my suitcase and wrapped it around the pillow. As I rubbed the pillow on my face, enjoying the feel of the pink silk on my skin, three girls charged into the room.

"Hi, I'm Madison. What on Earth are you doing with your pillow?" asked the plain girl with brown hair and thick rimmed glasses.

Self-conscious about how odd it must've looked, I said nervously, "I don't know."

An effervescent, bleached-blond boldly asked, "Were you imagining it was your boyfriend?"

"Boyfriend?" I replied to the girl wearing bubble gum pink lipstick and an overly plunged tee-shirt.

Mockingly, she said, "By the way, I'm Shelly."

"I'm Grace," said a bright-eyed girl softly. Her heart-shaped face was framed by strawberry blond curls. She had a sweet smile and wore a pale green cotton sundress.

I introduced myself as they barraged me with questions. "Where are you from? Was that your dad? Where's your mother? Was that your dad's car?"

After the initial fracas they turned out to be welcoming and I felt comfortable. I was confident that the four of us would become friends, even Shelly.

They gave me pointers about how the kitchen and dining hall were run. I appreciated their description of the work. Although I frequently dined with my parents, I never focused on what the waiters did. However, I did know the proper placement of an eight piece silverware setting.

We went to the main hall and prepped for dinner service. Madison called over, "Anna Lisa, don't make an assemblage of the flatware please."

Grace softly whispered, "We only use one knife, one spoon, and one fork."

There was a lot to learn. I felt overwhelmed, but Madison told me I did fine for a rookie. We went back to the bunk house and chatted some more.

~ ~ ~

The next morning we served breakfast. I swore I'd never take a glass of orange juice for granted again. I got stuck squeezing two gallons by hand.

Lunch was served poolside so I lathered my face and arms with sun block. I thought SPF 50 would do it. The guests ate quickly and dashed off because their afternoons were booked with hiking, boating, and horseback riding.

After we bussed the guests' tables a group of workers walked up. "Who are they?" I asked.

Madison said, "They're the wranglers. They come up for lunch after the guests depart."

Shelly shriveled up her nose, "And it's a good thing because they stink like horses and sweat."

Madison continued, "The girl in the designer straw hat is Tiffany Cachette. They call her Bev. It's short for Beverly Hills. Tiffany and her father drove here in a gold Escalade pulling a copper horse trailer. Look at those fancy boots, *Justin's*. They match her posh parade saddle which is covered with silver medallions. Her horse is a gorgeous thoroughbred, 18 hands tall, with perfect markings - *Queen Victoria of the Mother Land*. I mean, really, who names a trail horse after royalty?"

I responded, "That's so Beverly Hills. People there think they're hot stuff. Who's next to her?"

"That's Hoyle Garfinkel. He'll saddle up a horse for you if you head down to the barn. He's somewhat helpful. That is, as helpful as cowboys can be toward us non-cowboy types." The waitresses laughed.

I didn't get the humor so I merely smiled and energetically asked, "Is there a set time for this? Do I need to talk with him in advance?"

Shelly said, "They don't talk to us. Just show up and he'll have to deal with you."

"What's the scoop on the cowboy across from Hoyle?" I asked.

"That's Dash Baler. He has more rodeo prizes than anyone in the West. He works at ranches during the off season, always with the horses."

Shelly piped in, "And, that's his girlfriend, Candy Roper. You should see her trophies. She has this beat-up, old suitcase full of buckles and ribbons. Candy can hardly close it anymore. She left it on the porch of the dining hall one day and I rummaged through it. Candy and Dash can really ride. They make a cute redneck couple too. Don't you think?"

"I guess so," I said to be polite.

Madison took the conversation back from Shelly and pointed to a lanky brunette, "Lacey Honeycutt, the skinny one, is crowned Miss Cheyenne. That's *The Daddy of Them All Rodeo*." She continued, "The guy missing his front teeth is Skeebo Muley. I think the horse that kicked out his teeth also knocked him crazy. Skeebo rants about a noisy spirit and creepy things. He's into Native American legends and hopes they'll explain the voices in his head."

Shelly interjected, "Good luck."

Before Madison had time to tell me more, I asked, "Who's the guy with his boots on the table?"

"The tall one?"

I nodded.

"That's Hudson. He doesn't talk to anyone except wranglers. And, he rarely talks to them. I don't think Shelly or Grace has heard a *Howdy* from him, and I certainly haven't. He talks to his horse though: clicks, kisses, clucks, yeeha's, and aah's."

Shelly and Grace joined Madison in a roaring laugh. I smiled while I silently wondered why the tall one didn't talk. Maybe he was arrogant. Or perhaps he was shy. He looked like he was resting under his hat which was propped over his face. I observed him some more and concluded since he was tall and buff, he was most likely arrogant.

I went to the table to take their order. Tiffany Cachette ordered a garden burger with Swiss cheese, romaine lettuce, tomatoes, and Dijon mustard on a croissant. She added a strawberry smoothie with soy. Dash Baler ordered ham sandwiches with chips and Pepsi for himself and Candy. Lacey Honeycutt wanted a salad with low fat Italian dressing and diet Pepsi. Hoyle Garfinkel asked for a Philly steak sandwich with extra onions, French fries and Mountain Dew. Skeebo ordered a fried bologna sandwich on white bread with pig skins and root beer.

The shy one didn't look up. "What would you like, sir?" I asked. Slowly pushing up his hat, he looked at me and quickly took his boots off the table. He kept his eyes on mine. His eyes were entrancing. They were blue, not light blue, and not gray. They were the color of the mountain sky. His high cheek bones could have been chiseled out of stone, not marble because his skin was too ruddy for that. He was tan. Shiny beads of sweat gathered on his brow below blond curls.

He kept his silence. I couldn't speak. I just stared at him, paralyzed. His gaze captured me. The other wranglers looked back and forth at us like a tennis match.

Dash elbowed Hudson, "Ain't yuh gonna answer the lady? We're starvin'."

Hudson stuttered, "Y-y-yeah." He cleared his throat and said, "A hamburger, f-f-fries, and sweet t-t-tea." His tone was deep and full. I was stunned. He stuttered. That's why he avoided conversation.

I made my hands write, gripping the pen hard. I was afraid I would drop it. But more importantly, I had to hide my shaking. I turned and made my feet walk toward the kitchen to place the order. All seven pairs of eyes followed me. Mostly, I felt those mountain blue ones on my back.

I overheard Dash say, "What's with yuh, Range Man? Are yuh feelin' like yure gonna barf?"

Hoyle added, "He'll hurl if the heat rattled him."

Candy said, "It was a scorcher but he ain't never had no problem with heat before. Hudson, what's goin' on with yuh?"

They looked at him. That deep voice said, "Nothin'." The others dropped their questioning.

I brought the food to the table with help from the waitresses. The wranglers ate like they hadn't eaten in weeks. Even Lacey devoured her low fat salad. Then they slowly got up from the table, stretched, and walked contentedly over the hill. I watched them go.

There was something different about them. They weren't like other workers or guests. They were serious with us. Among themselves they joked and laughed, sometimes with their mouths stuffed full of food.

Madison and Shelly were right, wranglers keep to themselves. Except for ordering, they didn't look at us. It was as though we were invisible.

There was one exception. Hudson glanced back over his shoulder as he crested the hill. His eyes found mine. Although it was a short glance, it was intense. And, there was something wonderful in it.

Madison interrupted my thoughts, "Anna Lisa, how about it?"

"How about what?" I replied.

"Hellooo, I was talking about going swimming and hanging out by the pool before the dinner rush."

"Be sure to put on lots of sunscreen. The elevation and clean air can result in a mean burn," Shelly giggled.

"Right, sunscreen," I tried to fake as much enthusiasm as I could. My mind was still on those captivating eyes. Why did a simple glance, seem so powerful?

~ ~ ~

The pool was welcoming and cool. A brilliant sun glared down on us as we floated and bobbed. Three children played Marco Polo tempting me to yell *Polo*.

After our swim, we spread our towels on the grass and Madison ordered a platter of nachos with spicy jalapeños for us to share. She explained this was her second year at the dude ranch. "I earned top honors from Fontaine Bleau High and wanted to relax this summer with Brandon Templeton but he dumped me for a ditzy airhead. That's why I came back here. He's envious because I was accepted to Stanford and he couldn't get into Princeton."

"His loss," I told Madison. "You must be bright to make it into Stanford."

Shelly squealed, "Want to hear about me?"

"Sure," I said.

"I'm from Maine and a junior at Rady High. I'm dating the football team's quarterback, Bobby Bishop. He's sooo cute. I'm in varsity cheer."

I said, "You're probably good at that."

"Oh am I," she said with a whirly arm movement. "Dad and Mom are worried because Bobby and I are seriously in love. They sent me here to get distance between us. I warned my dad, if Bobby meets a new girl, I'll never talk to him again," Shelly whined.

"Don't worry Shelly," I said. "Only a few girls can wear a bikini like yours. Bobby won't dump you."

Shelly beamed, "Bobby loves this swimsuit. He says it drives him mad." She was smiling, "Anna Lisa, do you think he won't find anyone this summer?" It's the kind of question a girl asks to reassure herself, even if nobody answers. Shelly pouted, "Without cell service I can't send bikini pics to him."

Madison rolled her eyes. Shelly didn't notice. While she sulked over the lack of coverage, I asked, "We don't have cell coverage anywhere on this ranch?" Without this I was disconnected from Mother's sharp tongue. I was truly escaping. It felt wonderful.

The afternoon was passing quickly so we headed to our bunk house, showered, and got ready for work. That night there would be a campfire after dinner. The waitresses and I hastily cleared tables and prepped for breakfast. The kitchen staff noisily clanked pots and pans rushing to get there too. I was hoping Hudson would be there.

We followed a trail through the dark trees and came to a grassy clearing. I looked up. It was new moon. Against the black sky, the stars blanketed the night like silver glitter tipped onto black construction paper. I had never seen so many stars. The neon lights of Los Angeles drown out stars. I guess that's why they need to carve them in cold cement on Hollywood Boulevard.

Suddenly, a star shot across the sky. I closed my eyes and made a wish. Wishes are different at seventeen than they are at five. I reminisced about my youth. I wished for a doll, a kitten, a pink canopy bed, and a Cinderella costume with glass slippers. There weren't falling stars, so I tossed coins into our koi pond. I made those wishes come true by either saying them in earshot of my parents, or telling my nanny, Lady Mary. I knew Lady Mary couldn't keep her plump little mouth shut. She would tell Mother and poof, my wishes were granted.

The wish I didn't tell anyone was one about Mother's acceptance of me. Needless to say, it never came true. Mother preferred the easy way of demonstrating her so-called love. She bought material wishes. I should've told her my silent wish. It might have softened her heart.

Anyway, it was time to enjoy the present and look toward my future. That wish made in the mountain's dark night would be in my heart for evermore. I wouldn't tell a soul. If it came true, it would be because it was meant to be and I wanted it badly.

When we approached the campfire, it was blazing. A ranch hand called Pip Lavoz strummed the guitar.

Her voice was beautiful. She had a western twang with powerful projection. Trotter Blue put her in charge of organizing nightly campfires and leading guests in folk songs because she was fabulous.

Madison picked a row in the back and we followed her. It was perfect. I was far enough from the light of the fire to peruse the crowd and look for wranglers.

My heart sank. They weren't there.

CHAPTER TWO

6:00 A.M.

On the way back to the bunk house, Grace caught up with me and asked, "Are you a Christian?"

She took me off guard. I'd never been asked that. I needed to consider what the question inferred. I pondered, "I suppose so. I know there's a God or a Great Spirit. Los Angeles has too many distractions like worshipping money, movie stars, music awards, and then there are the new age things like crystals, chakras, and astrology. I never thought about what I believe in. It certainly isn't money. Why do you ask?"

Grace replied, "There's this cute little white church down the highway and I want to go. It has a sunrise service, so we could be back in time for work. You might find something there for you, Anna Lisa."

"Sure. We can go. It's about time I figured out what I believe. Thanks. What time should we leave?" I asked.

"Let's leave at 6:00 a.m."

Six a.m. came early. I could have easily rolled over and gone back to sleep, but I committed to go with Grace. So I slid into my skirt, blouse, and sneakers. That was my Sunday's best. I forgot to bring a pair of dress shoes. Looking in the mirror I thought, if God's there, and He's all He's touted to be, He won't care about my sneakers.

Grace and I walked to her car slowly. She remembered to bring the right shoes. It was slow going in heels on the uneven dirt path.

We drove out the driveway and it felt nice to be off the ranch. It was a break from the routine of kitchen and food service. Besides, it was beautiful. The sun hadn't yet risen over the mountains, but it told of its coming by glowing on the mountain crests crowning them with gold tiaras. Aspen leaves fluttered in the headlights and it was quiet on the road. Tall pines lined one bank of the two lane highway. On the other side there was a clearing for the church.

The church was small with an angular steeple. At the top was a sphere that looked like planet Earth. Perched on Earth was a tiny brass cross. I thought, Christians mount crosses everywhere. They put them on buildings and around their necks. This would be like the French putting guillotines on the Louvre or on a gold chain. Christians should have stuck with fish. I could wear a twenty-four karat fish.

The base of the steeple curved slightly. It reminded me of Asian temples which slant to dump demons off the roof. I asked Grace, "Do Christians believe demons fall from the sky?"

Wrinkling her forehead she answered, "Of course not."

Double doors with polished hinges were on the east side of the chapel. Outside, was a green lawn with manicured shrubs and a bordered stone path. Everything glowed in the coral hue of the predawn light, especially planet Earth and the cross.

We parked and walked into the church. The only light inside was cast by candles. Grace and I sat on a hard wooden pew in the second row.

Before the sermon began, the chapel doors opened and let in a bright ray of light. The silhouettes of seven people stood in the doorway. Four of them took off their hats. The guys let the girls go through first. As they stepped into the candle light, I stared in disbelief. They were wranglers.

They passed in front of us. As they did, Hudson looked over. His eyes met mine. If I wasn't imagining, and if it was possible, his eyes smiled.

The wranglers sat on the opposite side of the church in the first row. During the service they bowed their heads in prayer, sang along with the hymns, and swayed to the music. They quickly disappeared after the service.

Grace and I drove back and talked about the sermon and God. The morning's message was thought-provoking. It made me think about where I came from, where I was, and where I was going. I realized that I was like a boat without a rudder. I lacked faith and values to direct me. My life was one of self-indulgence, money, and the accumulation of material things. Dad was right, I was going to grow this summer. Thank God, I took the first step of leaving Bel Air. Here, I was free to open my eyes and heart to people with different values. I was free to listen to God's plan for my life without Mother rebuking my decisions.

Worshiping together was up-lifting. I hoped Grace and I could make it a regular part of our summer. I wanted to ask her if she noticed Hudson's glance, but realized a question like that would be off the wall. Grace was right. I found something there for me. I also found someone.

~ ~ ~

After breakfast, Trotter Blue called me aside. He said, "I've been watchin' yuh."

I froze. My thoughts darted to our activities that morning and the day before. Did he think Grace and I were sneaking off the ranch? Were we too noisy at the pool? Maybe my eye contact with Hudson hadn't gone unnoticed?

He continued, "I've been doin' this business a long while and I know if a bunch of gals ain't got no wagon boss, they'll be totin' stars on their aprons tryin' to do everythin' their own way. Before yuh know, they're tryin' to rule the roost. Truth be said, I like that in the ladies but this here's my business. It's my bread and butter. If I ain't got a top hand, things will end up lookin' like a hog ranch."

I had no idea what he said. I exhaled and softly said, "I beg your pardon, sir."

"Miss Anna Lisa, I want yuh to lead the bunch."

"The bunch? Waitresses, sir? Me, lead them?"

"Yesiree."

"Excuse me sir, but Madison has more experience than I do."

"Yep, she's a sharp shooter," he said.

"Why me, sir?" I asked quizzically.

"I said to yore pa the first day we met. I saw spirit in yore eyes. That makes yuh a top waddie. Go on now. Don't question what I decide. Now get. Lead them fillies fer me."

"Yes, sir and thank you, sir."

At lunch, I divvied up the poolside tables. "Shelly, take those four-tops and that two-top on this side of the pool. Madison, take the six-top and the rest of the two-tops. I'll give Grace those four-tops closest to the counter. I'll take that eight-top and the rest."

Wow, I thought. I was starting to sound like a lead waitress. It felt good that Trotter Blue trusted me to be in charge of the team. For the first time, I missed modern technology. I would have given anything to text Dad to let him know his faith in me was well placed.

The lunch crowd arrived and we were busy. The added responsibility made things seem busier. I wanted service to run smoothly and the guests to be satisfied.

After the crowd ate and left, I quickly bussed the eight-top table. The wranglers would be up for lunch. Since there were seven wranglers, only the eight-top, accommodated them.

Much to my surprise, the wranglers went to Madison's six-top. One wrangler didn't show - Hudson. I heard Hoyle tell Madison that in addition to his Rueben and Pepsi he needed a Roast Beef sandwich to go.

Monday, I assigned the tables the same way for lunch. Again, only six wranglers showed. Hudson wasn't there. It remained that way for the entire week.

Finally, I switched things so that I took the six-top. I had to find out why Hudson wasn't showing up. I figured the best person to start a conversation with was Tiffany. She was from Beverly Hills. I was from Bel Air. I thought it would be easy.

Tiffany ordered a vegetarian sandwich with avocado on whole wheat. I said, "You like that sandwich too? It's my favorite. It must be our California roots."

She sneered and gave me the evil eye. It didn't go well. There was no way she would talk with me. Madison heard me address Tiffany. She met me at the counter and demanded, "What was that about?"

"I was trying to establish rapport to understand these people," I explained.

"Are you crazy, Anna Lisa? Tiffany's least approachable. She only made her way into the group because she's an excellent horse woman. She has to constantly prove herself. With the slightest slip-up they'll isolate her. Cowboys are like wolves. They keep to their own pack. Did you notice? Not one came to the campfire? They don't mingle with outsiders. Cowboys won't even date girls outside their circle." Madison continued, "It's not explicitly written in the Cowboy Code but it's universal law for them."

All I could say was, "Oh."

Madison rambled on, "Anna Lisa, of all people I thought you would have read up on cowboys or Google them before you came here. I can see Shelly not researching this, but you? I assumed you checked out the Western History Association or the National Cowboy Hall of Fame."

"I didn't have a chance," I lied.

"Didn't you even check out the *Quarterly Corral Bulletin* or at least read Job French's The Westerner's Buckskin Guide? I'm taken aback by…"

"O.k., I get it, Madison," I replied defensively. She was right and I knew it. I was wrapped up in escaping from my mother's world. I didn't bother to look into the world I was headed to. I thought everyone was like me. There I was, stuck without modern technology to find out about cowboys and their Cowboy Code, or whatever Madison called it.

~ ~ ~

After lunch, I didn't want to hang out at the pool. I went to the main dining hall to prep for dinner. There were salt and pepper shakers to fill, ketchup bottles to marry, and tables to set.

The ranch chef, Sam, was in the kitchen. It was a great place to visit because he enjoyed passing out samples of his latest culinary concoctions. He noticed me and I figured I better address him, "Hi Sam. What smells so good?"

He smiled and puffed up a bit, "Chili con Carne, the good old cowboy kind based on beef and beans."

"I've had chili before but this one's aromatic."

"Ahhh," said Sam. "That's my secret ingredient."

"What is it?" I inquired.

Grabbing a jar with golden brown powder, he opened the lid and held it under my nose, "Smell."

I took a whiff, "Yum. It smells appetizing."

"You like it, Anna Lisa?" In an educational tone he continued, "It's Cumin. The ground seeds of a small plant related to the carrot family. Cumin's common in curry dishes, soups, and pickles."

I commented, "It smells earthy almost like sweat. It's musky and lovely."

Sam laughed, "You have spirited and imaginative taste buds Miss Anna Lisa. Sweat? There's corn bread in the oven. With your imagination it probably smells like ambrosia of the Gods."

I smiled, "I should set out butter and honey."

"Good thinking," Sam said in a complimenting tone.

I changed the subject, "Sam, how long have you worked with cowboys?"

"I've been a chef for Trotter Blue for ten summers. This is my eleventh one. During the off season, I teach cooking in New York. For me, the chance to challenge myself with palette pleasing recipes for large groups is a hobby. Imagine that. I get paid too."

"I see," I said disappointed.

Sam said, "If I heard your original question correctly, you wanted to pick my brain about cowboys. What's the matter Anna Lisa? Is their stick-to-themselves culture bothering you?"

"A bit," I admitted. "Today, Tiffany just about drilled right through me. I was only trying to chat with her."

"Anna Lisa, don't take it personally. Cowboys have their own way of socializing and I imagine Tiffany's adamant about maintaining her good standing with them." Noticing my distress, Sam continued, "Do you remember the old musical *Oklahoma*?"

"Yes," I replied. "The cowboys and farmers were rivaling factions."

Sam said, "They were but they've grown closer over the years. Today the rivalry is between cowboys and city-slickers. For a cowboy to fall for a city girl is as rare as finding the queen bee in a hive. If a cowboy intends to court a city girl, it's just about as dangerous too."

"Speaking of bees. . ." I feigned a smile, ". . .better get honey on the tables." Sam gave me enough insight for one day.

I noticed Trotter Blue had his office door open. He heard us talking. He stepped into the doorway and addressed me, "Lady Anna Lisa, how're the first days as my capataz of the waitresses?"

"It's fine sir," I surprised myself by following his question. I got it. The trick was to listen to the context. It depends on the situation like it does in Japanese.

"Yuh ain't doin' all the work fer them gals. Yure leadin'. Tonight's yore night off and Monday's yore day. Yuh ain't gonna show yore pretty little face around here on free time. Yuh hear?"

I happily spun around and bumped against Hudson. He grabbed my arms gently stopping me from hurtling into him. Holding me, he looked down with those beautiful eyes. The outer corners of his eyes had little creases dusted with dirt. His lips were full and he smiled.

Hudson must've been in the dining hall and overheard me asking Sam about cowboys. Ugh. My cheeks felt flushed. I know it showed. I had Mother to thank for giving me her pale, fine skin. Timidly, I apologized, "I'm sorry. I didn't know you were behind me." At that moment, I felt like crawling under a rock.

Trotter Blue broke the tension by saying, "Howdy Hudson. Glad yuh got word we need to flap our jaws." Hudson let go of me, stepped aside, and tipped his hat. His eyes had a twinkle in them.

They went into the office. The door was left ajar and I couldn't resist listening so I decided to stock the station closest to the office.

Trotter Blue said, "Hudson, I need yuh to gather yore cowboys and round up two hosses come Monday. Yuh'll find them at that churn twister, Woody Carson's place, one palomino, and one bay. According to Woody, they'll make mighty fine trail hosses. Remember, that old man's famous fer bein' full of windies. So watch out." Trotter Blue continued, "He'll charge a good penny. Yuh need to get prices down by a couple hundred green ones, yuh hear?"

"Yes sir," Hudson answered in a deep voice. I was shocked he didn't stutter.

Trotter Blue continued, "Yuh'll find Woody off the interstate near that lamb licker's field. He'll be in the big house behind the worm-fence."

Hudson replied, "Yes sir. I know where that is. Yuh can see the sheep from the interstate. Woody's dirt drive is past that field." Again, his words were clear and confident.

Trotter Blue continued, "Yuh got it right. By the way how's Little Missy treatin' yuh?"

Hudson replied, "She's doin' fine. Mighty fine. A real pleasure. She was gettin' a bit cantankerous there fer awhile. Actin' like she's got a baby on board."

Trotter Blue said, "Yuh ain't sayin' she's wearin' the bustle wrong?"

I gulped quietly and shuddered horrified. Hudson was married and expecting to become a father. Yikes. I felt faint and it wasn't altitude sickness. It was like falling out of a tree knocking the air from my lungs. I felt so stupid and confused. I didn't understand why he stuttered nervously with me but not with Trotter Blue. And he glanced at me and held my eyes. At church he did the same thing. Plus he smiled when I rammed into him.

Their conversation continued and I listened. "Some days I think, I've given it all, but I get back on her." My mouth fell open and I stifled a gasp forcing myself to listen quietly.

Trotter Blue asked, "Have yuh tried her with steel?"

"Hudson said, "Yep, sir, I have. I've gotten after her good. It ain't helpin' none."

Trotter Blue said reassuringly, "Just keep doin' what yure doin'. They all come around sooner or later."

Hudson said, "She'll be fightin' me as feisty as all get out. The good Lord knows she's strong willed." Trotter Blue chuckled like he understood females.

"She sure is pretty all fired up. Yuh know Trotter, it's a nice feelin' to have somethin' hot and spicy between yore legs."

Stunned, I set the honey jar down harder than intended. They heard the bang and looked at me through the crack in the door. I ran out of the dining hall straight to my bunk house.

CHAPTER THREE

THE WILD ONE

Thank goodness I didn't have to work that evening. It would've been impossible to focus. A long hot shower and time to think was what I needed. I grabbed my flip-flops and a towel. I knew aromatherapy would help so I shoved lavender body wash, rosemary/mint shampoo, sweet pea body lotion, and white tea spritzer into my shower caddy.

On the way to the shower, I passed Madison. She insisted I meet the new waitress, Caprice. Madison led me down the hall to Shelly's room. Grace and Shelly were sitting on a top bunk talking with the new waitress. I poked my head in. They grinned.

Madison said, "There she is, Anna Lisa." Caprice was seated on the top bunk across from Grace and Shelly. Madison introduced me to the red headed girl with big round eyes. I thought to myself, they were like frogs' eyes and with that red hair she could be as toxic as the Ecuadorian frog.

"Welcome, Caprice," was all I could muster.

Caprice summersaulted off the top bunk and landed sure footed on the wooden floor. She came over and shook my hand feverishly.

Shelly said, "Caprice is a wild one."

I replied, "Obviously."

Shelly kept talking, "You should see her jeep. She drives with the top down and doors off. The jeep is covered with stickers and netting. Collapsed lawn chairs hang from the roll bar."

I followed Shelly's babble as best as I could. Picturing the jeep was difficult. Shelly continued, "I know we're going to like Caprice and be good friends. She'll add lots of fun to this boring team. She's constantly telling jokes." Pointing her finger at me she added, "And the pranks! She dreams up good ones."

Why was Shelly pointing at me? Grace interrupted my thoughts, "You should see Caprice's films. They're on YouTube. She brought her laptop loaded with MovieSoftware so she can edit the films she'll shoot here at the ranch."

I feigned a smile, "Niiice." I was not in the mood to socialize, especially with a wild new person.

Shelly asked why I wasn't at the pool that afternoon and Grace answered before I could. "Didn't you notice? Madison was mean to Anna Lisa? She insulted her intelligence."

Madison said, "It wasn't intended as an insult. What I said was valid."

Then Shelly broke in, "Madison you have to feel with your heart and be sweet to people. You owe Anna Lisa an apology."

"Hey," I piped up. I didn't want them squabbling over my feelings. "I don't need an apology and there's no offense taken. But thanks."

Their bickering gave me time to think. I lied, "I wasn't at the pool today because it's my night off and I wanted to help the evening run smoothly." Changing to my team leader tone, I addressed Madison, "Please show Caprice where things are tonight. Assign the tables and be sure to introduce her to Sam and the others in the kitchen. It's getting close to serving time. Sam made Chili Con Carne with cornbread. It smells *delicioso*. I'm going to bed early. Good luck Caprice on your first night."

Caprice shouted at the top of her lungs and jumped punching her fist in the air, "Let's get it done girls!" Shelly was right. Caprice was a wild one.

~ ~ ~

The hot shower was wonderful. I soaped up with body wash and foamed the shampoo into my hair. I rinsed my hair and worked in the conditioner. The steam was delicious. Lavender and rosemary/mint filled the shower stall. The only thing better would have been a bubble bath.

Unfortunately, the bunk house tub was removed. Capped pipes stuck out of the wooden walls. Steel wool was stuffed in the rickety wooden floor where the drain hole had been. According to Madison, the previous summer was hot so the horses needed an extra water trough. It was handy having Madison in the group. Given her history at the ranch, she was full of information.

I dried off and made a turban out of my towel to wrap my hair. I rubbed sweet pea lotion over my body and topped myself off with white tea spritzer.

It was early in the evening, but I wanted to be alone so I pulled on warm pajamas, put in my ear buds, set the phone to Mozart's piano concertos, and crawled onto my bunk. I grabbed a book, <u>Pride and Prejudice</u>, -the ultimate book of romance. Not even that could keep my mind steady. I got off the bunk and made a cup of tea. I thought to myself, Dozy Chamomile would make a relaxing end to a crazy day.

I decided to paint my fingernails. I was looking for something subdued, yet challenging. A French Manicure would take my mind off Hudson. Lucille Beautant, the manicurist at Mother's spa, told me that if I kept my pinky pointed, making the white crescent would be easy. I took a sip of tea and attempted the pointed pinky technique. Sure enough, a perfect white crescent curved around the tip of my finger. By the time my fingers and toes were completed, I had dismissed all possibilities of getting to know Hudson. I fell asleep peacefully for the first time in a week.

CHAPTER FOUR

WILL YUH RIDE WITH ME?

The next morning, I dressed and took a short hike. The sun was rising over the great mountain to the east. Sunlight casted a warm coral hue as it crested the peak. Trees, flowers, grass, and my manicured finger nails glowed. Perched on a boulder, I watched the sun rise higher until the coral glow grew into stark brilliance.

Mother Nature's beauty stretched far and wide. The sunrise was my awakening from the fantasy of a cowboy romance. Peace put my feet back on solid ground and my head on straight. I walked to the ranch to prep for breakfast. I was relaxed and calm. The anticipation of romance had disappeared and I accepted it.

Later that day, I randomly assigned lunch tables. With Caprice on the team, our workload lightened. She was great with the guests. She had them smiling and laughing. Her playfulness raised our spirits. After the guests departed, we bussed our tables.

The clan of wranglers strode up to the eight-top in my section. I walked over with the breeze on my back. Hoyle looked up and said, "Man, yuh smell good!" My aromatherapy treatment was a bit overdone. Hudson gave Hoyle a boot kick in the shin under the table.

Hoyle yelled, "Ugh. I was only givin' the little lady a well-deserved compliment."

Hudson said in his commanding tone, "Mind yore own business."

By then I knew about the keep-to-your-own-culture, so I shrugged it off. I took orders with neutrality. I was proud of myself. After putting in the order, I stood with the other waitresses and turned my back to the wranglers. Their food was up. I served them and returned to the waitresses. We chatted and laughed at Caprice's jokes.

I heard the wranglers' chairs push back so I turned around and walked over to clear the table. Hudson remained seated. Dash asked, "Hey Boss Man ain't yuh comin'?"

"Naw. I gotta talk with Trotter Blue about somethin'. I'll catch up with yuh later."

I cleared the table even though Hudson remained in his chair. "Would you like something else?" I asked.

His mouth turned into a mischievous smile. What a flirt. Then, Hudson blushed in embarrassment that was visible through the grime on his skin. He looked in the direction of his buddies watching them clear the hill. Then he stood up and held out his hand, "I'm Hudson."

I shook his hand and replied, "Hello, I'm Anna Lisa Clay."

His hand was strong, callused, and big. He held mine just a nanosecond too long. "Won't yuh please take a seat?" he asked tilting his dusty russet hat.

Hesitating, I took the chair across from him. I was about to say *no kicking under the table*, but remembered Madison's lecture, so I stayed quiet.

"Where yuh from Annie?"

I gasped. Only, my dad called me by that cherished nickname. I fumed silently over the arrogance of this two timing, pregnant wife cheating cowboy, and the audacity of him calling me *Annie*.

"Bel Air . . . it's in Los Angeles," my tone implied *you ignorant redneck*.

He ignored my saucy haughtiness and asked, "Well L.A. how about yuh come ridin' with me tomorrow?"

Shocked, I replied, "I heard Trotter Blue wants the wranglers to pick up horses in the valley."

"Yeah, but I ain't goin'. I told the others I'd stay back and feed the ponies. They'll head down come sunrise. Anyhoo, Bev'll be there. That gal can negotiate like her born and bred city-slicker self. So how about ridin' with me?" I stalled, grasping for words while he sniffed the air. "Come to notice, Annie, yuh do smell mighty fine," he said with a twinkle in his eyes. If I didn't know more about his wife cheating ways, I'd find him charming.

I decided to come right out with it, "It's nice to invite me, but shouldn't you spend your free time with your wife, especially if she's not feeling well with the pregnancy?" Hudson furrowed his brow appearing confused. I said, "Don't look like you don't understand me. I heard it all. Trotter Blue asked about your *Little Missy*."

Hudson sat still, thinking. Then he chuckled. He stared at me and laughed loudly. Pounding his hand on the table he hollered, "Yure crazy L.A!"

"That may be so, but I won't interfere in a marriage. I've seen too much of it in Los Angeles. You don't know me, but I have more principles and class than that."

He bent over in hysterical laughter. My face flushed with exasperation. I was irritated and started to leave my chair.

Hudson said, "Whoa, Annie." He grasped my wrists and held me. I could have wrenched myself free but didn't because his hands were controlled and gentle. "If yuh please, plant yoreself in the chair. I'll explain." I sat down and he continued, "Trotter Blue and me were talkin' about Trixie."

"Trixie, your pregnant wife," I rudely butted in.

He stalled smiling, "Yuh really think I'd shove steel into a lady?" He couldn't stifle his laughter and roared as he replayed the script in his head.

"You're so crass. I know men can be vulgar, but, oh my God, you were talking to your boss about your wife as *something hot and spicy.*"

Hudson winced at the use of *oh my God.* "Annie, I was talkin' about Trixie. Trixie, yuh hear," he said brusquely.

"Who is Trixie? And steel? And don't forget about *Mrs. Hot and Spicy,*" I said in a huff, crossing my arms.

Smiling, he gained his composure and softly said, "You're beautiful mad."

I started to leave my chair and he said, "O.K, I'll tell yuh. Trixie's a three year old filly hoss. I'm breakin' her. At times, it helps to use spurs. That's what we call steel. Hot and spicy means she has spirit like yuh do."

I had to smile. I was way off. "Oh," I said humbly. "I'm sorry. I shouldn't have eavesdropped."

"Yuh got that right. But given yure sweet smellin', got principles, and as pretty as an angry kitten, I'll accept yore apology," he said. "Got a wild imagination, don't yuh, Annie? Must come from Hollywood…that's in L.A., yuh know," he said with a spark. Then he added, "Are yuh gonna ride with me or not?"

I smiled at him and took in those mesmerizing eyes, "I'd be delighted. What time would you like me?"

"I'd like to have yuh anytime," he said snickering as he toyed with my words. Then he added respectfully, "Annie come after yuh wake-up and eat. I'll be waitin'."

We stood up. "Until tomorrow then," I said.

He simply said, "Yeah." and walked toward the main hall to talk with Trotter Blue.

~ ~ ~

Turning around, I saw the waitresses with their mouths gaping. I forgot they were watching. I assumed Madison would give me another lecture. It didn't matter. I was glowing.

Amazingly my perspective went from disaster to tantalizing magnificence . . . *like Hollywood*. I chuckled to myself and walked toward the dining hall with the four of them marching after me. Madison demanded first, "Anna Lisa, explain what happened back there right now."

Grace added, "Hudson doesn't talk to anyone and …"

Shelly finished her sentence, "He was calling you friendly nicknames."

Caprice asked, "Why was he laughing? I'm the one with the jokes."

Madison sparred with me again, "Anna Lisa, you don't learn. The dumbest thing you can do is get a wrangler mad at you. Don't forget your boss is an old cowboy. He'll naturally side with Hudson."

"Madison," Shelly said in her coquettish way, "Hudson wasn't mad at Anna Lisa. They had chemistry."

Madison bellowed, "Shelly, what could you possibly know about chemistry? You probably didn't even pass the class."

Shelly screeched back, "I did so. I got an D+."

Rolling her eyes at Shelly, Madison barked at me some more. They hammered me with comments and questions. As long as they did there was no need, or possibility, to explain.

Facing Madison, I said forcefully, "Isn't this your night off? Go enjoy it."

She breathed in, huffed, shook her head, and stomped away.

Sam heard the commotion and called me into the kitchen. His bright eyes twinkled, "What'd I hear? Did you walk into the bee hive?"

"Oh Sam. Why does it have to be difficult?"

"That's life my dear."

I went through the motions of serving guests. The others didn't mention more about the luncheon incident. Without their leader, Madison, they were pleasant.

The three were going to the campfire after work. Although I wanted to retire and dream about riding with Hudson, I joined them.

Facing Madison alone in the bunk house was not appealing. It would be easier to avoid her if we entered as a group.

That night I dreamt of him. It was a mixture of pleasure and dread. There was a field and violet blue wind whipped through the air. A handsome, tall, male figure walked toward me. I could tell it was a wrangler because of the silhouette: wide shoulders, small waist, a cowboy hat, and boots. The wind pushed him back. He pressed against it to get close to me. Regardless of his struggle, he couldn't. I called to him and the wind drowned my words.

Waking in a panic, I looked at the other girls. They were sleeping peacefully. Thankfully, I didn't call his name or scream in my sleep.

CHAPTER FIVE

THE RIDE

Monday morning I slithered into blue jeans and pulled on a fitted amethyst tee shirt. Quickly, I braided my hair, brushed my teeth, and slipped on my Keds sneakers. I ran to the dining hall and hurriedly ate toast with boysenberry jam, gulped my tea, and stuffed two carrots into my back pocket. I dashed out the screen door letting it slam behind me. I ran toward the corrals. Thank goodness, the waitresses hadn't arrived yet. I had no desire to answer questions.

I approached the meadow, noticing a hill where the wranglers' bunk house stood. There was a large window and a porch with a bench swing. Off the porch, stones formed a fire pit. The bunk house overlooked an expansive meadow. Across the meadow horses milled about, munching on green Bermuda grass. I noticed two horses tethered to a nearby hitching post.

My heart raced when I saw Hudson. He was sitting on the fence wittling a piece of wood. I slowed my pace to look like I wasn't anxious to see him. Taking a deep breath, I walked calmly admiring the sight of him.

As I passed the bunk house, a strong wind kicked up. I found it odd because it had been still on the other side of the hill. The wind lifted the braid off my back. It was the same violet blue wind of my dream. Fear welled inside me and I fought an urge to run. I forced myself to keep a steady gait.

Once I reached Hudson, he smiled and said, "Good mornin',
Annie."

"Hello, Hudson." It was the first time I said his name. It had
a nice sensation as it rolled off my lips. He put his whittling down,
folded his knife and put it in the front pocket of his jeans. He looked
clean. I'd always seen him after a half day's work, sweaty and grimy
with smudges on his chest. Today, he was spotless and smelled
freshly showered.

He said, "Yuh ready, Annie?"

"Yes. I am."

Hudson said, "First we need to curry comb and brush them.
Yure ridin' this one." He gestured toward a beautiful white and
brown paint. Her jet black tail flowed to the ground and her white
mane was strikingly long. On her forehead was a shaggy bob that
reached her eyes. Her pretty brown face portrayed delicate features
and her eyes were spirited and alert. Hudson tossed something to me
and said, "Here, catch."

I grabbed the comb. He smiled and said, "Yuh can catch."

I wrapped my knuckles around the band and started combing
in the direction of her coat. He came over and said, "L.A. I see yuh
need a lesson. Put yore hand flat on the comb, under the band." I did
as he said. He put his warm hand on top of mine directing the comb
in a circular motion, lifting the hair. The feel of his touch stirred my
emotions. Removing his hand, he said, "Do it like that on her beefy
parts." He walked back to his horse and stroked mine as he passed,
"Don't worry Mariah she'll get the hang of it."

"What'd you say her name is?" I asked.

"That's Mariah. This guy's Phantom."

Phantom was a large gelding quarter horse with a muscular frame. He was a beautiful blue roan with a blue-white coat and a blaze over half of his face.

"Good name," I said. "The masked Phantom of the Opera?"

"Yure observant, ain't yuh, Annie?" Hudson noted.

I said, "You couldn't have named him." After that escaped my mouth, I could've kicked myself. It sounded like I thought Hudson was ignorant.

"Of course I named him. He's my hoss, ain't he?"

"And, Mariah?" I asked.

"Naw, she was named and broke by the finest cowboy west of the Mississippi. Yuh'll like her. She's got spirit, but she's well-mannered and willing to please. Phantom's a good old boy. He's sensitive to yore seat. Yuh can guide him around all day with no reins."

I commented, "He's handsome. Do you own Mariah or does she belong to someone else?"

"Yuh bet. I own Mariah and Phantom free and clear."

"Hudson, the day I arrived at the ranch Trotter Blue mentioned he sold a horse named Mariah to a great wrangler who *lived the Cowboy Code like it was carved in his heart.* He said, *a finer young man he ain't never seen.*"

Hudson muttered, "Is that so?" I saw color rise in his tan cheeks. "Yeah, this is the Mariah Trotter Blue's talkin' about."

"Then you must be that cowboy," I said to Hudson giving him a knowing smile.

He said, "Annie, don't tell yore pretty little head I'm great, because I ain't. What Trotter Blue's referrin' to is nothin' but the way I see life."

"Is *this way* what Trotter Blue calls the Cowboy Code?" I asked.

"Yep."

"Will you tell me the Code?"

"Sure. Let's get these ponies saddled and I'll tell yuh while we're ridin'," he said handing over a brush. He told me to brush Mariah in the direction of her coat. Then he handed a pick to me and told me to clean her hooves.

I bent over to clean her front hoof. I felt a hand grab my butt. His advance infuriated me. I whipped around intending to slap Hudson hard in the face. Instead I came face to face with Mariah. Half a carrot was sticking out of her mouth. I laughed and moved the second carrot to my front pocket.

I went back to cleaning the hoof while I heard Hudson call, "L.A. what yuh doin' down there?" He was grinning and shaking his head, "Stand up. Yuh gotta lift the hoss' hoof to clean out the frog."

"The frog?" I said. He lifted the hoof and showed me the underside. It was shaped like a frog.

"Some folks say it's the shape, others say it's a talisman. They got a story about killin' a frog, dryin' the skeleton, washin' it in a creek, and wearin' the pelvic girdle around their necks. Fer yore information, I ain't never worn no frog girdle," Hudson said smiling. "Now, pick it up."

I tried to lift her hoof, but it was impossible.

"Annie, come here. Stand with yore legs apart. To get her to lift, yuh gotta let the hoss know what yure intendin'. Slide yore hand down the leg like this." He did this as he leaned against me and popped my foot up. He took a look at the sole of my sneakers and said, "Gal, wearin' those shoes around hosses might get yore paw crushed."

I felt a flush of embarrassment. Hudson noticed and said, "Don't fret. Yuh ain't half as wacked as some guests. I had one doxy wantin' to ride in flip flops." Hudson let my foot drop gently. "Clean the front hoof on the left side first."

I tried with no success. Hudson chuckled. Then he came to help me. He bent his body over mine reaching for her leg. Hudson's face was so close I could feel his warm breath on my neck. He held Mariah's leg, while I picked out the muck and a pebble.

He said quietly, "That's it Annie. Ain't nice havin' a pebble yore slipper."

I could have managed the other hoofs, but I didn't mind his help.

Hudson took care of Phantom and disappeared into the tack shed. He brought out a saddle pad and a beautiful woven blanket of crimson, yellow, and violet blue. He noticed my admiration of the blanket.

"Woven by Utes," Hudson said. A sharp screech echoed across the meadow. The horses spooked and tugged at their halters. Hudson reached to calm them. "Yure alright. Easy now."

"What was that?" I asked nervously.

"It's a long story," he said. I looked intensely at him, but he ignored my stare. I decided to drop the subject. If people say *long story* it means they don't want to talk about it. I assumed this was true for cowboys too. He said, "That's a tale fer the next ride." He was planning another ride so he wasn't disappointed in my awkwardness or sneakers.

Hudson showed me how to place the pad and blanket high on the withers. Then, he brought a large saddle from the shed. The saddle was embossed with oak leaves and acorns. There was a circle around the letter *Y*. It had simple silver medallions with the same acorn design. The back was laced with a silver band. It was freshly polished and the leather was rich and shiny.

He placed the saddle on the blanket, reached for the cinch and fed a thick leather latigo through the *D* ring. He wrapped it around cinching it snugly. "Hosses are mighty clever. She's holdin' her breath so the cinch ain't tight. Then she'll blow out and the saddle will be as loose as yore granny's teeth."

"*Granny's teeth*. What kind of expression is that?" I laughed.

Hudson replied, "Paints a clear picture in yore head, don't it?"

He brought out a bridle with leather reins. He unfastened Mariah's halter. She lowered her nose toward the bit. Mariah took it readily. He flipped her ears through the bridle, fastened the chin and neck straps, handed the reins to me, and said, "Take a walk." I walked around and brought her back to Hudson. He tightened the cinch, wrapping it one more time.

I stuck my left foot in the stirrup hoisting myself onto Mariah's back. Hudson asked me to stand in the stirrups, "Yuh got some long legs on yuh L.A." I sat back in the saddle. He held my calf and his touch was intense. He moved my leg forward and adjusted the stirrup. He walked around and adjusted the other side. This touch was as potent as the first time he touched my leg.

~ ~ ~

Hudson swiftly mounted Phantom. Obviously, he'd done that thousands of times. He led the way down a trail. We came to a dirt road which was wide, but a far cry from the paved avenues of Los Angeles.

Hudson rode beside me explaining the Cowboy Code. I wanted the details so Madison couldn't one up me. "There are ten things we gotta understand, Annie. First, is honesty. Yuh gotta have integrity and be truthful. No goin' back on yore word. No matter what it is or what curves the trail takes. Yuh gotta live in truth."

"What if I don't want to deal with something so I fib to get out of it?" I asked.

Hudson answered, "A fib ain't honest. Yuh gotta deal with it fair and square."

I asked, "Would that include telling little white lies?"

Hudson replied, "White, blue, black. The color ain't gonna matter none. It's the principle. Are yuh ready fer me to go on?"

"Yes. Go ahead please."

"Second, yuh gotta help folks if they're havin' troubles. And yuh better not go around braggin', because people see it in yore eyes if yuh done good."

"Next yuh gotta listen to yore pa and ma. Gotta live by their rules. They've been there and know what's right and what's wrong. Yore folks already tried them wild notions yuh got in yore head while they were buckaroos. They're worth listenin' to."

I asked, "What if my mother doesn't understand me?"

"Annie, there ain't no ma that don't understand her kidlet. She may not like what yure doin'. But she knows yuh inside and out. Do yuh want to jabber about yore ma all day or can we move on? What number are we on, five?"

"I think it's number four," I said.

"So yure payin' attention even though yuh got contrary opinions," Hudson said and winked at me. "Four. No short cuts. Yuh gotta work hard until the job is done. Yuh ain't sittin' around bein' lazy, drinkin' soda all day. God gave yuh tools but it's up to yuh to build the barn. Any commentary?" he said mockingly.

"No," I smiled.

"Cowboy Code five. Respect. Yuh can't go interuptin' people while they're explainin' somethin'."

"Ooops," I said. "Sorry."

"Yure sayin' *sorry* must be a city-slicker code fer gettin' out of bad behavior," he said like he was reprimanding a child. "Respect ain't only fer folks yuh ride with, it's showin' consideration fer old timers too. Appreciate what they say and how they feel. Yuh gotta have the brains to know when they need to sit down or take a nap."

Hudson stalled, cleared his throat, and continued, "Then there're women.

"It's the ladies that birth us and do the nursin'. They patch us up when we get thrown from the hosses. Once we're grown, it's a woman that cooks our food, worries about us, keeps us on the right path, and beggin' yore pardon, Miss, keeps us warm at night.

We ain't takin' advantage of pretty gals because we know one day they'll be someone's' better half and some little kid's ma."

I didn't comment on this code.

"The seventh code is bein' kind to little children and animals. Yuh gotta be gentle and take good care of them. Like these hosses," he leaned back and stroked Phantom. "They depend on us fer feed, water, and exercise."

"Number eight, yuh gotta be clean and neat regardin' yore person. What yure sayin', thinkin', and doin' gotta be clean too."

I interrupted, "Hudson, how can you stay neat around horses? Today's the first time I've seen you clean and fresh smelling."

He cocked his head and asked, "Yuh notice if I'm clean and how I stink, Annie?"

"I didn't say *stink*. I said *smell*."

"So yuh notice?" he smiled.

"Yes," I said meekly with blazing cheeks.

"All right then. Yuh start yore day clean, and as Annie says, *smellin' fresh*, then yuh wash up come night fall, and yure *smellin' fresh* again. We're almost done with the codes. Can yuh hold on?"

"I'm listening," I said.

"Penultimate code," Hudson said. I looked at him with astonishment. "Annie, I bet yuh ain't got a clue that rednecks know big words too. It means *next to last*."

"I know what it means Hudson. I don't doubt you."

Hudson commented, "Watch yoreself. Yore body language says yuh doubt my smarts."

"Sorry."

"There yuh go again with *sorry,*" he winked one of those beautiful eyes. "Penultimate code. Yuh got this country, the good old U.S. of A. Yuh gotta love it because it gives yuh freedom. Yuh can't be burnin' no flag like them crazies do. Yuh gotta be patriotic and respect this land and its laws. Above all yuh gotta be willin' to fight fer her even if it costs yuh yore life. Yuh ain't no flag burner are yuh, Annie?"

"That's not my style," I replied.

"Here's yore final code. Yuh gotta be God fearin'. Gotta worship the good Lord. Yuh can't say His name in vain, like *Oh my God.* Hear me Annie?" I nodded. "Givin' thanks ain't somethin' yuh do only on Sundays. Yuh praise Him because He saves yuh from the bull, helps yuh rope the calf, and puts a beautiful lassie in front of yore eyes -even if she's got loads of brazin' commentary," he looked at me.

I was astonished. Cowboys' beliefs were insightful, honorable, and strong. Since they valued these simple, but weighty tenets, they created a unified set of individuals. I thought cowboys were a bunch of wild, hooting guys who kicked horses rodeo style. Instead, they formed a group with a culture rich in sensitivity, respect, and honor.

Madison knew this all along. Hearing it directly from Hudson was deeper than a Google search.

No wonder cowboys keep to their own. In their eyes we're untrustworthy flakes with shallow values.

~ ~ ~

Phantom started to trot slowly. The movement brought me back from my philosophical meanderings. "Yuh ready to trot, Annie? Sit down in the saddle and relax yore hips. Pretend yore hips are water sloshin' around in a wash tub. Now give her some clucks and squeeze her with those long legs."

I asked what *clucks* were and he said, "Like this." He smacked his tongue on the roof of his mouth and sucked in a bit. I clucked and gave Mariah a squeeze but she just walked faster. "Tap her belly with yore heels and keep cluckin'." Mariah finally began to trot. I was bumping up and down and grabbed the saddle horn. Hudson swung his horse beside mine. "My, oh my, Little Tenderfoot. What'd I say? Put yore mind on water. Yore hips are water. Slosh left, right, East Coast, West Coast. There yuh are. Let go of that nubbin. Holdin' on won't help yuh none."

I let go of the saddle horn and the more I relaxed my hips the easier it became. I kept the rhythm. But the moment I took my mind off slosh, coasts, and wash tub, I bounced again. "Annie, pretend yuh got a dollar bill under each cheek. Keep yore seat or they'll go flyin' off yore saddle."

Water, dollar bills, East Coast, West Coast, left, right. It was a lot to remember. And Hudson's gorgeous physique on Phantom didn't make it easier to keep my mind on sloshing.

He said, "How about we pick it up and lope? Yuh ain't gonna swish side to side, yuh gonna glide back to front. Kiss her and give Mariah a big squeeze."

He made the kiss sound to demonstrate. I imitated the kiss and gave Mariah a big squeeze digging my sneakers into her sides. She broke into a smooth lope.

It was exhilarating. The horses' hooves rumbled on the dirt road leaving plumes of dust behind us. I beamed. Hudson said, "Yuh like it, Annie?"

"I love it!"

After a long distance, Hudson slowed Phantom to a trot and down to a walk. Mariah followed suit. I found myself bumping hard the moment she slowed into the trot. I managed to stay on until she returned to a walk. Hudson stopped Phantom. I called to him, "How do I stop her?"

"Pretend yuh got pennies in yore back pockets. Exhale, sit on yore pennies hard, and say *whoa.*"

I did as he said and Mariah came to a stop in two steps. Hudson dismounted, and I followed his lead, or so I thought. "Annie, when dismountin', keep one boot, or one sneaker in yore case, in the stirrup until yuh reach the ground with yore other foot. Yuh can't blow both stirrups and jump. Yuh can get mighty hung up that way."

What looked easy was full of rules. "Would you like me to mount Mariah and try again?" I asked.

"Naw. Yure smart. Yuh'll catch on."

We walked the horses into a beautiful clearing surrounded by aspens and a river. The only sounds were trees in the breeze, birds, the river gurgling, and panting horses. We let the horses drink then Hudson wrapped their legs in hobbles.

He opened a bag that was tied to Phantom's saddle. Hudson pulled out a bandana, sat on the creek bank, and motioned for me to join him. "Hungry, Annie? I filled my yannigan bag with a few eats." He handed the bandana to me, "Open my old wipe. See if anything's to yore likin'. I tried to pack what a gal from Bel Air might eat."

"Thank you," I said pulling out grapes and cheese. He took the cheese and cut chunks with the same knife he used for whittling. He offered me the first chunk. The cheese and grapes tasted delicious after our hard ride. I said, "It's beautiful here."

Hudson nodded then he leaned back resting on one elbow and we talked. He wanted to know what my city life was like. He asked: where I went to school, how old I was, what pets I had, what I did in my spare time, why I came to work at the ranch, if I liked mountains, what the beach scene was like, my plans for the future, and so on.

I wanted to learn about him. He was mysterious and silent on the ranch. Alone with me, he was open and easy to converse with.

He surprised me by asking, "Are yuh homesick, Annie?"

"No," I replied.

"Ain't there anythin' yure missin'?"

"Well, I don't miss my cell phone or the country club chatter. If I miss anyone it's…"

He winced, "Yore boyfriend." I pushed his shoulder knocking him off his elbow onto his back.

"Oops," I said.

Propping himself up, he responded, "Don't worry yore pretty little self. I've taken harder falls."

"I was about to say I miss my father. He's the only one who calls me *Annie* like you do. At night, when he gets home, I hear his footsteps on the marble stairs. He checks my room to see if I'm still awake. I make sure I am. I ask him about his day and he tells me an adventurous story. Then he kisses my forehead and wishes me sweet dreams. I miss this." I paused, feeling a twinge of nostalgia. "And, I also miss lavender bubble baths."

He looked pensively at me then jabbed, "Ahah, I knew yuh'd be missin' yore luxury lifestyle."

"Well, what about you Hudson? What do you miss?"

"I miss Ma's home cookin'. I miss comin' home to a house that smells of supper."

"What's your favorite food?" I asked.

"There's nothin' like Ma's pot roast and apple pie," he smiled.

"When are you going home?" I asked.

His smile faded, "Ma died two years ago. I'll ramble and roam until I find a place to settle."

I swallowed hard, "I'm sorry."

"That's life Annie. God's good. Death is part of His plan. Ma's in a better place now. I'm on my own. Losing Ma forced me to grow up mighty quick."

"What about your father? Where's he?"

"Pa died fightin' fer our freedom. Ma kept the flag they draped over his coffin on her bedstand until the day she died. I got it now. Goes with me everywhere. Reminds me of what kind of stock I'm from and what's important. I got his truck too. Drivin' it brings back memories: huntin', fishin', laughin', and talkin' about bein' a man." He slid behind me, picked wild flowers, and tucked the stems into my braid.

The sun was warm and we raised a sweat riding. I took off my sneakers and rolled up my jeans. Hudson stared at my feet. "What're you looking at?" I asked. He gestured to my feet. "They're French," I said stepping into the water. "Come in Hudson. Take off your boots. The water's nice and cool."

He hesitated, then took off his boots, and socks, and shoved up his jeans. His feet were bright white. Given his dark face and hands, I expected him to have matching feet. Guys back home have beach tans which include their feet, except for the flip-flop lines. He stood facing me, "Annie, yuh do crazy things."

"Don't you wade in creeks?" I said as I stepped onto a rock to match his height. The rock was covered with algae. My feet slipped. I flailed my arms trying to catch my balance. Hudson grabbed me, wrapped his arms around my waist, and pulled me to his chest. He was solid and his arms were strong. Our eyes locked. Our lips were close. His breath was warm and sweet. I held perfectly still.

Then he put me on the bank and I said quietly, "Thanks for catching me."

"Anytime."

Phantom whinnied. Hudson and I glanced in the direction of Phantom's stare. There was a hue of violet blue and a figure ran through the aspen grove across the river. "Who's that?" I asked Hudson.

"Time to head out," he said. I could see in his face he was concerned. We threw on our shoes, gathered the hobbles, mounted the horses, and set out at a gallop.

We didn't talk on the ride back. At the corral, we dismounted and he said, "Don't worry about the hosses, I'll see to them." He added, "Annie, I had a darn good time with yuh. Ride with me again, will yuh? By the way, that was a fine dismount, even in sneakers."

"Thanks," I smiled and walked toward the girl's bunk house. On the way I saw the wranglers coming down the hill leading two horses. I was tempted to say *Hi* but remembered Madison's lectures. We passed each other in silence.

CHAPTER SIX

HONESTY & RESPECT

I changed into my bikini and went for a dip in the pool. Floating in the pool, I thought about my time with Hudson. I put my head back so my ears were submerged in the stillness of the water. My mind freely wandered over each word he said, every look he gave me, the touch of his callused hands, warmth of his strong arms, and the scent of his breath. The water was cool and the sun was as radiant as I felt. Not even the eerie screech in the meadow or the stranger in the woods could put a dent in my happiness.

That night I heard tapping on my window. I was afraid to pull back the curtain and see the violet blue hue of the stranger in the woods. The tapping persisted. I peered through a crack in the curtain. In the moonlight I saw Hudson throwing pebbles. Opening the window, I noticed the bunk house didn't have screens. "Are you crazy Cowboy? The girls' bunk house is off limits. Trotter Blue will call my dad, worse yet my mother. He'll send us home and . . ."

He stepped to the window placing his finger on my lips and whispered, "Annie, I ain't goin' in no girls' bunk house. No one's goin' home. Ain't yuh supposed to ask how my day was?"

I cleared my throat and formally said, "How was your day?"

"It was the best day of my life. I'm as pleased as a little dog waggin' two tails. I went ridin' with the sweetest damsel. She's as soft and fluffy as a goose-hair pillow. She's got fancy toes. Calls them Swiss - no, French. Anyhoo, some European country. Now yuh hear this gal's different since she's from a concrete forest - likes to wade in creeks barefoot."

Then he paused a moment and looked in my smiling eyes. He reached up, pushed a lock of hair off of my face and gently put his lips to my forehead. "Sweet dreams, Annie. Best close that window up tight so yuh ain't gettin' no bats in yore house."

~ ~ ~

The next morning I awoke and jumped off the bunk landing flat on my butt. "Anna Lisa, are you o.k?" Grace asked.

"I'm fine," I lied. It was too easy. Right then and there, on the plywood floor of that small room, I decided to work through one Cowboy Code a week, like Ben Franklin who tackled virtues one at a time. I started with *Honesty*, "Actually Grace, I'm pretty stiff and sore. I'm not use to country exercise."

Grace helped me to my feet. "You'll have a good bruise."

I said, "My bikini bottoms better cover it."

~ ~ ~

That day, Hudson didn't come to lunch. I had a notion it might be awkward for him to see me in front of the wranglers. Perhaps he worried I'd say something about our ride or perhaps he was merely working with the new horses. I asked Hoyle, "What would Hudson like?"

"He ain't eatin' here today."

"Oh, no?" I asked.

Naturally, the reply was a curt one, "Yuh heard me."

I wondered where Hudson was. He didn't mention plans.

After dinner I joined my friends at the campfire. Madison confessed, "Anna Lisa, I'm sorry for making a fuss about your chat with Hudson. It's none of my business. I like being your friend and I respect you."

I replied, "Madison, if you respect me, talk to me with manners. You're up on the Code. Try practicing it."

"Anna Lisa, I'm not a country bumpkin and I don't intend to become one. I'm a cerebral individual."

"Being country and cerebral are not mutually exclusive," I told her dogmatically.

"I see, now, you're an expert on cowboys? How'd you find cell range to research the Code? Don't tell me you hitched a ride with the wranglers yesterday."

"Never mind Madison. Let's change the subject. Pip sings well doesn't she? Do you like this song?"

She replied "I'm not fond of country music. I like jazz and classical. Country music is always about someone crying, sighing, or dying. And their grammar sucks."

"Madison, that's part of the culture. You know an identifier. It's their dialect. It doesn't mean they don't read or pass English 101."

"Anna Lisa, how *did* you become such an expert? You drove to the valley with them, didn't you?" she accused.

"No, I didn't. Let's drop it," I suggested. Trying to change the subject I asked, "Is registration for college soon?"

"You mean registration for Stanford University?" I think Madison liked saying *Stanford.* "I have until early September to select my Stanford classes."

Shelly, Grace, and Caprice came to sit with us. Shelly said, "Tomorrow's my day off. Do you think it'd be o.k. if I went on the lake tour?"

I said, "That's cool. Trotter Blue wants us to enjoy the activities as long as there's space."

"Yes!" Shelly cheered. "I know that cute guest from Florida is going. He was eying me at breakfast today. I'm going to wear my sexy bikini."

Shocked by the additional information I firmly said, "Shelly, flirting with guests is off limits."

"I see, Anna Lisa, you can flirt with cowboys, but I can't come-on to a guest?"

"Flirt with cowboys? Is that what you think?" It was all I could say if I intended to stick to the Honesty Code. After the campfire, I overheard Shelly complain about my double standard.

The four waitresses headed to the dining hall, probably for late night ice cream and a game of Uno. I marched past them, showered, and crawled into bed.

Sleep came quickly and deeply. Riding the day before wiped me out. Bickering with friends also tired me.

It was midnight before I woke to tapping on my window. I stretched, rubbed my eyes, and pulled back the curtain. There stood Hudson with pebbles in his hand. I opened the window.

With a look of amazement, he said, "Good evenin', Annie. City gals sure do weird things. What's on yore face, expensive night cream?"

"I didn't put on anything." I touched my face. It was gooey. I smelled my hands - mustard and ketchup. My palms were covered. Annoyed, I said, "That prankster. Smell, Hudson."

Hudson chuckled. He pulled his bandana from his pocket and wiped my face gently. Then he took my hands in his and wiped my palms. He said, "I thought only wranglers did that kind of stuff."

"Well, Caprice is a number. She's wild," I declared. Hudson put his bandana back in his pocket. I asked, "How was your day?"

He grinned, "I took the day off and drove to the city. I had a purchase to make and errands needed tendin' to."

It sounded like he was going to stop talking and I wanted him to stay longer so I whispered, "What's this city like?"

"It's modern, but in its time, it was a minin' boomtown. Folks from miles around come lookin' fer gold and silver. It was a crossroads fer cattle tradin' too. There are a couple of old hotels that go back to those minin' times, The Hearston and The Black Steer."

"Do you think famous cowboys stayed there?" I asked.

"Naw. Nothin' but rich ranchers and lucky fellows that found gold. Ain't nobody else got enough dough. A cowboy hunkers down in a field somewhere. If he's lucky he'll lay his bed roll in the hay of an old barn."

Hudson added, "Yuh know the shirt I wore ridin' with the snaps?"

"I noticed," I said flirtatiously.

"It was invented in the city, authentic cowboy." Then he calmly reached up and tilted my forehead toward him, "Yuh smell like somethin' I could eat." He kissed my forehead and said, "Sweet dreams, Annie."

I should've gotten out of bed to wash my face but I didn't want to wash away the feel of his lips on my forehead.

CHAPTER SEVEN

BOOTS

In the morning, I greeted the girls, "That was a good one." They were surprised I wasn't irked.

Grace nervously asked, "You're not mad Anna Lisa? I told them not to but they said I was a softy and didn't have guts."

"It's o.k. Grace. I don't melt from a little ketchup and mustard."

While we served breakfast I wondered what I should do with the news Shelly was hitting on a guest. I decided to let it run its course. Shelly might frighten the guy with her daring swimsuit.

Before lunch, I went to change my pillow case. I didn't want to sleep in the smell of condiments again. On my bunk was a box with a violet ribbon. There was a little envelope. On it was written *Annie*. I thought Dad sent the package so I anxiously ripped it open.

Written in pen was, *Will yuh ride with me? Hudson*. I had to catch my breath and read the card again. I untied the violet ribbon delicately and opened the box gently folding back the tissue. In the box was a pair of boots. Size eight. I slipped off my sneakers and tried them on. They fit. I stood there filled with euphoria, admiring my boots.

Grace poked her head in and said, "Wow, new boots Anna Lisa?" She continued, "They're Justin's! What kind of leather is that?"

"It's Iguana skin," I said.

Grace said, "Who are they from?" Before, I got to the card, she nabbed it. She put a hand across her mouth like she was stifling a scream.

"Please don't say anything to Madison or Shelly. Promise me you won't say anything to anyone," I begged.

Grace said, "Your secret is safe with me, Anna Lisa. Hudson must like you. Do you know how expensive those are? He probably spent a week's paycheck on them." Grace gave me a hug, "Anna Lisa, I'm happy for you."

"Thanks," I replied. I took off the boots and slid them under the bunk with my flip-flops. I put on my sneakers. The note was placed out of view under my pillow. I pulled my hair into a pony tail, securing it with the violet ribbon. Then, I changed my pillowcase.

At the poolside, I prepped for lunch. Guests arrived and I drifted around the tables. Given my elation, it was hard to concentrate on the mundane routine of lunch orders. Somehow I managed to get things straight.

When the guests departed, seven wranglers approached the eight-top. Hudson sat closest to where I stood. I saw him glance down at my feet. Then he looked at my hair. "Nice ribbon," he said.

I felt my face blush and said, "Thank you. I love ribbons. I love beautiful shoes too." The wranglers look down at my feet. My old sneakers didn't impress them. They looked at me like I was idiotic. Hudson and I imperceptibly shared the secret.

~ ~ ~

At dinner, I wore my new boots. Thank goodness Madison, Shelly, and Caprice didn't notice. Only Grace did. She was great. She discretely pointed at my feet and threw me thumbs up with a sneaky smile.

Dinner was almost over when Sam called me to the kitchen. "Do you know Greek mythology?" he asked.

"I love the myths," I replied.

He said, "Good. Tell me about Persephone." Given his odd request, I assumed Sam hit the red wine intended for the Marinara Sauce. He should have asked me about Bacchus.

"Persephone was the daughter of Demeter, the Goddess of seasons. Hades fell in love with Persephone at first sight. Every year he would take her for one season to live with her as his bride."

"Exactly," Sam said. "You know Greek mythology well." In a stern, sober, and professor-like tone, he continued, "Be wary, Anna Lisa, three months is plenty of time to fall in love. You need to ask yourself if the lifestyle is right for you. Is the guy from a culture you're willing to embrace? Is he worthy of your love?"

"Sam, I'm losing you," I said.

Sam chuckled, "Call me Messenger Hermes. There's a cowboy on my kitchen porch. He wants to see you after your shift." Sam winked, "You can head out now if you like. I'll do my chef stroll through the dining hall and if your tables need anything, I'll see to it. Go now, before your coach turns into a pumpkin."

I threw my arms around his chubby chef build and gave him a hug. "Thanks Sam, I mean Hermes," I smiled, and hurried toward the back door.

Sam called, "Watch out. Don't get stung."

I peered through the kitchen window and saw Hudson leaning against a porch post whittling. Moonlight shined on his hat shading his eyes. All I saw were his gorgeous lips and a piece of straw sticking out of his mouth. Mariah and Phantom were tethered to the hitching post next to him.

He saw me and pulled the straw from his mouth, threw it to the ground, stuffed his knife and whittling project into his pocket, and said "Good evenin', Annie. We got us a full moon. Good night fer a ride. Glad to see yure wearin' those boots."

"Thank you for the lovely gift," I said beaming. "Hudson, it's too much. You shouldn't have bought grandiose boots for me."

"Maybe, but a gal of yore breedin' ain't likely to be fond of no stogies."

"Stogies?" I said with a question in my voice.

Hudson laughed, "Ain't they teachin' no vocabulary at yore highfalutin school? Stogies are old, beat up boots thrown to the down and out waddie."

"Well, these are beautiful. Look they fit perfectly. How'd you guess my shoe size?"

"It's a good thing yure a crazy Californian who blows her shoes to wade in rivers."

"You looked in my sneakers?" I said in astonishment.

He smiled like a child that was up to no good, "Yep. And they didn't stink none either. Let's roll out. Yuh need a leg up?" He interlocked his fingers and held them toward me.

I asked, "How am I supposed to ride without a saddle?"

"Yuh'll catch on mighty quick. Step yore fancy boot in my hands and I'll throw yuh up." He hoisted me and I landed square on Mariah's back. "Now scoot to her withers." By the time I finished scooting, Hudson had mounted Phantom. He clucked softly and we started walking.

"Annie, it's easier to learn ridin' bareback. Yuh feel each step. This'll help yore seat in the saddle. Want to trot?"

I replied, "Hudson, I don't know about that."

"Do yuh trust me?" he asked. "Ain't nothin' to be scared of. Look between her ears and yuh'll stay balanced."

I gave her clucks and a squeeze. She was easier to squeeze without the saddle. The boots helped too. Hudson stopped talking as we trotted past the wranglers' bunk house. Half way across the meadow, a violet blue wind kicked up. A sharp snap hit Mariah's rump. It couldn't have been Hudson because he was beside me.

Mariah took off like a Ferrari. She ran full out. She was cutting curves without slowing. My heart was racing. She ran through the trees not heeding the trail. I ducked to avoid low branches. Thank goodness for moonlight illuminating the forest.

I heard Hudson call "Rein her in. Choke up on yore reins. Turn yore hoss. Hold on Annie." There was nothing to hold on to but her mane. I grabbed a handful of hair. "I'm comin'. I'll be at yore flank soon." We sped out of the trees onto the dirt road. By now I was holding on to anything I could find, reins, mane, neck, mane again. As Hudson got closer, it sounded like a stampede. Phantom was next to me and I could feel him against my boot. All of a sudden, Hudson flung himself off Phantom's back onto Mariah.

He pressed against me lunging forward, grabbing her reins. "Whoa girl. Easy now." Hudson slowed Mariah and brought her to a stop.

The horses were panting. Mariah was sweating. I was shaking. Tears streamed down my face. Through my sobs, I heaved, "Let me down. Let me go."

Hudson gently said, "Shhh. Yure safe. Relax into my arms."

"I'm scared. I want off," I sobbed.

"Annie, the hoss ain't gonna try nothin' while I'm on her back. Trust me."

I snapped at Hudson, "I trusted you back there and look what happened."

He winced, "Slow yore breathin'. Lean back." Hudson held me and reached around catching my tears with his finger. He brought his tear laden finger to his lips, "Yure as salty as yure feisty." His unexpected comment, relaxed me and I had to chuckle. "Yuh ride like yuh were born with ponies. Did good stayin' on. I was sure yure gonna take off on an unscheduled flight around that first bend. Yuh got a mighty impressive seat."

"Impressive seat? I was out of control. The only thing saving me was doing what you said, *look between Mariah's ears.*"

Hudson said, "Yuh listen good. Got obedience too. I like that in a lady."

"Hudson, please stay with me on Mariah," I pleaded.

"Your wish is my command," he said grabbing the reins of Phantom to trail him along.

We didn't turn up the narrow trail. "Where're we going?" I asked.

He stated, "We'll loop around. I ain't gonna risk takin' yuh past our dice house."

I asked him why Mariah spooked. He told me I didn't need to worry about it and that I had enough fright for one night. Then he said softly, "Unwind. Enjoy the moonlight."

I calmed down and was able to appreciate the moon shining on the trees. It turned the pines into glistening silver needles and cast shadows across the trail. I enjoyed being held by Hudson.

It took a long time to reach the girl's bunk house and he asked, "How do yuh feel?"

By then I was over the fright. One moment I was crying hysterically, the next moment I was content in his arms. He slid off Mariah. "Lean forward and swing yore leg over," he said. The drop was further than anticipated and I hit the ground hard. Hudson caught me before I fell back. He said, "Annie, our moonlight ride ain't what I planned. Please, don't throw me out with the hog water."

"If that means give up on you, no way," I said. "I was hoping you wouldn't throw me out with pigs, or whatever."

He smiled softly, "Never." Tilting my head up he kissed my forehead and said, "Sweet dreams, Annie." Hudson jumped on Phantom, called, "Yeeha," and loped toward the corral. Mariah trailed behind.

CHAPTER EIGHT

SHORT SHEETS & TALCUM

In the bunk house, I splashed cold water on my tear swollen face. I took a cool shower then tried to crawl into bed but got tangled in the sheets.

"Ugh, Caprice," I said in exasperation. Right when I needed sleep, I had to undo the folded top sheet and remake my bunk.

"Where'd you take off to, Anna Lisa?" Madison asked as she stood in the doorway.

"Nowhere of importance. It gave you and Caprice plenty of time to pull your prank. Short sheeting a bed is an old one, Madison. What'd I do to tick you off?"

"It's not what you did, it's what you aren't doing. You're disappearing and not hanging out with us anymore."

Madison was right. I'd been so engaged in thoughts about Hudson, I hadn't thought of my friends. I said, "Let's go swimming tomorrow."

Madison said, "Sounds good. I'll tell Grace and Caprice."

"What about Shelly?" I inquired.

"Boy, are you out of it. Shelly's hanging with Scott."

I asked, "Who's Scott? That guest from Florida? So her swimsuit was a success."

"You bet." Madison replied.

"Has Trotter Blue noticed?"

"Not yet. Tomorrow Shelly's going hiking with Scott, so she'll be out of sight. I don't know what Trotter Blue would do if he found out."

"What do you think could happen?" I asked nervously. I was the lead waitress so I had responsibility over the matter.

Madison said, "I'm not certain, but last year one of the kitchen hands, Easton Timberlake, picked up on a guest. She was a cute college student, out here from Wisconsin with her parents. Trotter Blue saw Timberlake kiss her one night. He marched over to the wranglers' bunk house, stuffed Easton's things in a duffle bag and dropped it in the parking lot. He let him make one phone call. His parents wouldn't pick him up, so that night Easton slept under the stars. The wranglers heard about his troubles and brought him a sleeping bag and some food."

That sounded like a cowboy. Regardless of fault, Easton Timberlake was in trouble so they helped. "Madison, how does Trotter Blue feel about workers pairing up?"

"Why do you ask Anna Lisa?" she said with a brazen smile.

"Just curious. You know his policies better than I do. Trotter Blue has strong principles."

Madison answered, "Definitely. But, Meadow Hazelhurst and Wade Brawley met here. They're still together and on the management team. Look at Dash and Candy. It's clear they're a couple. Pip and Buck Huntsman are also a duet. Then there's the engagement of Imogene Tuttle to Quade Remington. Trotter Blue realizes it's a long summer and romance is bound to happen. After all, it's the hot season."

I laughed. It felt good to laugh with Madison for a change.

She continued, "Don't let Mr. Blue's age fool you. He's aware of who's hitting on whom. I think he enjoys match making. Co-workers don't bother him. Going after Easton is different. It means he watches out for his clientele. Trotter Blue rightfully protects his female guests against advances from male employees."

Madison headed for bed. I hit my pillow and was out.

We had fun at the pool. I missed spending time with the girls. We laughed at Caprice's jokes. Thank goodness she had a tremendous repertoire, otherwise it would get mundane. Caprice broke out her video camera and started to compile her next video for the web. I wasn't thrilled about being in it, but it was fun clowning around.

Shelly returned from hiking and asked to change her free night because she wanted to go out with Scott. "Shelly, I can't change your night off."

She yelled at me, "Oh my God, Anna Lisa you have the worst double standard. I want to see Scotty and you think we didn't notice you and …"

I was worried about what she had noticed, so I cut her off, "Wait a minute, Shelly. I suggest you find someone to switch with permanently."

Shelly asked Caprice to swap evenings. "That's fine with me. I'll work Wednesdays," Caprice said. I made a mental note to watch for pranks on Thursday evenings.

We headed to the girls' bunk house to shower for dinner service. I showered quickly, because we spent too long lounging by the pool.

I grabbed my hairdryer, pointed it at my wet hair and a plume of white power covered me. I shrieked. I heard the girls laughing and turned around. Madison, Shelly, and Grace were huddled around Caprice, smiling. Caprice was beaming and filming at the same time. The talcum powder gave her good footage. I was tempted to turn my hairdryer on them, but realized that would cause all of us to be late for work. I headed back to the shower knowing I'd have to be a good sport to maintain their respect. Since there would be no time to dry my hair, I wrapped it into a tight bun.

After dinner service, we went to the campfire. We stayed until Pip stopped playing the guitar and the guests departed. I whispered to Madison, "Thank goodness Shelly had enough common sense to stay away from the campfire. When does this guy leave?" Madison shrugged.

Although it was late, I took time to blow all of the talcum powder out of my hair dryer. I undid the bun in my hair. My hair fell in big curls. Then I made a cup of chamomile tea and crawled onto my bunk. I cracked the curtain and watched. The moon was still full enough to make things visible. I waited for the sound of pebbles.

Something moved in the distance. As it came closer, I could discern the silhouette of Hudson. It was identical to the image in my dream. I opened the window.

He noticed and dropped the pebbles. "Good evenin', Annie. Ooowee, what'd yuh do to yore hair?" He smiled and brushed a lock off my face, "Look at them curls shinin' in this moonlight."

"How was your day?" I asked.

"Trixie's startin' to understand what I want. Dash and Candy are workin' her now. Hoyle and Bev took Shelly and a male guest riding this evenin'."

I interrupted, "Do you think Trotter Blue knows?"

"Naw. Hoyle's mighty discreet and Bev won't talk. That Bev though, she's good with the guests, got them thinkin' she's a real cowgirl. This ruffles Lacey and Candy's feathers. It's Skeebo I worry about. He's havin' a hard go of things. Keeps talkin' about visions. We all know strange things happen at the bunk house. But Skeebo's screamin' in his sleep, swingin' his arms and legs around like a wild man."

"What do you mean strange things happen at the bunk house?" I questioned.

Just then, Grace stirred and said, "Anna Lisa, is that you?" I could count on Grace to keep things secret. Hudson whispered in my ear quietly. He was almost indiscernible. I felt his restrained breath in my hair, "Sweet dreams, Annie." He pressed his lips to my forehead and ran his fingers through my hair.

"Good night, Hudson. Sweet dreams," I whispered.

CHAPTER NINE

KINDNESS TO CHILDREN

The next morning I waited on the Copper family. The father and mother were cheerful. They had two children, Bobby, ten and Pamina, seven. Pamina asked, "Are you a cowgirl?"

Bobby said, "Pamina, she isn't a cowgirl. She's just a plain old waitress." Mrs. Copper told Bobby to watch his manners.

"It's o.k. I'm working on being worthy enough to be a cowgirl. Bobby's right. I'm still a *plain old waitress*." I explained, "Not everybody knows it, but cowboys are a respectable bunch. They follow a code that is honorable and steeped in tradition."

Mrs. Copper said, "Really? Bobby and I went on a trail ride yesterday. The cowboys seem like grimy, dusty, sweaty people."

I said, "That's because they're working with horses. Rest assured, they clean up well. It's one of the Codes."

Pamina whined, "I want to see them, Mommy."

Mr. Copper said kindly, "We know, Sweetie. Remember, your wheelchair can't go on that dirt trail."

I knelt down, so I was eye level with Pamina. I saw disappointment in her eyes and felt moved. "Pamina, I can't promise anything, but if I could arrange for a cowboy to come here. Would you like that?"

Bobby butted in, "Get that big, tall cowboy. I think his name's Hudman."

VIOLET RIBBONS

"Hudson's the lead wrangler," I clarified.

Pamina asked, "Do you think he'd come to visit me?"

"I'll try. Maybe he could bring his horse." Pamina gave me a big smile.

Madison cornered me at the waitress station. "Anna Lisa, what do you think you're doing? Don't get that little girl's hopes up. Oh my God, Anna Lisa, you are out of touch with reality."

"Madison, it's worth a try. Didn't you see her sadness? Her brother does cool things and she's left out."

Madison huffed and stomped away.

After breakfast, I knocked on Trotter Blue's door. "Howdy, Lovely Anna Lisa. How's life treatin' yuh?"

"Rather well, sir."

"So I hear. Why yuh visitin' an old geezer like me? What's on yore mind?"

I said, "There's this little girl, Pamina Copper."

"Ah, the sweetie in the convertible," he said.

I replied, "She wants to meet a wrangler. Her brother's been on the trail and she's left out. Is there a way for her to meet a cowboy or cowgirl and perhaps pet a horse?"

"Angel Eyes, when yuh gonna quit amazin' me? Yuh got a heart of gold concernin' yoreself about that little tike." He thought for a long moment. The lines in his dry skin became more severe. He slowly spoke like he was putting a plan together as the words rolled off his lips. "If we get Candy in the big western saddle, we can lift little Pammy onto the hoss."

"Would that be Mariah?"

"Naw, too much spirit. I recommend we saddle the senior mare, Old Faithful. If yure serious about this, talk to the gal's folks. I'll take care of Candy and Old Faithful."

That was surprisingly easy. I planned to talk to the Coppers at the campfire.

~ ~ ~

The sound of clanking pots and pans came from the kitchen, "Hello Sam."

"Hi Anna Lisa, what's new?" he said as he tried to find the right lid for his sauce pan.

"Nothing much. I was wondering if I could bake a pie this afternoon, that is, if it wouldn't interfere with your dinner preparations."

"You won't interfere and I'd enjoy the company. What type of pie?"

"Apple," I said.

"For apple pie, I have a delicious recipe." He looked at me with a twinkle in his eye, "If you don't have your own."

I had never baked in my life. If the Clay's wanted dessert, we sent Joseph, our estate hand, to the French Boulangerie. Sometimes the apple turnovers were still warm when he returned.

"Your recipe would be great. Do you have a copy of it?"

"In my head, but I can recite it to you as you go."

"What's my first ingredient?" I asked.

Sam was full of insight. He told me the secrets of making the crust flaky and keeping the apples tart yet lightly sweet. He taught me how to make the pie aesthetically pleasing so it looked like it was made with care.

He also taught me how to preheat the oven, keep the dough from sticking to the rolling pin, and how to make slits in the top so the pie wouldn't explode while it baked. I didn't realize baking took so much time and effort. After a couple of hours, I had a beautiful apple pie. He told me to cool it in the mountain air on the ledge of the kitchen window. He said the country air was the trick to a home-style taste. I set it carefully on the ledge.

I asked Sam if he made pot roast. He asked, "Anna Lisa, do you like pot roast?"

"I don't think I've ever had it, have you?" Sam shook his head. It was time to prep for dinner service.

~ ~ ~

After dinner I rushed to the campfire. I saw Mr. and Mrs. Copper with the children and sat next to Mrs. Copper.

Quietly I told her, "I talked to Trotter Blue today…"

Mrs. Copper interrupted "It's o.k. Pamina has a strong character. Muscular Dystrophy has given that to her. She's learned to deal with disappointment. Pamina moves on to other interests."

I said, "But Mrs. Copper, Trotter Blue's in agreement. He wants me to find out if it's acceptable with you and Mr. Copper. Candy would place Pamina in the big saddle in front of her. Candy would sit in back and hold Pamina the entire time. The horse is a calm old mare and Candy's a tremendous rider."

"That's wonderful. Of course it's o.k. She'll be so happy." Mrs. Copper flung her arms around me. She turned to her husband. He was smiling and gave me thumbs up. It felt good see them happy. Cowboys understand the human psyche. Kindness to little children is a glorious feeling.

I went to the kitchen to pick up the pie and a fork. I wrapped the pie in silver foil and then slipped a kitchen towel over it. I didn't want the girls to see it and ask questions. After stuffing the pie under my covers, I showered.

Hudson's nightly visits were becoming a cherished routine. "Howdy, Annie," he whispered. "Yuh smell like apples. Yuh gotta have an entire salon of shampoos."

I stifled my desire to laugh, "How was your day?"

He didn't have much to say, "I'm sorry Annie. Nothin' interestin'. I hope I ain't disappointin' yuh."

"I understand. Some days are mundane." I grabbed the pie from under my sheets, "I baked this for you."

His face lit up. He unwrapped the kitchen towel and pulled off the silver foil. He looked like a little boy at Christmas opening a package. I handed him the fork. He ate a bite and stood still, saying nothing. "Is it that bad?" I asked.

"Bad? Tastes like the pie Ma baked," his eyes glistened. "Have some," he said loading the fork and putting it in my mouth. It was good.

Hudson, looked me in the eyes and said, "Thank yuh, Annie. Yure the sweetest critter I ever met." Hudson put his hand behind my head and pulled me toward his lips giving me a sticky kiss on my forehead. "Sweet dreams, Annie." I watched him go, shoveling forks full of pie into his mouth.

CHAPTER TEN

BATS

I fell asleep and the violet blue dream started. I heard screeches and felt dozens of little feet on my head. Things were crawling around and slapping me in the face. I woke up and let out a scream. Bats were in my hair. My cry sent them flying through the room waking Grace and Meadow. They shrieked and jumped out of their beds. I ran down the hall. "Caprice your pranks have gone too far. I don't know how you screwed up their echolocation but you have to stop these things now."

Caprice woke from her sleep and said groggily, "Anna Lisa, you've got a bat in your hair." I reached up, pulled it out, and threw it at her. She screamed.

"It's not funny is it Caprice? Knock off the pranks and get rid of these creatures."

"Anna Lisa, I didn't do this."

"Right," I chirped.

"You have to believe me. This is beyond what I can do. I don't know what's happening, but I swear it wasn't me. Honest." I stared in her eyes looking to see if her pupils dilated. Dad's aikido master said when a lie is told, pupils dilate. Caprice's remained still.

Caprice grabbed her video camera, "This will make good footage. The light is weird. It's sort of blue, sort of purple."

I told her, "Sometimes the wind's this color."

Madison said, "That's because the moon is waning. Didn't you study earth sciences?" We opened the doors and shoed out the bats. Caprice filmed.

After the excitement I was unable to sleep. If it wasn't Caprice, what was it? Perhaps it was the scent of apple pie and these were fruit bats. But, I wouldn't recognize a fruit bat if it did land in my hair. Odd things were happening in violet blue. There were things Hudson hadn't told me, happenings too frightening. And Skeebo saw things in his mind. I shivered and double checked my window. I crawled under my covers and fought the unease running through my body. I practiced yoga breathing to quiet my mind and tried to find sleep.

~ ~ ~

The next morning, I felt awful. Sleep was a necessity for me. I stretched and felt through my hair to make sure no living things were romping around. Then it hit me. This was the day Pamina was to meet a cowgirl. I hurried to the dining hall, wanting to have the Copper's table.

"Good morning," I greeted them.

Pamina's father asked, "Good morning. Is everything still a go?"

"Yes, sir," I confirmed happily.

Pamina said, "I am so excited. I can't wait."

I knelt to her level and said, "Eat a big breakfast because it's the most important meal for a cowgirl." I thought to myself, they eat big lunches too.

After breakfast, the Coppers hung around the dining hall, waiting. I was starting to worry about Candy possibly rejecting the plan or forgetting.

Madison pulled me aside, "Where's your trusted cowgirl? I told you not to meddle. You head no warnings, Anna Lisa."

I cut off her lecture, "Relax, Madison. She'll be here."

Trying to quell my doubts, I reminded myself Candy is a cowgirl and lives by the Code. Just then, Candy crested the hill and rode to the edge of the veranda. I went to Pamina and said, "Here's your cowgirl." Holding open the screen door, Pamina motored through and sped down the ramp toward Candy. I had to run to keep up.

Candy said, "Howdy, Anna Lisa. I hear this was yore idea." I braced myself, expecting her rebuke. Surprising me she said, "Glad yuh thought it up. Shows yuh got substance." Candy continued, "We'll be certain little Pammy has a grand day." She turned to Pamina and said, "Yuh gotta be Miss. Dandy Pam."

Pamina smiled and said, "What's your horse's name, Candy?"

Candy replied, "Her name is Old Faithful,"

Pamina said, "Anna Lisa gave me a carrot from the kitchen. Can I give it to her?"

"That'd make her as happy as a flea in a doghouse. Watch yore fingers." I grabbed Pamina's hand and held it flat. Candy watched and said, "Anna Lisa, where'd yuh learn how to do that?" I ignored Candy and helped Pamina slowly offer the carrot.

"She likes it," Pamina squealed in her charming voice.

Candy said kindly, "Come ride with me."

"I -I can't walk," said Pamina shyly.

Candy said, "That's alright. Old Faithful will be proud to walk fer yuh. Anna Lisa, give our little friend a leg up."

I lifted Pamina from her wheelchair. She was lighter than expected. Her leg muscles had waned. Candy held her securely and put the reins in Pamina's hand. Candy covered Pamina's grip with her own hand. They turned toward the meadow.

Late that afternoon Candy and Pamina loped to the poolside. I heard Pamina giggling. She called, "Anna Lisa." I went to help her dismount. "Bye, Faithful." I held Pamina so she could nuzzle the horse's neck. "Bye, Candy."

"See yuh later, Miss Dandy Pam." Candy turned Old Faithful and galloped toward the corral.

I set Pamina in her wheelchair, knelt down, and asked, "How was your day cowgirl?"

"Anna Lisa, it was so much fun. Look, the Rodeo Queen signed a picture for me." She held up a picture of Lacey. Lacey's hair was styled in brown ringlets. She wore a white cowboy hat with gems. Her nails were manicured and painted berry-pink. She had on the right amount of make-up and wore a long sleeve, snap button, fringed shirt with a sash draped across it. I thought, cowgirls clean up amazingly well. Pamina waved a ribbon. "Candy gave me this. She said I earned a blue ribbon today. The silly cowboys threw ropes at Pepsi cans. They called the hoops a Mexican sounding something."

"That's the Spanish word *lasso*," I told Pamina.

She said, "How'd you know? You're just a plain old city waitress." From the mouths of babes and drunks, it was true. I still had Codes to confront.

Pamina continued, "The big cowboy, Hudman, showed me how bull riders tie ropes. He said that's why he has cow puss on his hands. He had me feel his hand. It's rough and hard."

"Oh, calluses," I chuckled.

Pamina rattled without noticing. Madison passed us and I told Pamina at full volume, "I'm glad your day was fabulous." Madison glared at me. She heard my tone of self-importance. After I said this, I realized the Humility Code was going to be hard to master. Nevertheless, I was determined to conquer it. Pamina gave me a hug then motored toward the guest houses to find her family.

~ ~ ~

That evening was my night off. The weeks were passing quickly. There were no pranks from Caprice, at least, none toward me. I decided to take a luxurious aromatherapy shower and replace my nail polish. I chose Passion Flower Orange.

I wanted to read. So I made a cup of tea, painted my nails, and opened the book. Given the bat drama the previous night, I was short on sleep. I drifted off on page one. I woke to, the sound of Hudson's pebbles. Carefully, I peered out the window looking for bats. "Howdy, Annie."

"Hi," I said drowsily.

Hudson asked, "Did I wake yuh?"

"No. I mean, yes, you woke me."

"Yuh fell asleep with yore pulp novel on yore belly. I'm sorry, Darlin'. Go back to sleep."

I was stunned Hudson called me *Darling*. "Don't go. I need to ask something." I smiled sleepily, "How was your day?"

He chuckled softly, "Mighty good. Dandy Pam visited. Candy rode with her around the meadow. They trotted and loped. The gals showed off crupper tricks and we talked about rodeos. She's got a cute little laugh."

"What are crupper tricks?" I asked.

"Fancy riding on the hoss' hips," he replied.

"You gave her a great time." I said. Hudson didn't acknowledge my remark.

He said, "Trotter Blue says there's a special lady behind this plan." I smiled but didn't take ownership. I blew the Code many times between my braggadocio life in Los Angeles and my big mouth with Madison. If not for the Cowboy Code, I wouldn't know that humility was a peaceful, pleasant state. Hudson was right. People see the good you do.

I said to Hudson, "I understand from Pamina, a cowboy named *Hudman*, taught her how to tie a rope for bull riding." I winked at him. He gave a little smile and said nothing.

"Let's ride Monday," Hudson said. "Bring yore swimmin' suit. I got somewhere special to take yuh."

"Same time?" I inquired.

"Yeah." He leaned over and kissed my forehead, "Yuh got a beautiful heart, Annie. Sweet dreams."

"Good night, Hudman."

CHAPTER ELEVEN

COWBOY CAMPFIRE

Waiting for Monday, made Sunday seem like forever. Grace and I headed for the little white church as usual. I was learning more each Sunday about virtue and love. I also learned how to pray. I had tons of baggage to unload and one enchanted prayer request.

When we returned, the Coppers sat in my station. Mr. Copper thanked me profusely. Bobby talked about his newest super hero, Hudman and Pamina couldn't control her stream of exaltations regarding Candy and Old Faithful.

Lunch for the guests came and went. The wranglers sat at the eight top and I was their server. Not smiling at Hudson was difficult. We knew so much about each other. Pretending our friendship didn't exist was like stifling hiccups at a five star brunch with a harpist playing in the background.

Fortunately, Candy broke the invisible tension, "Good afternoon, Anna Lisa."

I looked like I saw a ghost, "Hhhi Candy. Pamina had a terrific day." Candy merely smiled.

They wolfed their food, stretched, and headed for the kitchen to pick-up supplies for the overnight horseback ride. They wouldn't be back until noon. I assumed Hudson forgot his guest camp-over commitment or worse yet, he forgot about me. It was a kick in the gut.

During dinner service Sam called me aside, "Anna Lisa it's not like you to mope. What's wrong?"

Looking up from the plated filets, I said, "Sorry. It's bad news. I'll try not to let it show." I faked a smile and turned to serve the guests.

The steaks had marinated for five hours in red wine, garlic, and cumin so an appetizing aroma filled the dining hall. A husband and wife were happily chatting when their spoiled brat rudely interrupted whining for steak sauce. Reminding myself of the Code, I smiled and said, "One day you'll be big and tall like your Daddy and your taste buds will be grown up. For now, I'll get steak sauce for you. Would you like ketchup too?"

"That'd be cool," he piped.

I headed to the kitchen and overheard Sam talking with someone. It sounded like Hudson so I stopped outside the swinging doors and listened. Sam asked the voice, "Do you like home-style pot roast?"

The voice replied, "It's my favorite, why yuh ask bean master?"

Sam continued, "What's your favorite pie?"

The voice replied, "It's good old U.S. of A. apple pie." There was more, but it was muffled. That nosy chef was testing how friendly Hudson and I were.

Sam said, "Relax, I'll get the message to her." My next order was up. Sam poked his head over the food ledge and saw me listening through the cracks of the swinging doors, "I have a message for you but you obviously heard."

"Tell him I'm busy, but ask him to wait. I have to question him before he leaves."

Sam said, "Leaves?"

I responded, "Ask him to wait, pleeease."

Sam smiled, "I know guys, Anna Lisa. If it involves a pretty girl, he'll wait."

I hurried the plates to the tables. Things wrapped up quickly. Dessert was S'mores at the campfire which helped guests depart quickly. The waitresses loved S'mores night, so they joined the guests around the campfire. I couldn't care less for milk chocolate served with a burnt marshmallow.

I opened the back kitchen door. Phantom was eating grass and Hudson stood on the porch, whittling. He looked up from his whittling. His eyes glowed in the light from the kitchen. If he wasn't so gorgeous, it would be easier to stay mad. "Hey Annie," he said without an element of apology in his tone.

I told him, "So our ride's off. I was looking forward to it." He asked me what happened. In an equally curt voice, I replied, "How are you getting back from the guest camp in time?"

Hudson said, "I ain't goin'."

"Really?" my reply was stupid. If Hudson said he wasn't going, he wasn't. "We're on then?" I asked in a softer tone.

He nodded, "Do yuh have plans this evenin'?"

I replied, "Sleep."

He inquired, "Would yuh like to join me at the campfire?"

I was surprised, "I thought wranglers never went to campfire night. Don't tell me you love S'mores."

He chuckled, "Naw. I hate them soft gooey eats. Do I look like a Girl Scout?"

"Not in the least," I said admiring him.

"Yuh noticed wranglers ain't goin' to no city–slicker sing along. Yure comin' to my campfire at the dice house. What do yuh say?"

"I'll go," I said coolly. It wasn't easy hearing him say *city-slickers* in that condescending way.

Hudson jumped on Phantom's bare back, "Annie, use that stump to haul yoreself up." Hudson directed Phantom closer. He didn't tug the reins. He didn't kick.

"How'd you get Phantom to line up with the stump?"

"It's lookin' where yuh want yore hoss and pressin' a little. Ain't magic."

I said, "It looks like magic."

He smiled, "Climb up here with yore magician." I stepped onto the stump, put my hands on Phantom's back and heaved myself up, swinging a leg over. Hudson called, "Yeeha." Phantom lurched into a canter. "Yuh best hold on little possum." I threw my arms around Hudson's waist to avoid sliding off Phantom's rump. I could feel the strength of Phantom's muscles under me. I nudged close to Hudson. We fell into a comfortable rhythmic lope.

Hudson's abdomen was incredibly firm. "Do you do crunches?" I asked.

"Do I what?" he said.

"Sit ups. Your abs are solid," I said seriously.

"Abs?" he said with a chuckle.

Thinking I needed to explain, "Abdominal muscles."

"Annie, I know what abs are. Comes from bein' a workin' man." Hudson slowed Phantom to a walk, but I didn't release my hold. He took his free hand and held it over mine. He struck my hand against his abs. "Solid has a rock," he said. I knew he was smiling.

He seemed to enjoy my company and I enjoyed his. Rationally, I understood our friendship, but it was emotionally painful. Hudson only brought me around when ranch hands weren't there. That night, their absence was convenient.

"Why aren't you on the camp over?" I inquired.

"I wanted to spend time with yuh," he said. I smiled. He added, "Besides, they got plenty of wranglers: Dash, Hoyle, Lacey, Candy, and Bev. It's an itty bitty group of guests."

"What about Skeebo?"

"Skeebo and I'll lead next time."

I dismounted landing square. This time, I anticipated a long drop. Hudson glided off and tethered Phantom to the post near the wrangler's bunk house. A light was on inside and I could see Skeebo talking to himself. "Skeebo's here?" I questioned.

"Yeah. Ain't he livin' here?"

I didn't answer. Skeebo's being there was a step in the right direction. At least one wrangler would know about me.

Light from the window revealed a stack of kindling, dry grass, and logs in a rock ring off the porch. Hudson knelt down, lighting the dry grass. His match lit the darkness. The fire caught quickly and cast a golden hue over him.

"Take a seat and get yoreself comfy," he said motioning toward the porch swing.

I sat down and Hudson asked if I'd like something to drink.

"Do you have mineral water?" I asked hopefully.

"Sorry, got Pepsi."

"No thanks. Plain water's fine."

He went into the bunk house. I saw him pull a glass off the shelf and wipe it with his shirt. He filled it with water and was heading back to me when a violet blue wind whipped hair in my face and slammed the swing against the wall. Lights in the bunk house went out. It was a dark night but an iridescent cloud floated overhead. Letters formed, *LONADIES*. The only light came from the strange cloud and the fire. Suddenly, the wind dowsed the fire and the cloud vanished. Everything was pitch black.

Jumping off the swing, I ran to the bunk house. The fierce wind held the door shut. I ran from the porch hoping to escape. The wind followed me into the meadow. I tripped on a log, fell to the ground and got a mouth full of dirt. I heard Hudson call, panicked, "Annie."

It took all my strength to stand. I opened my mouth calling for Hudson, but the wind muffled my voice. I pushed forward with no success so I turned and ran with the wind on my back. Then something grabbed me. Between the blinding air and the forceful hold, I was confronted with blurred violet blue wretchedness. I swung and kicked to free myself from the hold when Hudson's voice breached the uproar, "Easy, it's me." He picked me up and carried me into the bunk house. The door slammed behind us.

Hudson set me on a bottom bunk. I sat there shaking, crying. I sucked in dirt and coughed. Dirt mixed with my tears and crusted my mouth. He held me steady. The wind was howling, slamming the swing against loose wall boards. "What is it?" I demanded through sobs. "Tell me," I yelled forcefully.

Lighting a lantern, Skeebo ranted, "It gets angrier than a bull synched tight when she's around. Yuh believe me now Hudson?' It's gotta be that Cheyenne name."

Muddled, Hudson queried, "*Annie* is a Cheyenne name?"

Skeebo yelled, "Hudson it's her middle name, *Lona*."

Hudson said, "Who ever heard of a name like Lona?"

Skeebo explained the name translates to *beautiful*. Hudson said, "Well, her folks got her name right."

Frustrated, Skeebo shouted, "It hates the Cheyenne."

Hudson bellowed, "Skeebo I gotta get Annie out of here."

Skeebo said in a panic, "Yuh can't go now Hud. Didn't yuh see the cloud? LONA DIES. It's gonna kill her."

A dread surfaced in my stomach. I could feel blood flow from my head. I thrust my head between my knees but it didn't help. I fainted, falling to the floor.

I came to on a wrangler's bunk. The lights were on and the wind was quiet. Someone had taken off my boots. They wiped the dirt from my mouth and covered me with a quilt.

The quilt was handmade from faded scraps of material. The colors and patterns formed a beautiful design. Embroidery on the underside of a corner swatch read, *Made with Love for my Son, by Irie Rose Evermore.*

My eyes roamed the room. There was a table with a deck of cards. Wooden pegs on the walls held ropes, cowboy hats, and a gun in a leather holster. A rifle was propped by the door. Across the room, a tin coffee pot sat on a pot belly stove. Their bunk house was rickety like mine. The only difference was a kitchenette. *Kitchenette* wasn't quite the word for the rust encrusted stove, dirt caked sink, and old fashioned refrigerator with a latch handle.

Skeebo was pacing, muttering to himself quietly. His eyes caught mine. He said, "Trail Boss, she's awake."

Hudson took two strides and was at my side. "Aw, Sweet Thing, yuh had quite a scare. How yuh feelin'?"

"How do you think I feel?" I snapped. "I was flung like a tether ball, whipped by my hair, tripped in a hole, and nearly choked on dirt. I was almost killed and no one will explain why." He looked stunned by my sharpness. I took a long breath and composed myself, "I'm scared, Hudson."

He put his hand to my cheek, "I ain't blamin' yuh, Annie."

I challenged him about the guns and why they didn't use them. He curled his lip, "Ain't no way to booger it up with a gun, Annie."

Skeebo added, "If there was, we'd pull iron faster than hell could scorch a feather on a bird's a…"

Hudson snapped, "Watch yore tongue, Skeeb. We got a lady here."

I broke the tension between them when I asked, "Why do you have guns?"

He looked baffled and said, "Yure askin' about that black-eyed Susan?"

"I guess so," I said.

Pointing to the wall he said proudly, "This blue lightnin's mine and Skeebo brought his smoke pole."

I confronted him, "You're proud of owning guns?"

"Of course - we got plenty of ammo too. Ain't they teachin' yuh about no second amendment in California? Annie, it's about time I get yuh back to yore bunk house." He lifted me over his shoulder like a sack of potatoes and said, "Skeebo get the door. This Missy's goin' home." Hudson swatted me on the butt.

"What was that for?" I barked.

"I couldn't resist yore liberal bedonkeydonk."

I said, "My what?"

Hudson murmured, "Never mind."

Phantom was still tethered to the post. I pulled my leg over and leaned forward resting my head on Phantom's neck. I inhaled the musty smell of his mane. It was a comforting aroma. Hudson mounted behind me, grabbed the reins and moved Phantom to a slow walk.

At the bunk house, he slid off, helped me down, pushed my hair back, and gave me a kiss on my forehead. "Sleep well, Ms. Liberal Activist. We'll talk on the trail."

I went in the girls' bathroom and looked in the mirror. My face was clean, but my body was covered with dirt. I grabbed my caddy and entered the shower letting hot water flow over me like a relaxing therapy.

VIOLET RIBBONS

I crawled into bed, closed my eyes, and tried to quiet my mind. My thoughts wandered to the violet blue centers of the columbines Hudson put in my hair. I thought about our first ride with the sun on him, the sweetness of grapes, the cold water, and his grip on me. I drifted to sleep.

CHAPTER TWELVE

THE SWIMMING HOLE

I woke early, stiff, and aching. The others were sleeping. I slithered into my favorite bikini. It was pale green with cream colored hearts and petite ruffles on the top and bottom. I pulled on jeans, then, slipped on my Cache tee-shirt, socks, and boots. I stuffed a towel and tube of sun screen into my bag. My hair was knotted but I managed to assemble it into a braid. I brushed my teeth and shuffled out the door toward the dining hall.

Hudson was sitting on the rail of the veranda. Beside him, two saddled horses watched. He looked up from his whittling, "Mornin', Annie."

"Good morning. Mariah gave up on my grooming already?" I said jokingly.

"Naw, I don't want yuh around our doghouse. We're avoidin' trouble."

I felt relieved. "Have you been waiting long?" Hudson shook his head. "Can you give me a minute? I'll grab a croissant and some juice."

"Take yore time, Annie."

I asked if he'd like anything. He smiled, chuckled, and said, "From the mess hall? Naw."

I ate quickly and stuffed two carrots in my bag. As soon as I returned, Hudson was on Phantom. I mounted Mariah. There was something different about Mariah's saddle. It had a wide leather strap. "What's this?" I asked.

"It's a night latch," he replied.

"Do I tie my bag to it?" I asked.

"Hand yore bag over. I'll attach it to my tie strings. Yuh ready rider?" I nodded. He didn't explain the night latch. I decided to ask later.

Hudson took the trail that avoided the wrangler's bunk house. He didn't address the mysterious matter. It was early so I didn't mind.

He asked, "Want to get that hay burner trottin'?" I squeezed Mariah. Then Hudson transitioned to a canter. With a kiss, Mariah did likewise.

It was a beautiful morning. The aspen glow broke into sunshine. It was early enough to avoid overheating the horses and ourselves. "How far are we going?" I asked.

"Farther than a croissant will fuel yuh. I got fixins in the war sack." Hudson motioned to the bag strapped to Phantom's saddle. He continued, "Even got sparklin' mineral water."

I smiled, "You remembered. Thanks."

"Of course I remembered. Respectin' a woman's wishes is important business fer a cowboy. Most gals ain't worth yore time. They only want yuh because yuh ride the rodeo or wear a cowboy hat.

"Yure different, Annie. Yuh want to find out what makes me tick, my culture, my pa, my ma, why I own guns," he winked. "That apple pie had me grinnin' like a skunk eatin' cabbage in the moonlight. I'd nab a fancy water fer a gal that can bake like that any day." He added, "Besides, if all yore wantin' is expensive bubbly water yore an easy keeper. Pleasin' a lady is one of God's gifts."

I looked at him. Guys back home wouldn't mention *God's gifts* when they're hitting on a girl - talk about stalling a teenage boy's engine. Hudson was different, odd, but adorable.

We rode quietly through a meadow bursting with red and yellow flowers. Several deer grazed at the edge of the forest. Hudson whispered, "Look, Annie." A large buck with a huge rack placed himself between the herd and us. A fawn bounced joyfully between the deers' legs while they munched green plants. We continued down the trail around the mountain. Hudson pointed out the birds of prey including a bald eagle. Then he told me to look up. High in a pine was a collection of sticks. It was a nest six feet in diameter. He said, "Annie, we got penthouses too. Our's are made of sticks."

I smiled.

Soon, the coolness of the morning disappeared and the sun was blazing hot. I started to feel weak. Hudson read my body language and said, "Why ain't yuh wearin' a hat? It keeps the sun off and the heat down."

"I forgot my Dodgers cap in Dad's car." He brought Phantom next to Mariah, took off his hat, and put it on my head. I breathed in. His hat smelled like horses, sweat, and him. It was wonderful.

He asked, "That help?"

"Yes. Thanks," I stammered lost in the aroma.

We left the dirt road and entered a wooded forest. Hudson said, "The trail's overgrown. Folks ain't comin' here no more. It's thicker than a mule's tail. I should've put yuh in leggin's."

I asked about leggings and Hudson explained they're leather chaps which protect the rider's legs. "Watch yoreself on the branches, Annie. Don't want yuh to poke them beautiful eyes." We had to duck to avoid the overhang. The horses walked slowly as we moved branches aside. I was glad to have Hudson's hat which kept pine needles off my face.

Struggling with the thick brush, I asked, "Is the rest of the trail like this? How much farther? I hope it's just around the bend. Is it?"

"L.A. yure like a little jackaroo. *Are we there yet? How far we gotta go?* At least yuh ain't hollering that yuh gotta pee."

"Actually, I do need to urinate," I said.

"Urinate? Hah! Is that what yuh call it in the city?"

I retorted, "It's the medically correct term, Hudson."

"Maybe so, but it's gotta be a bear on a little kid. *Ma, I gotta urinate.* By the time the kid masters the word he'll have wet his britches. Why ain't yuh just callin' it pee?"

"Hudson, why are we talking about body excrements?"

He laughed again, "Body *excrements.*"

"Enough. If it pleases you, I'll say it your way. Hudson I need to *peeeee.*"

"Get off yore pony and find a bush."

I dismounted and headed for some well screened bushes. Returning he said, "My, oh my, city gal's turnin' country, peein' in the woods."

"I'll admit it's beautiful." At the country club the lady's restroom has marble floors, automatic faucets, lavender liquid soap, hand lotion, mouth wash, feminine products, and cloth towels. But it doesn't have aromatic pine trees, or pine cones, and needles that crunch under your feet.

"Listen Annie, do yuh hear it?"

I listened carefully. At first I only heard the leather of our saddles. Then I heard it. "A waterfall." Hudson smiled at my delight.

The brush opened lighting a grassy clearing in the middle of the thick forest revealing a waterfall. It was glorious. Not for its size, but for its serenity. It had carved a spherical deep blue pool. Mist hovered over the water. There was a flat, large boulder on the bank, perfect for basking in the sun. It was stunning.

We dismounted and let the horses sip water. Hudson untied hobbles from our saddles and set them. Handing Hudson his hat, I thought about shopping for a hat if I could get to town. It made sense if we were to ride all summer.

I pulled off my tee shirt. Hudson stood motionless, staring at me in my bikini top. "Aren't we swimming?" I asked.

"Yyyeah, we'll swim," he stuttered.

I pulled off my boots and tucked my socks in them. I shimmied out of my jeans, folded them and stacked them on top. I shook out my tee shirt to remove the pine needles and placed it on the pile of clothes.

Lathering my legs and arms with sunscreen, Hudson still stared. I teased, "Didn't your parents teach you it's not polite to stare?" He blushed and looked away.

I finished sun screening. "Hudson, please get my back."

"Yuh bet," he said. I handed him the sunscreen and pulled the braid off my back. He methodically applied the sun block. Starting at my shoulders, I could feel his rough, callused palms carefully spreading the lotion. He got to the small of my back and let his hand rest there while he asked, "How's that Annie?"

"That's nice. Here," I said holding my hand out for the tube of sunscreen, "I'll get your back."

He took off his boots, socks, jeans, and shirt. His shoulders were immense. They looked wider without a shirt. His chest was well defined. His abdomen was ripped. Michelangelo's David couldn't compete with Hudson's striking looks. I was relishing in the exquisiteness of his body when he said, "Ain't yore ma tell yuh it ain't right to stare?"

I laughed at his lively remark, "Touché." He took off his hat and placed his boots on the rim. "Hudson, that's weird. Why put your boots on your hat?" I said in a pompous tone.

"Annie, I ain't askin' yuh why yuh make a neat little stack of yore garments like we got snakes that'll sneak into your britches. We ain't got no snakes in these parts. Now, boots on a hat makes sense. It keeps it from blowin' away. Yuh learned today how important a hat is. I'm ready fer that sunblock."

Turning his back to me, I squeezed a good amount of lotion into my hands. I tucked the tube in the side of my bikini bottoms and rubbed my hands together until the lotion was warm. I started at his shoulders. They were too bulked to resist massaging. Then, I went up his neck pressing my thumbs along the vertebrate. I continued down his spine with my thumbs. He let out a moan, "Annie, where'd yuh learn to do that?" He exhaled peacefully.

"Lance taught me."

I felt his muscles stiffen, "Whose Lance? Yore boyfriend?"

"Boyfriend?" I chuckled, "He's my masseuse."

"Yuh let a man touch yuh like this?" Hudson demanded.

"Of course. He's a professional masseuse. Haven't you had a professional massage?"

"Naw. Even if Lance is professional, the guy's gotta go wild when he touches yuh. Men see yuh and blow their bullets."

I enjoyed the interesting compliment. I would have lingered in it, but his tension rose. I said, "Hudson, Lance thinks his partner Lester is beautiful. Relax. Let me get rid of your lumbar tightness."

Hudson whispered, "How can a gal with dainty fingers, massage like this? Yuh better take good care of yore pinkies because I'm gonna need bushels of sunscreen this summer."

I reached down for more sunscreen with one hand and asked, "Is this too hard?"

He let out a satisfied moan. I smiled and explained the key to massage is to add lotion keeping one hand on the body. This is relaxation message, not Rolfing. Hudson said, "Rolfing? Sounds like a cowboy hittin' the bars too hard."

I laughed, "Rolfing is deep massage that evokes emotions. Some people cry."

"Yuh gotta have a roll of money big enough to choke a cow if yuh gonna pay someone to make yuh cry. Yuh metropolitan folks are crazy as popcorn on a hot skillet."

I massaged his large muscles rigorously. He moaned again. "Do you still think this city girl is crazy like popcorn?" I asked jaggedly.

"Yeah, I do. Popcorn with melted warm butter and salt, served in a crystal bucket."

Hudson knew how to charm me. I thought if I were to fall in love, I'd choose this man.

"Ready fer a swim?" Hudson said lifting me in his arms as he jumped. We plunged into the water.

I screamed, "You're an animal. It's freezing." He was smiling from ear to year, laughing his fabulous laugh. I looked at him, admiring his smile. "How deep is it?"

"Ain't got a clue because yuh can't touch the bottom."

I sank under the water to test how far I could go. I shot up quickly shivering, "It's cold down there."

"Like I said, yuh can't touch the bottom. Yure quiverin', Annie." He held open his arms and I swam to him. The only warmth came from his skin. "Float on yore back. The sun'll warm yore front and keep yore toes out of the cold." We floated holding hands.

Hudson pulled me toward the waterfall. We went under surfacing on the backside.

The sun's light formed diamonds in the falling water. I pressed against the rocks and found firm footing. Hudson placed his hands by my shoulders. We held each other's eyes. I was captured by his gaze. This private nook was the perfect place for a first kiss. I waited motionless. He didn't move.

"Scuttle up the ledge to that grotto," he said. I carefully climbed the rocks while Hudson followed. We sat there in silence.

Since we didn't talk and he wasn't going to kiss me, I thought we should address the mysterious events, "Hudson, you promised to explain things to me."

He said, "Let's go in the sun. We'll chat while we eat."

Carefully crawling down the ledge, Hudson held out his hands to steady me. The water seemed colder now. We swam under the waterfall and climbed the bank.

He pulled two towels from the saddlebags. Hudson opened one and draped it around my shoulders. Even though it was bristly, his gesture was nice. The towel had warmed in the leather saddle bag. "Thanks," I said.

He wrapped his around his waist. Hudson sat next to me handing over a vegetarian sandwich with avocado, water cress, and provolone. He put a roast beef sandwich and chips in the grass in front of him.

"Here's yore classy water," he mentioned opening it as he handed it to me. I was thirsty so I took several sips.

"Would you like some?" I said holding the bottle to him.

"Thanks, I got Pepsi," he replied pointing to the lunch bag.

We ate and talked between bites. "It ain't easy to explain. Skeebo hears things. Some think if yuh bored a hole in Skeebo's head yuh wouldn't find enough brains to grease a skillet, but it ain't like that. Each of us knows there's somethin' mysterious goin' on. Skeebo's the only one crazy enough to talk about it. He ain't no closer to understandin' nothin' today than two years ago. One thing we know, whenever yure around it goes screechin' like a plucked jaybird. Ain't never throwin' a ruckus like this before. Always comes with a violet blue color. That's it, Annie. Ain't much of a story."

I was agitated, "This is all you have to tell me?"

Hudson said, "Pretty much, although Skeebo says Native Americans got loads of spiritual places in these parts. He thinks it's related. Why yuh got a Cheyenne girl's name?"

"I don't know. Before Skeebo told me, I had no clue where the name came from. How long has this been happening?" I asked.

Hudson responded, "Trotter Blue recons about twenty years. Ever since he built that shack we live in. It might be a rare case of St. Elmo's Fire."

I asked, "What in the world's St. Elmo's Fire?"

Hudson explained, "Some call it Fox Fire. They say it's a type of electricity. It's kinda blue and jumps from cattle horn to cattle horn. Sometimes from rider to rider. I ain't seen it but a couple times. Makes yuh jump like a speckled-legged frog. Yuh wanna run but yore stuck standin' still."

"What's behind the St. Elmo name?" I asked.

Hudson said, "St. Elmo's the patron saint of sailors. Shipmates see it too. I imagine sailors are as lonely as cowboys. We're like teetotalers in a saloon."

Mesmerized by this phenomenon, I asked, "Really? If I ask a sailor or another cowboy, would he know about this?"

"Annie, yuh questionin' what I tell yuh?"

I said, "It's farfetched, Hudson. I've never heard of this."

"Yuh ain't believin' me," Hudson said roughly. "Annie, I ain't the kind of guy to tell big fish stories."

I touched the back of his hand, "You're right, I'm sorry." We finished our lunch. I spread my towel. Hudson spread his next to mine. I closed my eyes thinking about his description of St. Elmo's fire, the happenings at the ranch, and my dreams. The warm sun and lunch relaxed me. Before I could muster the energy to comprehend the mystery, I drifted to sleep.

The dreams started. This time they were pleasant. I dreamt Hudson was stroking my arm lightly with the tip of his finger. He stroked the back of my hands and each of my fingers. Then his fingertip traversed up my wrist to the inside of my elbow. The dream continued. He caressed my forehead, down the bridge of my nose and my cheeks. Then down my neck and circled the small hollow between my collar bones. His finger lightly stroked my stomach tracing my navel. I felt his touch down the length of my legs, to my toes, and up again to my waist. He traced me with the most delicate of touches. The dream was vivid. I relaxed deeper.

As though through a fog, I heard Hudson say, "Annie, yuh awake?"

Finally, I slowly and drearily woke. Hudson was propped on one elbow. I stretched, "Was I asleep for long?"

"Naw," he smiled.

"I slept like the dead," I said.

He flinched, "Don't say that."

"Hudson, it's just an expression."

"I don't like it none. Better to say yuh slept as peaceful as a babe in its ma's arms or try as restful as a lizard on a hot rock."

"A peaceful baby has a better image. But a lizard? I don't know about that one. Either way, it was the loveliest sleep I've had in a long time. Did I snore?"

He smiled, but shook his head, "Yuh were smilin' in yore sleep, Annie. What'd yuh dream of? It must've been good, given how yuh was grinnin'."

"I could hear water, birds, and the soft breeze blowing through the trees. I felt a finger on my skin. It was lovely."

He smiled and moved off of his elbow onto his back. We relaxed in the sun.

Once our swim suits were dry, we pulled on our jeans, shirts, socks, and boots. While I was dressing, Hudson joked, "And what yuh call them toes, Egyptian, Swedish? It's gotta be Brazilian."

"They're Passion Flower Orange. Do you like the color?"

"Hot dang, they're nice lookin' toes. Bright and sassy like yore attitude." He gave me a coy smile and twirled a blade of grass between his teeth.

The horses led us through the overgrown brush as the sun revealed the lateness of the afternoon. Clouds blew in and it started to rain. Hudson and I stopped under the canopy of a large pine tree. This was another perfect setting for that first kiss. Hudson took my hand and held it in his. We waited for the storm to pass and continued on the trail. When we hit the dirt road we loped to make up time. We meandered up the trail to the meadow. Hudson said, "Race yuh."

"Right," I said with annoyance.

"Come on L.A. I'll give yuh a hundred yard lead." Although I highly doubted my ability to win, I was up for a competitive challenge. I mimicked Hudson's *Yeeha* and kicked Mariah.

She galloped up the hill. Phantom was breathing hard to catch her lead. He passed Mariah. We entered the meadow laughing and hollering. I don't think I ever hollered in my life. In Bel Air the voices are subdued and boring. Hudson was hooting and cantering around the meadow. Suddenly, he stood up on Phantom and circled around me. "Cowboy, you're crazier than I imagined."

"Oh yeah? What did yuh imagine? A red neck, mush pup that falls fer apple pie, swimmin' holes, and passion flower toes?"

"I imagined you possibly had a wild side. I just never expected this."

"Think again, little Annie. Imagine some more because I've got lots of wild sides and wild surprises."

He landed back in his saddle and came close to me and said softly in his gorgeous deep voice, "I had the best day with yuh."

I smiled, "Likewise."

We dismounted and he looked toward the bunk house. I followed his gaze, afraid St. Elmo's fire was acting up. Dash, Lacey, Hoyle, and Bev were standing on the porch staring at us with their arms crossed and their mouths half open.

"Oops," I said quietly. "I'm sorry Hudson."

"No need to be sorry. It's me who's off my mental reservation." He whispered, "Yuh can't be sorry fer being good company and lovely to look at."

"I better head back now," I said.

"Yeah, I'll take care of the ponies," he said.

I marched past the wranglers. Their eyes followed me. I held my gaze firm and didn't acknowledge them.

CHAPTER THIRTEEN

OBEY LAWS

Back in the girls' bunk house I saw Madison. "Anna Lisa, what's on your head?" she snapped.

"My head?" I knew I gave Hudson back his hat. "I don't know."

She pulled my braid to the front of my face and continued, "You don't know the Colorado State flower?" There were Columbines tucked into my braid. I thought to myself, he's full of surprises. I wanted to smile, but Madison was standing in front of me with my braid in her fist. "Those are protected flowers. You can't go picking them and adorning yourself like you're some goddess of nature who's above the law. You can be fined or jailed. Anna Lisa you're starting to act as ditzy as Shelly."

"Madison, calm down. Between Caprice's pranks and your insults, I wonder why I bother to be your friend," I retorted.

Madison replied, "I'm trying to keep you out of trouble. And Caprice is merely having fun."

"Hi girls," Caprice called. She was standing in the doorway filming us.

"Great Caprice. If you put this on the net and get me arrested, I'll have my attorneys judge your wages for the rest of your life," I said firmly.

Caprice said, "Relax, Anna Lisa. Where's your sense of humor?"

"Sense of humor? Yeah right," I murmured as I stomped toward my room and grabbed my soaps. In the steamy shower, I thought about the tensions between the waitresses and me, and the strains between Hudson and the wranglers. The planets were definitely aligned in Ares. Hudson and I only found peace when we were alone.

That night pebbles clinked against my window. I wasn't expecting Hudson, given our wonderful day, plus being busted by the wranglers. "Evenin', She-Who-Sleeps-Smilin'," he called softly.

"Hudson, why'd you put contraband in my hair?" I quirped.

His smile faded, "Annie, that ain't what yure supposed to ask. What's buggin' yuh?"

"The Columbines are protected flowers," I snapped.

He shrugged. Shocked by his nonchalant response, I said in a snarly tone, "I thought the Cowboy Code required you to obey laws."

"Yuh bet."

"Then why'd you pick the Columbines?" I grilled.

He said casually, "The law says yuh ain't to pick more than twenty-five a day. That's twenty-four hours."

"I know a day is twenty-four hours," I sassed.

"Ain't trustin' me yet are yuh? Yuh better because I don't want nobody questionin' my character. How am I supposed to feel with yuh judgin' me? Annie, yure a fine gal, but somethin's missin'."

A wave of panic rose in me. I was afraid Hudson was going to pull away.

I was trying to think of something to say when he broke the silence, "Yuh gotta know I'm a simple guy. Yuh can trust me."

With shame, I replied, "I was listening to friends. Trusting's hard for me, but I'll try."

"Ain't no sense tryin', Annie. Yuh gotta do it. I know deep down yure mild and sugarcoated. Eventually, yuh'll come to trustin' me. Now where's that question I expect from my Sweet Annie?"

Filled with relief, I asked, "How was your day?"

He said, "It was a humdinger of a day. There's this crazy city gal who's as pretty as a little red wagon. She rides, swims, and races like one of us."

Smiling, I interrupted, "How'd it go with the wranglers?"

"Yuh were perfect," he replied. "Yuh stomped off mad enough to eat the Devil with his horns on. Ain't even say *good day*. They thought I was irritatin' yuh somethin' awful. Yuh had them convinced I made yuh madder than a bobcat in water."

I asked, "If I'd been outgoing, would they've thought I was your friend?"

"More than that, they'd think yuh was my gal," he replied.

I sighed, "Your culture is difficult to figure out."

"Naw, ours is simple. It's yore's that's confusin'. Good night, Annie." He passed his fingertip from my shoulder to the inside of my elbow and down my forearm. Hudson noticed my tremor and kissed the underside of my wrist. Then he kissed my forehead. "Sweet dreams."

"Good night, Hudson. Thanks for the wonderful day."

~ ~ ~

The following day Hudson didn't show for lunch. I asked Skeebo if Hudson's order was to-go. To my amazement, Skeebo replied in several sentences, "Naw. He's gone to town. Said he's in need of shearin'."

"Shearing?" I responded. "What's that?"

"He's visitin' the barbershop." I faked indifference, but was disappointed. I would miss those blond curls.

Madison looked when she heard the chatter. She glared at me. Candy noticed and scowled at Madison who turned away swiftly.

That night I went to the guests' campfire with Grace. I don't know why I didn't hang out with her more. She was the kindest of the girls.

While Pip tuned her guitar I asked Grace about her car. "I forget to start it regularly. Dad says if I don't, the battery will die."

"Let's go shopping in the city Monday. That'll take care of the battery for a while," I said.

Grace replied. "That sounds like fun." I told her I wanted to buy a western hat. Grace said she'd look for a gold nugget pendant. She saw pretty ones on the way in. I reminded her to talk with Trotter Blue about getting Monday off.

CHAPTER FOURTEEN

CHIEF SPIRIT WARRIOR

Pip wrapped-up her singing and a tall, husky, Native American man centered himself in front of the fire. He had long, sleek hair and deep set eyes. His skin was dark with slight folds revealing his years. He said, "I am Chief Cheyevo, one of the elders of the Hopi tribe. I come to tell you about Native American history."

Skeebo was in the crowd, slanting forward, and listening intently to Chief Cheveyo. I was glad to see Skeebo. I needed to talk with him and planned on cornering him after the chief's presentation.

Chief Cheyevo spoke in a powerful, captivating voice, "My name means Chief Spirit Warrior. You'll find Native American names come from nature. For my people, nature includes animals, plants, rocks, rivers, and mountains. It also includes spirits, stars, planets, and the sun."

Chief Spirit Warrior continued, "My people are not of this land. I know of this region because I'm not only a tribal elder, I'm a professor of Native American Studies at the University. It's important we don't master merely our own tribal heritage. We must understand the interrelationships of all tribes and the plight, suffering, and cultural richness of each. Where you're sitting was once occupied by Utes. The tribe was forced to move to the Southwest. For Utes, this has been a long suffering."

Chief Cheyevo continued, "Pokoh was the old man who created our world. According to legend, Pokoh formed each tribe out of soil. He traveled to different areas and created more tribes. Pokoh wanted each tribe to reside on the soil from which it was created. They were also to die on that same soil. It was a deep sadness for the tribes to move. Its profundity is not something the White Man, who buys and sells land, can comprehend. Pokoh was giving and brought many gifts to each region. Utes were mountain gatherers and hunters. They hunted elk and deer. All parts of the sacrificed animal were utilized. What was not eaten immediately was desiccated. It was saved for times the spirit was angry and did not provide for an easy hunt. Bones were formed into knives and needles for sewing. Hides were treated and used for breechcloths, leggings, and shirts for men. For women, deer hides were used for dresses. The dresses were usually fringed as were the shirts of warriors. Their clothes were decorated with teeth and beads. Tribal members told rich and mystical legends. There are still many storytellers today who keep the legends alive."

Chief Spirit Warrior proceeded to tell a legend of Totem Gifts from the Northwest. After the chief ended his legend, Skeebo went to him. The two were engaged in intense conversation and they glanced at me.

Grace said, "Anna Lisa, it's getting late and I still need to shower."

My eyes were fixed on Skeebo, "Go ahead. I need to talk with someone." Grace didn't ask who. She respected my privacy.

When Skeebo broke away from the chief, I called, "Skeebo, may I talk with you?"

"Sure, Anna Lisa. Wasn't that fascinatin'?" he asked.

"Yes, did it provide you with additional insight?"

"Naw, it's the same old details – Utes – Animals - Mystics. Like the other ranch hands yuh probably think I'm so narrow-minded I could look through a keyhole with both eyes at the same time."

"No. I think you're sensitive to the mystical realm. Maybe you have a sixth sense or can channel. Plus you've done research. Please tell me what you know. Has this mystery thing ever communicated with you directly?"

He sat on a log and motioned for me to have a seat. I sat quietly and waited for him to talk. Dad said after you ask something you wait silently. The first person to talk loses. Dad was referring to signing contracts, but I apply it to all situations.

Finally, Skeebo spoke, "I sometimes hear a gal's voice. Now, yuh think I'm off my rocker fer sure."

"Skeebo, I don't think that. Continue."

"This gal's voice ain't sayin' nothin' I can understand, but she cries."

"You mean cry, like crying tears?" I asked.

He nodded, "Most times they fall on Hudson and wake him. He swears it's a prank; someone spittin' on him."

"That's disgusting," I said.

He laughed, "That's the difference between guys and gals."

I returned to a serious tone, "Skeebo, do you think it might be a ghost? Perhaps an unhappy female ghost?"

"I reckon so. Yure the first to believe me."

Ignoring his remark, I asked, "Why does she get angry with me?"

He said he didn't know and that it doesn't mind Lacey, Bev, and Candy. I looked surprised and said, "The only difference between the female wranglers and me is they're cowgirls and I'm not."

Skeebo said, "That ain't the only difference. One, yuh got a Cheyenne middle name. Two, they ain't the apple of Hudson's eye."

"What?" I looked at him with doubt.

Skeebo continued, "He's smitten on yuh. I'm certain Anna Lisa because Hudson and I go way back. I got his crazy ways down pat. His ma practically adopted me because my folks kicked me out."

"They kicked you out of your home?" I asked with surprise.

"Yep. After my accident, they disowned me. Told me to pack my bags and scat. Pa said *Yuh ain't never comin' back, son.* They'd been savin' fer my schooling since I was a little tike. I'm the first one in my family settin' to get a college degree. I snuck off and registered fer Junior Rodeo. They found out and were madder than a bull behind the gate. They thought patchin' me up wasn't worth it. Didn't think I could learn nothin' after that bull kicked me in the noggin. Hudson, seein' I was in trouble, brought me to his ma's house. The fine woman tended my injury, saw to it that I got therapy, gave me a roof over my head, and fed me well."

I interrupted, "Pot roast and apple pie?"

"How'd yuh know?" he said with surprise.

"All the years I know Hudson, he ain't never been a talker. Since he locked eyes with yuh, he ain't shut up. He's talkin' and whistlin'. Last night he was singin' in the shower and he ain't got a voice like a gut-gored buffalo either. Sings pretty good. The night he invited yuh to his campfire, he was preparin' all day: swept the porch, set the fire, tightened the rickety old swing, and washed the window. Then, he showered, put on some manly smellin' stuff, and clean clothes."

I asked, "You've never seen him like this?"

"No, Miss. He's a changed man. Ain't never been in love. I was thinkin' he ain't never gonna settle. Thought he'd be a bachelor forever. It ain't like the gals don't hit on him. He's tall, blond, and has all his front teeth. But none of them ever tickled his fancy. He ain't never been fond of no one until yuh come along." Skeebo continued, "I tell yuh, Anna Lisa, Hudson's got giddies."

I was shocked, "Giddies? What's that, some type of S.T.D?"

Skeebo looked perplexed "S.T.D? Yuh mean S.T.P. - like fer yore engine?"

I said, "S.T.D, *Sexually Transmitted Disease*."

Skeebo's face tensed, "Giddies ain't no disease. It's that funny feelin' yuh get in yore stomach when yure in love, or nervous on a ragin' bull. It makes yuh feel good and woozy at the same time."

"You mean butterflies, Skeebo."

"Butterflies, moths, whatever. Anna Lisa, Hudson's my best friend, and I owe my life to him and his ma. God bless her soul above.

"If yure messin' with him, yuh better knock it off. If yure fallin' in love, that's a different story. But, if yuh ain't serious and yuh want to be Miss Free Wheelin' L.A, takin' on a cowboy romance - don't. I ain't gonna sit here and watch yuh drag him through hell. Yuh might as well get out now."

I was stunned by his seriousness and replied, "Skeebo, I'll never drag him through anything but paradise. He's lucky to have a friend like you."

He stood up and stretched. I said, "Good night, Skeebo."

He said slowly, "Let me see yuh to the girl's bunk house safely."

These cowboys never ceased to amaze me with their gentlemanly ways.

CHAPTER FIFTEEN

50X

The next morning after breakfast, Grace ran to me, "Anna Lisa, there's another package on your bunk." She smiled, "It's tied with a violet ribbon."

I ran to the bunk house with her. Sliding the gift card from under the ribbon, I carefully opened it. It read, *Will you ride with me in the hot sun? Hudson.*

I untied the ribbon, set it aside, and opened the box. It was impossible not to squeal. There among the violet tissue was a stunning cowboy hat. It was the color of desert mist with a three piece buckle band. It didn't have the gems of Lacey's hat. But, it was tastefully adorned with shining silver pieces. Grace asked to see it and looked inside the rim.

"Anna Lisa, this is 50X."

I responded flatly, "So?"

"It's 50X beaver fur. It's a quality hat. He must have spent another week's paycheck on you."

"Shhh, Grace, here they come." I gently, but quickly, put the hat upside down in the tissue and shoved the box under the bottom bunk. I put the card under my tea mug and tied the ribbon around my head like a headband. The other girls passed and went to their rooms talking and laughing.

Grace asked me, "Do you still want to go shopping Monday?"

"Because I have a hat, doesn't mean we can't shop. Girl time sounds perfect. It'll be fun." Grace smiled. Grace was unpretentious and sweet. I asked her, "What're your parents like?"

"I don't know. I don't remember them. We were in a car accident, when I was a baby. I was the only one who survived."

"I'm so sorry," I said softly.

"My adoptive parents had a difficult time getting me. They wanted me after the accident, but my mother's sister, Millicent Sharp, stopped it. Millicent took me in. She wasn't married and was working sixty hours a week as Vice President of International Marketing for Bexton & Kemp. After a few months, and several changes of nannies, Aunt Millicent realized that a child needs a father and a mother. She contacted my papa and mama. They were ready to go to China for a private adoption. They had plane tickets for Hong Kong but they heard I was available so they dropped their plans, and started the adoption process again. They say the best day of their lives was when Millicent relinquished guardianship to them."

"Wow," I said.

Grace said, "My adoptive mother is kind. Since I called my birth mother *Mommy*, she insists on being called *Mama*. She says in case I have a flashback or a dream, she wants me to identify and savor that relationship as separate from our mother daughter relationship. Isn't that thoughtful?"

I smiled, "It's selfless."

"I'm in high school, so Mama has gone back to Special Ed teaching. I remember her reading to me and playing games. She would pack a picnic basket and we would eat in the fort built by Papa. Papa works a lot but he always finds time to go camping on weekends. They taught me to appreciate the beauty of the wild. That's why I chose this summer job. I'm saving for college."

I nodded to let her know I followed her story. "Grace, you have a great attitude. You're the sweetest girl I know, yet your early childhood was tragic."

"Anna Lisa, do you realize how blessed I am? I have parents who want me. They begged my aunt. Not a day goes by without thinking about what they've given me. Imagine how life would've been if I were shifted between nannies and daycare."

~ ~ ~

That evening Hudson tossed pebbles at my window, "Evenin' Annie. What yuh drinkin' at night?"

I said lifting my cup, "Do you want a sip? It's herbal tea - organic chamomile."

"Naw. Sounds too Californian fer me," he puffed up his chest.

I laughed. "Thank you, for my hat. You shouldn't have, Hudson."

"Don't yuh like it?" he asked.

"I love it," I said.

"Then I should've," he said smiling.

"Your haircut looks nice, but I'll miss your curls."

"I knew yuh'd say somethin' girly. Trotter Blue was complainin' about my long hair. Said I was lookin' like a hippie. Told me to get cropped. Annie, he's the boss. I gotta respect the man," he said firmly.

Hudson was cowboy, neat, clean, and respecting older people.

"How was your day?" I asked.

He said, "It was fine. I cashed in at the pool hall last night. Do yuh shoot pool, Annie?"

"Me, shoot pool?" I said with an air of snobbery. "No."

Hudson said smiling, "I'll take yuh to Rory's Pool Hall. How about Friday night?"

My first date was to a pool hall. I heard Mother's voice in my head protesting. Hudson broke my thoughts, "Before then, come by and I'll steam yore hat."

"Steam my hat?" I questioned bewildered.

He said, "Yuh ain't gonna wear it without a good shapin'."

"I didn't know it needed to be shaped, Hudson. It looks beautiful the way it is."

"I imagine on yore pretty little head it does," he said looking at me. "I'll customize her wee a bit." Hudson leaned over, kissed my forehead and said, "Sweet dreams, Annie."

"Good night, Hudson. Thank you again."

"The pleasure's mine. Good night, Annie."

~ ~ ~

After dinner service, I pulled my hat from under the bed and walked to the wranglers' bunk house. The fearful memory of the last visit was fresh in my mind and my adrenal glands were on high alert. I walked fast through the dark forest. Before I realized, I was running. My feet slipped in the damp underbrush. A branch caught my shirt and I screamed. I ripped free lunging further into the darkness. The porch was there before I knew it and I thudded into the closed bunk house door. I heard Lacey scream and Hoyle cock the shotgun.

Dash called, "Who's there?"

"It's me," I panted. "Anna Lisa."

Dash opened the door, blocking my entry, "What in heaven's name are yuh doin' here? Yuh sounded like a herd of longhorn yearlin's in a brandin' pen." He was gruff and unwelcoming.

Hudson shoved Dash aside and said, "She's here fer me."

"What yuh doin' with a glitzy city-slicker like that?" Dash said in a disapproving tone.

Hudson ignored Dash. He motioned to me, "Come in. I'll set the kettle."

Dash said to Hudson, "What yuh gonna do? Serve her tea and crumpets. That's what she's used to." Dash held his Pepsi can and stuck his pinky out like he was holding a fancy tea cup. Then he belched.

Skeebo was the next to speak, "Shut up, Dash."

"Whoa, Skeebo. Yuh friendly with city folk?" Dash chided.

"She's Hudson's guest. Show respect," Skeebo snapped. That quieted Dash and he plunked down on his bunk.

Hudson noticed my panting and saw my torn shirt. He asked quietly, "Did somethin' frighten yuh in the woods?"

"It's dark and I was afraid," I said.

Hoyle said sarcastically. "Of course it's dark. We ain't got no city lights. And there ain't no fancy motion detectors. Were yuh expectin' a big Hollywood sign and street lights to show yuh the way?"

Hudson addressed Hoyle sternly, "Yuh know better than to be inhospitable. Where're yore manners?" Hoyle recoiled at the rebuking.

The kettle whistled and Hudson said, "Let me have yore hat."

I handed it to him and Candy said, "There's a nice one." She peered in the rim, "50X. Wahoo. Must've cost a fortune."

I didn't know what to say. I looked at Hudson. He said, "Fer a city gal, she's got good taste in country."

He put the hat on my head and studied it carefully. He observed me from the front, back, and both sides. Taking the hat off, he held it over the steam. He shaped it nimbly bending it this way and that. He worked as deftly and seriously as the sculptors in Laguna Beach. He let it cool, holding it carefully in his big hands. Then he handed it to me. I put it on my head, from front to back, the way I'd seen Hudson put on his.

He asked, "How does she look?"

Skeebo said some form of onomatopoeia that sounded like approval.

Candy said, "Wow, Anna Lisa, if I ain't knowin' better, and if yuh kept yore mouth shut, I'd take yuh fer a country dandy."

"Thanks, Candy," I said, blushing.

Bev and Lacey turned and walked toward the girls' quarters. Naturally, Dash and Hoyle ignored the affair. Pointing at a door, Hudson said, "Take a look at yoreself in the looking glass in our bath house." I passed through the door. There was a mirror. Moreover, there was a bathtub. Without expressing envy I turned to the mirror. The hat was stunning. Hudson tipped the four inch brim to frame my face in front and back. He put a bigger dip in the cattleman crown. He molded two side brims so they would keep the sun off my face and neck while maintaining their shape. He walked up behind me and said to my reflection in the mirror, "Yuh like it?"

"It's fabulous. Thank you."

"Yure welcome. Now, let's get yuh home before these disrespectin' outlaws give yuh more beef. Dash, Candy, mind escortin' Annie back to her dice house?"

Dash sulked while Candy said in good spirits, "Will do, Boss Man." Dash tried to open the door but it was jammed. Hudson thought he was pulling a prank so he pushed on it.

Pointing at the window, Skeebo stuttered, "Lllook." Violet blue mist rose up the window. Soon the entire bunkhouse was enshrouded in eerie color. The lights went out and I felt a tug on me. The door suddenly opened and I was outside.

I heard Hudson call, "Annie. Where's Annie?"

Dash said, "She's out."

Hudson ran for the door. Anticipating it was still jammed, he pushed it harder than necessary. It slammed against the outside wall echoing across the meadow.

The wind pushed me away from the bunk house. "Hudson," I cried.

The wind pushed me up the face of a bluff. Hudson grabbed my foot but my sneaker slipped off and he lost his grip. I was shoved higher up the steep ledge along a mountain sheep trail. I was high on the bluff and the mist was thick. I couldn't see the meadow below. Leaning into the face of the mountain wall, the gale force wind battered me. I felt around for a hand hold. Finally, I found an outcrop. I gripped it and pushed my body flat against the rock wall. The wind howled at my futile effort, blowing until I lost my balance and tipped off the ledge.

Time stopped. The fall slowed my mind. Illuminated with precision were his mountain blue eyes, our horses, the mountain vistas, aspen glow, sunsets, rain storms, rivers, and the swimming hole. My heart raced with the memory of Hudson's nightly talks, his kisses on my forehead, and his morals. What I achieved this summer passed before me: freedom, friends, values, and God. The aroma of pines overpowered my senses. In the arms of Mother Nature I would die, yet I prayed God would save me, avoiding Dad's devastation, and Hudson's shattered heart.

My thoughts stopped. The fall ended. I was alive. I landed on something soft, meaty, warm, and human. Hudson and Skeebo had stood next to each other breaking my fall. The wind screamed and spun away from the pile of arms, legs, and torsos which were commingled. A flash of bright violet blue lit the sky and disappeared.

Hudson moaned. I knocked the wind out of Skeebo. He was silent. I could see in their faces, my landing hurt.

"Annie, yuh o.k?" Hudson moaned.

"Yes," I said.

"Thank you Lord Jesus, Annie's alive," Hudson said lifting his head then letting it fall. I clambered off my human lifesavers and held out my hands to help them. Neither one took a hand. They stayed put, moaning.

I knelt down and stroked their sweaty foreheads, "You saved my life." They groaned again. "What can I get for you? Ice? Help?"

"Nothin', Annie. Keep strokin' my forehead," Hudson said letting out a deep sigh.

The other wranglers ran across the meadow to the base of the cliff. Hudson said in a weak voice, "Dash, Candy, get Annie out of here."

I protested, "No, I can't leave you like this."

Hudson moaned, "Hoyle will see to us. Go now."

Dash grabbed my arm forcefully and whipped me around, "Ain't yuh caused enough trouble?"

My voice shook, "I didn't want anyone to get hurt. If I knew, I wouldn't have come."

Hudson found his voice and said, "Dash, leave her be, or tomorrow, I'll kick yuh so far it'll take a blood-hound six weeks to find yore stink."

As we went up the path, I overheard Candy whisper to Dash, "Anna Lisa's heart's in the right place. She ain't able to help it none she's city farmed." Dash didn't say anything. At my bunk house, Candy looked me in the eyes, hugged me, and said, "Take good care of yoreself, Honey."

The following day passed without circumstance. Wranglers came for lunch. Hudson and Skeebo moved slowly. Hudson had a black and blue egg on his head. Swollen veins pulsed through it. Skeebo had a black eye.

I didn't want the waitresses to overhear, so I bent between the two of them and whispered, "You two look horrible. I'm evermore grateful than you could imagine." The other wranglers stirred at my whispered concern. Hudson smiled then winced from the pain.

That night Hudson came to visit. I had the window open, so he wouldn't have to find pebbles and fling them. "Evenin', Annie. Brought yore hat. Found it lyin' in the meadow. Still got her shape. Here's yore shoe."

"Thank you. How do you feel?"

"Got bruises. Nothin' new," Hudson said. "Got through the day. Could've used one of yore massages, maybe a Rolf. I ain't goin' nowhere near Lance, but yore fingers would do me good," he said forcing a smile.

"I made fenugreek tea. It's good for bruising. Take a sip."

He took a sip and spit it out, "Yuh drink this stuff? It's nastier than mule's pee. What'd yuh call it?"

"Mule urine?" I answered. He laughed. I insisted he drink the tea, "It will help."

He held the cup to his mouth and chugged, "Yuck. Annie, do I still got a date with my medicine woman tomorrow?" I looked at him. "Why yuh questionin' me with yore eyes?"

"Are you sure you're up for this?" I asked. "I'd understand if you want a rain check."

"I'm sure." He leaned over and kissed my forehead. His lips were still warm and moist from the tea. "Good night, Annie. Dream sweetly."

"Good night, Hudson."

CHAPTER SIXTEEN

RORY'S POOL HALL

Friday evening finally arrived. The day seemed long and trivial. Sam insisted I taste his meager attempt at corn dogs.

"Sam they're good. They're below your epicurean expertise, but I'm learning posh isn't always best. Children will dig them. Parents will be glad their children are happy while they enjoy your Vichyssoise and Beef Wellington. May I have another one before I head out?"

"Where're you going, my dear?" Sam handed me another corn dog and I took a bite.

"I'm going for a drive in a big green truck."

Sam looked sternly at me and said, "Is the cowboy stirring the beehive? Hasn't he knocked it over yet?"

I shushed him, "Don't tell anyone Sam. It's our official first date."

Sam asked, "Where's he taking you?"

"He's taking me to Rory's," I said smiling.

"The pool hall?" Sam asked with surprise. "Things are different here than in New York."

"They're different from Bel Air too. Isn't it wonderful?" I said.

"Anna Lisa, you certainly have joie de vivre," Sam chuckled.

I heard the kitchen door open. Hudson stuck his head in, "Annie, I thought I'd find yuh near the grub. Look, the egg on my head's gone."

I smiled, "I'm glad. Would you like a corn dog?"

"Yeah," he took a bite. With his mouth full he commented, "Sam, ain't bad fer a bright light chef."

Sam laughed, "Have fun tonight. I need to tend to the pâté."

Hudson walked me to his truck, a 1974 Ford 250. It was green, faded, and rusty with bull horns on the hood. He opened the passenger door. I had to grab part of the cab to hoist myself onto the bench seat. The old saggy seat was covered with a beautiful Ute Indian blanket. Dog tags dangled from the rear view mirror.

"She ain't much to look at. But she runs. She's got a built 394 and she'll pull any horse trailer up these hills doin' 70 mph. She's four gears plus a granny." Hudson revved the engine, pulled out of the parking lot, and said, "If yure too warm, yuh can open them wind wings. What do yuh drive, Annie?"

"I don't have a car. Dad said he would surprise me one day. But I got a baby blue moped for my birthday with a matching helmet. It gets me to the beach."

Hudson tuned the radio, "Yuh like country?"

I said, "Country's cool." Reception was lousy in the mountains. Music rasped in and out until we reached the foothills.

We pulled into a crowded parking lot behind a simple, square building. An orange neon sign read *Open*. Painted in black against pale blue stucco was *Rory's Pool Hall - Yawl Welcome Day or Night*.

Hudson killed the engine. It sputtered. He jumped out and went to open my door. The step was high. Hudson held out his hand, palm up. I placed my hand in his and he helped me down. He slammed the door and kept hold of my hand. Hudson led me to the backdoor and we entered the hall. It was dimly lit. Cigarette smoke hung in the still air. Fake Tiffany lamps shined on tables illuminating kelly green felt and brightly colored balls. There were a few cowgirls but it was mostly guys. Hudson led me through the tables and I noticed men pausing from their games to look at us.

Someone called out, "Hud, bringin' yore gal so yuh ain't bettin' tonight?"

Hudson said, "Got that right."

He steered me to a bar where a man with thick, red hair greeted him jovially, "Hudson, back already? Who's this pretty little thing?"

Hudson, turned to me and said, "Annie, this is Rory, he owns the joint and likely rigs the bets. Rory, this is Anna Lisa."

My cotillion training kicked in and I said, "I'm pleased to meet you."

Rory dramatized, "The pleasure's all mine, Miss Anna Lisa." He pulled out a frosty Pepsi can handing it to Hudson. Hudson leaned over the bar toward Rory and quietly asked, "Got any sparkling mineral water?"

Rory replied, "Got soda water, that do?"

Hudson looked at me for an answer, "Yes, please. That'll be fine."

Rory feigned a pompous tone and asked, "Would you like a twist?"

"That'd be lovely," I replied. Catching myself talking in my dialect, I adjusted and said, "Thanks." I excused myself and went to the lady's restroom.

I headed back to Hudson and Rory. They were watching a table absentmindedly engrossed in conversation. I overheard Rory say, "Hudson, yore gal's a beauty. Where'd yuh find her?"

"She's workin' at Trotter Blue's."

"This ain't like yuh. Yuh never brought a filly here. She's gotta be special."

"Never met no one like Annie. She's got me purrin' like a blind cat in a creamery."

Rory said "Leave it to a female to put flavor in yore grub. Met her pa?"

"Hell, no. We ain't at that stage. It's gonna take time because I ain't about to frighten her off. She's too good of a catch to pull in the line fast and wildly."

Rory said, "Sure got city written all over her. She's got a nice hat and boots, but that's about it."

Hudson said, "I gave her those as gifts. I ain't able to tell her to wear a long sleeve snap button shirt. Buyin' one of them would be too personal. Don't yuh think?"

Rory said, "Yeah. Besides, she looks damn good in them jeans and tank top."

Hudson grabbed Rory's collar. "Whoa, Hudson. Easy. I ain't realized Cupid's got yuh so bad. Yure plumb struck in love." Rory became serious, "Hudson, let me warn yuh, because yure more than a customer, yure a friend. I've seen city gals messin' with cowboys' hearts. They get back to the metropolis and drop the cowboys like fleas. Fer these girls it's adventure with a dude. They ain't got no stickin' power like our gals. I'm warnin' yuh, don't get entangled..."

I didn't want Hudson to listen to more of Rory's advice so I cleared my throat, "Ahem." They turned around and looked at me. Rory's translucent Scottish skin hid nothing. He turned red, matching his hair.

Hudson asked, "Ready fer a lesson?"

Rory said, "Take table seven. We got nearly a full house this evenin'."

Hudson paid Rory. He put his arm around me and escorted me to the table. Hudson said, "The balls are in number order and yuh line them right there." As he placed the balls in the wooden triangular frame he said, "Annie grab a cue stick."

"Q stick?" I asked confused.

"There on the wall," Hudson said pointing.

I asked, "It's Q, like Q in the alphabet? Like Q-tips?

"Yeah. Whatever," Hudson said.

"What does it stand for?" I asked.

"Geez, Annie, I don't know. Nobody asks what it stands fer. There yuh go again, like a kid. *What's it stand fer? Why they call it that? Are we there yet?* And don't tell me yuh gotta *urinate.*" He poked my ribs and laughed. I had to laugh with him.

It was a treat to be away from where we worked, ate, and slept. Hudson tossed a cube of something toward me. I caught it. He said, "Yuh gotta chalk the cue stick tip and no I ain't got no clue where chalk comes from, only know it helps yore stick from sliding off the ball."

He noticed I was clueless. Grabbing my hand, he covered it with his and rubbed the tip of the stick. He stood close showing me how to wrap my index finger around the cue stick and slide it. "That's right. Shoot the white ball to break the others."

I hit the white ball. It tapped the others. Hudson lined them up again. Huddling up behind me, he took hold of my hands and shoved the stick fast. The balls shot all over. A striped ball rolled into a pocket. "They ain't goin' to crack, so there's no need to be dainty."

We were having a wonderful time, laughing, and smiling. Hudson deliberately knocked my stripes into pockets so the competition would be closer. Each time, he winked and said, "Aw, nuts."

Hudson kept an eye on three biker dudes waiting for a table. They were dressed in dark colors. The biggest one wore a leather jacket, black jeans, and black boots. Another wore a black long sleeve shirt and leather vest. The third one wore a black tank top with a chain hanging from his belt. He had tattoos on his arms. They looked mean and stared at us.

It was my turn to try for the eight ball. Hudson intentionally scratched a couple of times. I hit the ball so hard it flew off the table and rolled under the chair of the biggest biker.

"Excuse me, my eight ball rolled under your chair. May I retrieve it?" I asked.

He sneered and eyed his buddies the moment he heard my city accent, "Not at all. Help yoreself." He stayed seated.

"It'd be easier if you stood up," I suggested.

"I ain't standin', Missy. Reach under there and grab the ball."

I hesitated, bent down, and reached between his boots to get my ball. When I had the ball in my hand, he clamped his legs and pinned my arm. I squirmed and tried to free my arm, but he pressed his boots tighter. He and his buddies started laughing. He bellowed, "Hey Itchy, look I got a hot city gal with a ball in her hand."

Itchy said, "Snake, you lucky turd."

Snake said, "Trout, do you think she'll grab my ass next?" They laughed their obnoxious, boisterous laugh.

Then Trout said, "Ooowee, yore mama. I'm next."

Hudson saw me squirming to free myself and heard the vile things coming out of their mouths. He was enraged, "Let the lady go."

Snake stood up, knocking me to the side. At least my arm was free. I stood next to Hudson coddling my arm. Snake growled, "Hey, aren't yuh the pile of crap who stole my money?"

Hudson said curtly, "I ain't stealin' nothin'. Yore luck ran muddy and yuh kept puttin' spot cash into circulation."

Snake replied, "Bullshit. Yuh steal money and dare show yore face around here. Got yoreself a fancy city gal because yure wallowin' in the mother load that belongs to me."

Rory walked over. Snake sat down and I thought this altercation had come to an end. Hudson was taller and more muscular than Snake. Perhaps Snake found some sense in his brain to back off. All of a sudden, Snake grabbed me and held me on his knee. "If yuh hadn't stole what belongs to me this creature wouldn't be frolicking, laughing, and rubbing up on yuh like yure her stud."

I instinctually raised my knee and came down with the heel of my boot on his toes. I broke loose. Snake wailed. Hudson wound up his fist, swinging the minute Snake bent down to grab his throbbing foot. It missed Snake but landed squarely on Itchy's jaw.

Rory said, "Hudson, take Anna Lisa and get out of here, fast."

Hudson, grabbed my hand and we practically flew out the back door. We ran to his truck. He opened the driver's door, heaved me up, revved the engine, and sped off. I slid to my seatbelt and buckled it. He was driving like a mad man.

I stammered, "Will they come after us?"

"Naw, Rory'll hold them fer awhile. We'll be dustin' them. Don't worry." He looked at me. "Annie, yure shakin'," he said. "Yuh ain't use to this are yuh?"

I snapped, "Is this normal for you guys?"

He said "It ain't normal. But a good lookin' urban gal like yoreself in a pool hall is as unexpected as a fifth ace in a poker deck."

I flared, "You think being abused by those biker dudes was my fault?"

He said, "Ain't yore fault, Annie. It's mine."

"You stirred up a beehive by taking me on a date. Great," I said astringently.

Hudson said softly, "Yure worth it, Annie. I'm sorry yuh had to go through that. How's the arm. Yure coddlin' it."

I said honestly, "It's sore."

Hudson motioned for me to slide next to him. I undid my seatbelt and slid over buckling the center belt around me. He slowed the truck. I felt at ease not racing through mountain roads. Then he took one hand off the wheel and put his arm around my shoulders. I let myself lean into his body. It had been a nerve-racking incident. His protective touch eased the stress in my mind and body. I drifted off to sleep.

We pulled into the parking lot at Trotter Blue's ranch. Hudson killed the engine. He rubbed my cheek with the back of his fingers, "Yuh fell asleep."

"I'm sorry. I'm not used to drama," I explained.

He opened the truck door and grabbed my hands helping me hop out behind him. We walked toward the girl's bunk house. Hudson slowed our pace and said, "Annie, it was a nice evenin' until those cusses messed things worse than a hen in a pile of cow dung."

"It was. You're a good teacher and playing pool is more fun than I expected."

He said calmly, "I'm glad. It was my pleasure to teach yuh. And, by the way, it's called *shootin'* pool." He bent over. I was expecting a kiss on our first date. But, he didn't. Instead he kissed my forehead, "Sweet dreams, Annie."

"Good night, Hudson."

In the girl's bunk house, I saw Madison, "Hi Madison, what's up?"

Madison looked at me and demanded, "Anna Lisa, where have you been?"

"Why? Did I miss something exciting?" I asked.

Pointing at my shirt, she said "Look at you?" I looked down at my shirt. It was covered with blue chalk.

I replied, "I was shooting pool. Guess I was sloppy with the chalk."

She was surprised. Madison said awkwardly, "You play pool?"

I took the opportunity to correct her, "Yes. Madison, it's called *shooting* pool. Why do you ask?"

"It's un-Bel Air." Madison piped.

I said, "You're right," and walked away. The best way to deal with Madison was to admit she was right. I was tired of her arguments. Moreover, I hated her judgmental attitude.

Grace was in our room. "Hi Anna Lisa, did you have a good time?" she leaned forward, anticipating romantic scoop.

"I loved playing, I mean, shooting pool."

Grace asked, "Is that where he took you? How cute. How creative. Guess what, Anna Lisa, I have bad news. I can't go shopping Monday. Trotter Blue has important guests coming, a big wig father and son. I wonder if it's a senator or maybe the governor of California. He wants things to run smoothly."

"That's too bad. I thought of something else I want to buy," I said.

Grace asked, "What's that?"

"You know those shirts with long sleeves and snap buttons?" Grace nodded. "We'll have to go another time."

"Anna Lisa, why not take my car and go? It'll be good for the battery. I have a G.P.S. in the glove compartment. You won't get lost."

"Thanks Grace." I added, "I'll miss your company. I'll take good care of your car."

Grace said, "I'll wait to buy that gold nugget."

~ ~ ~

The next day I avoided Madison and Caprice and spent my time with Grace and Shelly. We went for a hike to the river. We sat with our feet in the water and talked about college plans.

Grace was applying to St. John's College in Santa Fe, New Mexico. She had also visited a couple of state universities in California. Grace was an avid reader and excellent writer. She was looking for a good liberal arts school.

Shelly planned to go to cosmetology school in Florida, especially since she met her new squeeze. She said, "Scotty's at the University of Miami, Medical School. I have to be near him."

I said snickering, "Perfect weather for swimsuit attire." I imagined her flaunting along the boardwalk of South Beach.

College talk reminded me I was sitting for the S.A.T. in October. I had forgotten about school.

I decided, I would take the S.A.T. review book out of my suitcase and work through a few pages each day.

After a shower, I made tea, grabbed a pencil, the review book, and crawled into bed. It was lumpy. I was leery about what I would find. Slowly lifting the mattress I found a half dozen pool balls on the springs, all solids. At first, I thought Hudson was playing a prank on me, but that wasn't like him. It had to be Madison in cahoots with Caprice. Madison knew I was shooting pool.

I worked on seven pages of the review book. When everyone was asleep, I snuck to Madison's room and placed the balls where she would jump from her bunk in the morning. I went to my room and tucked into bed.

CHAPTER SEVENTEEN

SHOPPING

Pebbles pinged on my window. I slid it open.

"Evenin', Annie."

"Hello, Hudson. How was your day?"

"Dash, Hoyle, Candy, and Lacey come back from Cheyenne Frontier Days. Dash took top twenty. Candy got a buckle in barrels, and Lacey passed her Miss Rodeo tittle to a new dandy. Hoyle's team was first to saddle the wild hosses. He's got a good technique bitin' the hoss' ear."

"Did you say *biting the horse's ear*?" I asked in surprise.

Hudson smiled at my ignorance, "Honey, how else yuh gonna cinch and mount a wild animal without it throwin' yuh to the funeral parlor?"

"Hudson, why didn't you go with them?" I asked.

"'Another time. I'm attendin' to more important things," he said with a wink.

"I thought it was your passion. I won't keep you from what you love."

Hudson said cocking his head, "Yuh ain't keepin' me from what I love. I got no desire to head out now." I looked disappointed. "Don't fret, Annie. There's gonna be heaps of rodeos. There's a P.B.R. I got my eyes set on come December."

"What's a P.B.R?" I asked.

"It's a bulls only rodeo," he said smiling. "What do yuh want to do tomorrow?"

"Grace can't go shopping, but she's loaning her car to me. She has a G.P.S. so I'll find my way around," I said lightly.

"I don't want yuh wanderin' alone, Annie."

I was taken aback by his control, "I'm a big girl, Hudson. I'm going."

"I'm comin' with yuh," he asserted.

"You like shopping?" I questioned.

Hudson flashed his coy little smile, "I've done pretty good so far ain't I?"

"Yes, you have. You probably went in bought the item and came straight out. I'm not shopping like a guy - hunter style. I plan to mosey along, take my time. Look at everything, and I mean everything. Then I'll try things on and try more things on. Then I'll try the first thing on again to compare it with the other things. I'm a gatherer. I don't want to feel rushed because you're rolling your eyes and checking your watch."

"Yuh think I'd do that?" he asked.

"I know you'd do that. You're a guy,"

Hudson sulked slightly, "Will yuh show me what yure tryin' on?"

"I'd love to have your opinion," I replied.

"I give yuh my word. I won't do no eyeball rollin' unless yuh look so good my eyes can't bear it. I won't wear no watch. Can I come?"

I smiled, "Ok, but if I hear you huff in boredom, I'll leave you at the curb."

"I promise. I won't be huffin' none. Sweet dreams, Annie," he whispered and kissed my forehead.

~ ~ ~

I woke to a loud thump and heard Madison wail. Others in the dorm rushed to help her. I ignored the incident, dressed, brushed my teeth, put on mascara, lip gloss, and headed for breakfast.

Grace entered the dining hall, "Hi Anna Lisa, did you see what happened to Madison?"

"I heard it. She'll have a good bruise," I said snickering. Grace looked at me shrewdly.

She handed her keys to me. The silver keychain had a cross, an anchor, and a heart. Imprinted in it were the words *Faith, Hope, & Love* - perfect for Grace.

I walked to the parking lot. Leaning against Grace's bright yellow bug, was Hudson. He'd lowered the top. "Mornin', Annie. Yure lookin' mighty fine."

"Good morning, Hudson. You're serious about joining me. Do you want to drive?"

Hudson replied, "I can't, Annie. It's Grace's car and she's expectin' yuh to drive. Yuh ain't gonna break her trust."

I looked at him, "You decide everything with cowboy panache."

He smiled.

We left the dirt road and hit the highway. My hat flew off. Before I could move, Hudson nabbed it. He put it on my head and cinched the cord under my chin. Shocked, I asked, "How'd you do that? You got to my hat before I could and it's on my head. Do you read minds or foretell the future?"

"Naw, I think it comes from bull ridin'. Imagine yure sittin' on a two thousand pound steer loaded to the muzzle with rage. The second it moves, yuh better brace yoreself. Yuh read the beast's body and react fast or it'll throw yore head against the rail while yure still in the well. If yuh ain't anticipatin' the shute openin', yuh'll get thrown further than a Death Valley buzzard can smell a dry canteen. It'll kick yuh in the head and yuh'll end up like Skeebo half departed and hearin' voices."

"Does Skeebo ride anymore?" I questioned.

"Yeah. Once yuh got rodeo in yore blood yuh can't stop. Yuh want the challenge and pain. Yure addicted to the blood, grime, and dust. The way yuh tie the rope and where yuh set yore spurs dwell in yore brain. If the crowd roars, yuh got an eight second ride. It's like nothin' else. There's a heap more to bein' a rider than sittin' and lettin' yore spurs fly." He kept talking about rodeo explaining the details with intense passion. It was his love. It was his life.

Finally, the G.P.S. interrupted, *turn left in point five miles.*

I told Hudson, "You're amazing."

He smiled. I could see he was proud. I thought this was a simple life. Much to my surprise it was full of principles, power, and rodeo.

Hudson broke my thoughts, "Light's green." I followed the G.P.S. to the mall and parked.

"Are you sure you're o.k. shopping?" I asked.

"Trust me. I'm here ain't I?" We walked to the entrance of Neiman Marcus. Like a perfect gentleman, he opened the door.

"Thank you."

"My pleasure."

I wondered if it would be his pleasure after four hours of power shopping. I stopped at the perfume counter. He read the names: *Wicked, Pagoda, Pearl, Neon, Lust, Lilacs, Dawn, Silvia, Chase, Fidelity,* and *Truthful Musk.* Hudson said, "Try Truthful Musk." The clerk sprayed the card stock. "Why's she sprayin' the paper? It's gonna smell different on yore skin mixin' with yore sweet aroma."

I laughed, "Bull rider *and* perfume expert. You're better at this shopping thing than my girlfriends."

"I told yuh I'd behave," he said taking the shapely bottle and spraying Truthful Musk on the inside of my arm. I rubbed my arms together to warm the perfume and held my arm out to Hudson.

He took a long whiff and said, "This is the right one."

"I'll take it," I whipped out my credit card. Hudson offered to carry my package.

"I could use some moisturizer." We found the counter. "I'll take a jar of day cream with S.P.F. 15." The sales clerk handed a tiny four ounce jar to me. It cost seventy-six dollars.

"Annie, what yuh put on yore face, platinum?" I smiled at his comment and waved my card in front of his face. He carried this package too.

We walked the mall, in and out of stores, and none of them had cowboy shirts. Hudson must have read my concern, "Annie, what else yuh lookin' fer?"

I looked him in the eyes, "A long sleeve, snap button shirt."

He blushed slightly, "Yuh heard me and Rory talkin'."

I smirked, "Every word."

"Annie, yuh ain't only sassy, yure feisty, and determined. Most gals hear someone tellin' their buddy to dump the cosmopolitan chick, she'll hit the road. Not Annie. Yuh dig in. Gonna get country. Gonna get more country than country. I gotta handle yuh like a loaded gun."

We went back to the car and pulled out of the parking garage. He said, "I know where yuh'll find that snap button shirt." The light turned green, "Turn here. There's the shop, *P.J. Bull's*. Pure, authentic country wear. Are yuh hungry, Annie?"

I nodded.

"Let's get some barbeque before we head to P.J.'s."

Hudson told me to park anywhere. Grace's car was perfect for the city. It fit everywhere. Hudson took my hand. His was warm and firm. I looked at him and he gave me a smile. We tucked into a little hole in the wall restaurant.

Hudson said, "This here's the best barbeque in the State."

The little wooden sign read *Brendory's Smokehouse – Lip Puckerin' B.B.Q.* Hudson brought me to a window table for two.

"I'll be right back." He returned with a basket of chicken covered in a rich, burgundy sauce. The smell was sweet and pungent. I hadn't realized how hungry I was. My stomach rumbled. Hudson, looked at me. He went back for two plates and another basket. That basket held cornbread, a jar of honey, and little squares of butter pressed between cardstock and paper.

"Annie, I don't think they got mineralized water here, but they got sweet ice tea."

"Ice tea's cool." We slurped tea and stuffed tender chicken into our mouths. I buttered my cornbread and attempted to open the jar of honey. Hudson took it from my hands and opened it. He dipped his finger in the honey and held it in front of my lips. I opened my mouth and licked his finger. A chill rushed down my spine. He noticed and smiled.

P.J. Bull's was around the corner. Hudson held open a rickety door and I stepped inside onto the wooden plank floor. The store was fabulous. Its walls were decorated with framed, autographed pictures of rodeo riders and dandies.

I picked out three snap button shirts. One was white with violet and blue flowers on the yoke. It had silver snaps. Another was covered with red roses on the yokes and had faux ruby snaps. The last one was black with gold snaps. I tried them on.

Hudson approved, "Which one yuh gonna buy?"

"All three," I said heading for the cash register.

He said, "Annie, are yuh checkin' the tags?" I shook my head. He said, "That's a pretty penny yure holdin'."

"You like them, don't you?"

"I do. I could sit here all day and watch yuh come out of that changin' hall."

I spotted a dress. It was gathered over the shoulders into delicate straps. The skirt was layers of chiffon - kind of like Marilyn Monroe's dress in *Some Like It Hot*. But this one was black. "Wait, I have to try this on."

He plopped back in his chair. It fit like it was adjusted by my tailor. I stepped out cautiously. "Where yuh gonna wear that?"

"That bad, huh?"

"It's more like, that good," Hudson said smiling.

Returning to the dressing room, I spotted a pair of bling denim shorts. I grabbed my size and tried them. "Annie, are yuh tryin' to drive all the dudes mad or just me?"

I said, "This means you like the shorts, right?" Hudson nodded. He was patient and flattering.

I changed into my clothes and when I came out Hudson wasn't in the chair. I found him in the men's department. He meandered among the shirts. He held one up, looked at the tag on the sleeve and started to put it back.

"Try it on," I said. "Come on Hudson, try it on. I'll wait."

He said, "Did yuh see the price?"

I pleaded, "Please try it on for fun. Try it on for me."

He sluggishly agreed. He walked out of the dressing room in the blue shirt. I gawked. He looked like Atlas. At least the way I imagine Atlas to look. The mountain sky blue shirt matched his eyes. The snaps were mother of pearl with specks of electric blue, bronze, and gray. "What do yuh think?" he asked.

I stumbled on the words, "You're gorgeous."

He smiled, which added to his fabulous appearance. Exiting the fitting room he hung the shirt on the return rack. I went over and grabbed it. I ran to the checkout with my three shirts, dress, shorts, and his shirt.

He caught up with me, "Annie, I ain't..."

I shushed him, "It's my gift to you." I pulled out my credit card ready for the transaction. He was protesting. I said under my breath, "Hudson, you promised to behave. Please accept my gift."

Hudson said, "Roxanne, don't ring up that shirt."

Pointing her finger at Hudson, Roxanne said, "Sonny, if the lady's givin' yuh a gift, yuh better appreciate her gesture and generosity. After all, she'll enjoy the way yuh look. Yuh ain't the only one gettin' pleasure from that shirt." Roxanne winked at me.

I wondered how Hudson knew her name. "Excuse me," I asked, "Do you sell boots and hats?"

"Yes, Miss, the finest," she glanced at Hudson. They shared a telling look.

He didn't hold my hand as we walked to the car. True to his nature, he carried the packages. We got in and started to drive. Shops were closing. I said, "I didn't have time to find a gold nugget for Grace. It would've been a nice way to thank her for loaning her car."

Hudson replied, "It ain't that yuh didn't have time. Yuh didn't make it a priority."

Ouch, that stung. He was right.

I pulled over and grabbed the G.P.S. I typed *Jewelers*. Hudson said, "There's one around the corner." I sped around the block, parked, and ran to the door. It was open. The shop keeper said, "Howdy, Hudson. What can I do fer yuh, today?"

I whispered to Hudson, "How do all the clerks in this city know you?" He grinned.

"Little Lady's lookin' fer...," I cut him off because in the case was a lovely gold nugget held in a bezel for a neck chain.

"I'll take that one."

Hudson nudged me, "Ain't yuh gonna ask what it costs?"

"Does it matter? Grace loaned her car to me and because of it I had a wonderful day with you. That's priceless."

The jeweler boxed the nugget and I presented my credit card.

We stopped to fill Grace's car with gas. He wouldn't let me touch the pump. He insisted on washing the windows alone.

On the morning drive Hudson was full of rodeo tales and explanations. Returning to the ranch, he didn't talk. I reminded myself guys need space, but this didn't quell any worries. Silence wasn't his modus operendi with me.

We turned off the highway onto the dirt road leading to the dude ranch. The sun was setting. It coated the horizon with orange and red hues which glowed on wild flowers, aspens, and Hudson's skin. I parked the car and said, "What a spectacular sunset. Come with me to my meditation place. It's a boulder I hike to in the morning before sunrise. The aspen glow is priceless there." He got out of Grace's bug and followed silently. I said, "Climb with me."

"This is where yuh come to pray, Annie?"

"Do you like it?" I asked.

He nodded, "A sight like this is why we're here."

I grabbed his hand, pulled it across my shoulders, and leaned into him. He didn't object, but he was rigid and unemotional. We watched the sun fade into its nest of gold, and I said directly, "Hudson, what's on your mind? Was there something I said, or did in the city?"

Reluctantly, he said, "Annie, I'm concerned." He looked down, like he was ashamed of revealing his emotions. I moved in front of him, holding his hands in mine. It was the same way Dad use to hold my hands when he wanted to know what was bothering me.

He looked into space, "Today I realized me and yuh are different folk." I thought to myself, this took him awhile to figure out. I didn't say anything and listened. "It's a bigger problem than I like to admit. Don't get me wrong, we're havin' a good time, and I want to spend my days with yuh."

I prompted, "What's the problem? I dragged you shopping, but…"

He cut me off, "It ain't that. I worry I ain't gonna keep up with yore expectations." He continued, "Yure from money and yuh got class. Yuh waved that platinum credit card around, buyin' this, and buyin' that like it was nothin'. Annie, I ain't got that kind of money. I ain't never gonna give yuh what yure used to, unless I take title in the P.R.A."

I asked, "What's that?"

"The Professional Rodeo Association. I couldn't please yuh if I were in the top ten," he looked at me. I saw frustration in his face. I also saw sadness.

I looked into his eyes, "Hudson, I'm not looking for money. I'll admit, what I spent today on my parent's credit card won't even be a blip on their statement. But I don't need that. I only want to make enough money to live comfortably, not ostentatiously. You've shown me places and things I never knew. Look at the values you taught me. I'm a richer person now. Money can come and go, but character is permanent. And talk about pleasing me, your charm, beautiful eyes, and outrageous body are more than I could dream of. Don't let my family's money scare you off."

He chuckled and said, "Outrageous body? Annie, I ain't deservin' yuh."

I said, "You're wrong. I don't deserve you. Can you be happy with the time we have together now?"

"Yeah. We got today. It's a blessin'," he said.

We jumped off the boulder and he hugged me. I was hoping for that first kiss, but it didn't happen.

We walked to Grace's car, grabbed the packages, and locked it. At the top of the hill, Hudson stopped and took off his hat. I thought he saw a mountain lion or a violet blue figure. I followed his eyes. He was looking at the flag being lowered for the evening. He didn't walk again until it was taken off the pole, folded, and placed in the shed.

"You're so cowboy," I said playing with him.

He smiled broadly with his robust, glorious laugh ringing through the clear evening air. We passed the veranda where Trotter Blue was sitting. He saw us smiling, laughing, and joking. He also saw Hudson's arm around my shoulders. This didn't faze Hudson. He said, "'Evenin' Trotter. How goes it?"

"Mighty fine, Hudson. I can see all's good with yuh," Trotter Blue gave that mischievous smile guys share when one of them is with a girl. Some things are not different between country and city.

Farther down the path we passed Shelly, Madison, and Caprice. The girls gawked. I thought, they won't let this pass without bombarding me with commentary.

I looked through the bags and found his shirt. "Annie, thanks fer my gift."

I replied, "It was my pleasure. Thanks for coming along, and lunch."

He mimicked my city accent, "It was my pleasure." I poked him laughing. He pushed my hat back and kissed my forehead. "Sweet dreams, Annie." He bent over and whispered, "I'll be thinkin' about what yuh said back there."

I whispered, "How do you feel about it?"

Hudson said, "Like I found a little bit of heaven in you."

I smiled, "Good night, Hudson."

I went in the girl's bunk house and found Grace. She said, "I see you took your human G.P.S. to the city."

"Hudson's a good device," I said laughing. "You have the coolest car, Grace. It was great for city driving." I volunteered, "I'm the only one who drove."

She smiled.

"We picked this up for you," I said holding out the golden nugget.

She threw her arms around me, "Anna Lisa, it's perfect. Thank you. How much do I owe?"

"Nothing. It's my gift," I sat down and told her about the mall, our lunch, and P.J. Bulls.

CHAPTER EIGHTEEN

PAXTON

In the morning I put on my snap button shirt with the violet and blue flowers. Madison approached me, "Go ahead Madison, let me hear it. But, no matter how much reproaching you do, it won't change a thing."

Madison said, "I want to tell you, I understand."

"You who give me flack about my ignorance and contact with wranglers *understands?*"

"Yes me. Brainy, me. Let's hike after lunch and I'll explain," Madison said.

I couldn't wait to hear what she had to say. After we bussed the lunch tables, I directed Shelly and Caprice to take care of the wranglers.

Madison and I grabbed our canteens and headed for the trail south of the ranch. "Anna Lisa, I realize I've been a jerk. I was trying to protect you."

"Protect me? From what?" I questioned.

Madison replied unemotionally, "Dating a cowboy."

"Hudson and I are close. I guess you could call shooting pool a date. Why the lectures and jibes?" I asked.

Madison held her head down and said, "Last year, I fell in love with a wrangler.

"Anna Lisa, it was a heart wrenching mistake. There was this hunk of a wrangler, Paxton. I went on a trail ride with guests and he led the group. There was something appealing about him. I knew it was impossible for a city girl to break into the wrangler click so I used my intelligence. These guys value work and they can use a little cash. I asked Paxton to give me horseback riding lessons and I would pay him. Twice a week between lunch and dinner, he gave me lessons in the meadow. Paxton also gave me lessons on my day off. There went my college savings. We were becoming a couple. Trotter Blue learned about it and summoned me to his office. He said I needed to break it off with Paxton or he'd send me home."

I interjected, "Trotter Blue said that?"

"It gets better. He told me I didn't have the temperament to handle a cowboy. He said I was an *intellectual academic* and should focus on Ivy League guys. I was livid. This old man wasn't going to tell me who I should and shouldn't fall in love with."

I interrupted, "I thought Trotter Blue would understand humans can't turn on and off emotional pull."

Madison continued, "I became careful about seeing Paxton. Then it all came to a head. Paxton invited me dancing in town. We were having a good time. I went to the restroom and returned. I couldn't find him. I looked in the booths. In the last one, he was necking with a cowgirl. I was mad. I pulled her off him and confronted them. The sleaze said, *Why if it ain't a ragin' city gal? Look Pax she's so mad she could swallow a horned toad backwards.* I was about to punch her jaw and silence her sassy drawl but Paxton jumped between us.

"He headed out the back door with her in tow. I ran after them. She sarcastically grinned and waived as they drove off. There I was in town. No Paxton and no way to get back to the ranch. I called Trotter Blue and explained I was stranded. When he came to get me, Trotter Blue told me Paxton was married. His wife was living in the foothills with their twin baby girls. He said he couldn't fire that *Hell Rouser*, although he wanted to time and again. He sent Paxton's paychecks directly to the wife, so she and the babies were taken care of. Trotter Blue didn't fire me, but he said, *I think yuh learned yore lesson the rough way. Next time, listen to this old timer or yuh'll be sent to yore home ranch.* Anna Lisa, I don't know if Trotter Blue warned you about hanging with a wrangler. You might get yourself sent home."

I said, "I'll find out soon because Hudson talked to Trotter Blue yesterday while his arm was around me. Madison, what have I done?" The last thing I wanted was to be sent home.

At dinner service, someone tapped me on the shoulder. It was Trotter Blue, "After yure done here, come see me." I was shaking.

Madison came over and said, "What did he want?"

"I guess I'm being sacked. What should I say, Madison?"

"Tell him you won't see Hudson anymore."

"I can't say that. That's a lie."

Madison said, "So lie. If you don't want to go home, lie."

I instructed Grace to clear my tables and knocked on the office door. I opened the door slowly. "You wanted to see me sir?" I said nervously.

"Yeah, I did. Yure lookin' mighty country with yore shirt, and boots, and I seen yuh in that good lookin' hat. Yure dolled up country on the outside. How's the inside comin' along Little Darlin'?"

"It's going well, sir. The girls and I are a team. They respect my leadership. They pull pranks on me, but I understand they want to poke fun at my authority. I don't fuss about it." I added a few Cowboy Codes, "I catch my white lies. Instead of saying them, I say something honest. I'm showing more respect to others. I'm nice to the little kids and I treat Mariah well. I bring her carrots. Have there been complaints?"

He smiled, "Naw, everythin's fine."

"That's good," I exhaled. "Is there anything else, sir?'

"Miss Spirit Eyes, tell Hudson he needs to see me come Sunday. There ain't no rush." Trotter Blue added, "He's a good guy. The best yuh'll meet in these parts. He's got one heck of a heart. I took him under my wing like a surrogate pappy. Now, I don't want nothin' bad to come to him yuh hear? He looks big and burly, but he's sensitive inside. Yuh hearin' me Young Lady?"

"Yes, sir, every word."

He added, "By the way, them country clothes look good on yuh."

"Thank you, sir. I'll see you tomorrow."

Trotter Blue said, "Night, Spirit Eyes. Vaya con Dios and all that good stuff."

I smiled and left the office.

The waitresses were huddled on the other side of the door trying to overhear the conversation. Madison asked, "Did he sack you?"

"No, Madison. I'm still your boss. Get out of here before he catches you snooping."

CHAPTER NINETEEN

HEALING POULTICE

That night Hudson didn't stop by my window. It was his night off. He was probably at Rory's betting on pool. I prayed he wouldn't run into those gritty bikers.

After breakfast, I ran to the wranglers' bunk house to find Hudson and deliver Trotter Blue's message as promised. Dash and Hoyle were sitting on the porch. Hudson was on the swing practicing roping on upright tree stumps.

"Hudson," I called with eagerness. My enthusiasm died when I saw his eye was swollen and black, "What happened?" He didn't speak so I turned toward Hoyle and Dash. They were in no better shape. Hoyle's eye wasn't swollen, but it was dark purple. Dash had a swollen lip and bruised cheek. You could see fist marks on Dash's face. "What happened to you guys?"

Slurring over his fat lip, Dash said, "Hudson had unfinished business at Rory's. Me and Hoyle helped him take care of it."

I looked at Hudson. He glanced away. Uninvited, I sat next to him, "Was it Snake and his buddies?"

"Yeah," Dash answered, "Yuh think we look bad. Yuh should see them foul a…"

Hudson interjected, "Watch yure mouth." He motioned to me with his head.

"I beg yore pardon, Miss," Dash slurred, spitting unintentionally over the *p* in *pardon*.

Examining Hudson's gouged knuckles, I asked, "What did Rory say?"

Hoyle replied, "He didn't mind because we took it outside to the parking lot."

Lifting Hudson's hand gingerly, I said, "You didn't have to do this for me. I prayed last night you wouldn't run into them."

"You pray?" Dash asked with surprise.

"Yes, do you think God only takes care of country people? He watches over urbanites too," I said.

Dash and Hoyle looked at me with pensive stares. I ignored them and addressed Hudson, "Let me see your eye. What can I get you, ice? I know, a yolk-coriander poultice. I'll make it now." I stood up and a gush of violet blue wind pushed me off the porch away from the path to the dining hall.

Pushing back with no success, I yelled, "Hudson help." All of a sudden a rope slipped over my body tightening around my thighs. With my legs bound, I hit the ground. Someone heavy landed on my back knocking the breath out of me.

"Hold on Annie," said Hudson's deep voice. "I got yuh." Under his weight, I couldn't breathe. I gasped. "Sorry," he said lifting his chest.

The wind screeched and dissipated. Calm returned to the meadow. Hudson rolled off me onto his back. I buried my tear filled eyes into his chest releasing fear and tension. Hudson cupped my head in his hand and held me. Someone loosened the lasso.

"Good ropin', Hudson," said Dash. "Looks like yuh caught a pretty municipal calf."

I was amazed how cowboys bounce back from violence. It was as though nothing happened. Hudson told Dash, "Shut yore fat lip. Annie's still upset."

I didn't want to move, but I did and said, "I'll make the poultice now," I started to get up from the ground and pain rushed through my thighs. A hole in my jeans revealed a nasty scrape on my knee. I said, "Now, I know what calves feel like."

"I ain't used to ropin' humans. Reckon, I pulled the rope too tight," he said helping me to my feet. "I'm gonna escort Anna Lisa to the kitchen. She's determined to make one of them civilized witch doctor potions."

I corrected, "It's poultice, not potion. You don't drink it."

Hudson smirked, wincing, "Wellll excuse me."

I climbed onto Phantom's back behind Hudson. I pressed against him and wrapped my arms around his waist anticipating speeding off like last time. He didn't. We slowly walked. With one of his hands, he held my hands in place. He didn't mind my tight hold. I rested my head on his back.

I told him the message. Hudson didn't seem surprised or worried that Trotter Blue wanted to talk with him.

We tethered Phantom to a hitching post outside the kitchen. Sam was prepping lunch, "What are the two of you up to?" He saw Hudson's eye and said, "On second thought, I don't want to know."

I grabbed a stainless steel mixing bowl, filled it with warm water and dish soap, and then thrust Hudson's hand into it.

"Soak those knuckles, while I make the compress for your eye. Sam do you have coriander?"

"There, among the spices," Sam replied.

"And eggs?"

"In that refrigerator." I asked if he wanted to keep the egg whites. Sam said he'd add them to the next day's omelets. I cracked the eggs separating the yolks. Next, I stirred in coriander. It formed a pasty consistency. I rolled three yolk-coriander patties.

I handed one to Hudson, "Hold this against your eye for as long as you can. If you're comfortable on your back, let gravity hold the compress. Where's your bandana?"

Hudson said, "In my pocket."

"Excuse me," I said, reaching into his pocket.

"Anytime," he said with a naughty flair. Sam shot him a look.

I said, "I'd jab you now, but you're already sore." I pulled a blue bandana from his pocket and wrapped the patties for Dash and Hoyle.

Hudson said, "I tease yuh about yore home remedies, Annie, but my eye's feelin' better. Not well enough fer no jabs, but better. Got more funnel-geek tea? That'd taste good now."

"Fenugreek? Here," I said handing a tin to him. "Take these herbs to the others and make an infusion with boiling water. It'll help Dash and Hoyle too."

Sam leaned toward me and whispered "Dash and Hoyle too? What happened?"

I said, "My personal knights took care of my honor. As you can see, the battle was fierce."

Hudson offered, "Wasn't her fault. It was mine."

I looked at Hudson in astonishment, while I lifted his hand from the bowl, and dried it carefully in a paper towel, "I better get to work. Will you be o.k?"

"I'll be fine, Annie. How about yore knee?"

"I'll take care of it after work," I said.

That evening pebbles bounced off the window pane, "Evenin', Medicine Gal."

I smiled.

Although he felt sore, he came to talk. "Yuh gained respect from Dash and Hoyle. We're feelin' better. And Hoyle's eye ain't dark violet blue no more. It turned puke gray."

I smiled, "I'm glad. That's a sign of healing."

Hudson's tone got serious, "Dash thinks I'm crazy invitin' yuh to shoot pool. Says a date's gotta be a real nice place. Annie, will yuh accompany me to Studs & Sass come Friday?"

I replied doubtfully, "Studs & Sass is a nice place?"

Hudson told me it was, and assured me there wouldn't be *no biker scum*. "What will we do at this fine establishment?" I asked.

Hudson said, "We'll be boot scootin'."

Confused, I said, "Boot scooting?"

I could tell he wanted to laugh at my ignorance, "Yuh know, boot scootin', two steppin'. That kind of stuff." I still looked muddled. He said, "Dancin'."

"Dancing's wonderful," I said happily. "What should I wear? How nice is this place?"

"Wear yore dress. I'm puttin' on my new shirt."

I said, "Hudson, I don't have dress shoes with me."

"Wear yore boots."

"Boots with a dress?" I bantered.

"Yuh'll look as pretty as a little heifer in a flowerbed."

The week passed slowly. This gave me time to think about things. Here's a guy who has a value system that runs through his veins. He's strong, incredibly handsome, and smells great sweaty. He came to my defense and wouldn't let me take blame for problems I caused.

It was as clear as the Rocky Mountain air, Hudson was a real man. He had better things to offer a woman than money. As simple as he claimed his life to be, he lived it with fullness.

Hudson and I connected effortlessly. At first, I thought the wranglers posed a problem, but this concern was waning. I gained Candy's acceptance after she learned I was behind Pamina's ride. Skeebo opened up after we talked about his ghost theory which I believed and respected. Hoyle and Dash accepted me after I alleviated their aches and pains.

The only two left were Tiffany and Lacey. Tiffany was a lost cause. As much as she wanted to be a cowgirl, Hudson said, *Bev still puts her left boot on first - a cowboy sign of bad luck.* Lacey was my stumbling block. She was a true bred rodeo queen. I needed to know what made her tick. Was she thoughtful like Candy, crazy like Skeebo, or stuck-up given her rodeo title? I knew I couldn't approach her directly, but I needed her approval in order to be accepted by all the wranglers.

I was preoccupied with being on the same wave length with them. Maybe it was because I admired their principles or maybe it was more personal. Hudson and I wouldn't have to hide. If they knew about us, things could progress, and perchance he'd kiss my lips. So what was I going to do about Lacey?

CHAPTER TWENTY

HONKY-TONK

After a week of anticipation, Friday night arrived. I styled my hair in curls, put on my new dress, socks, and boots. I looked in the cloudy bathroom mirror. The combination would take getting used to. I grabbed Truthful Musk and put a spritz on my neck, arms, and dress hem.

Hudson knocked on the girls' bunk house door. I flung the wooden door open, almost knocking it off the rusty hinges. Light from inside fell upon him. I couldn't breathe. He wore the blue shirt, jeans, boots, and a big gold buckle. He held his russet hat in his hand.

"Evenin', Annie. Where's yore hat?" he asked.

"Hudson, a hat with this dress? You're not serious."

He said under his breath, "Annie, that's a two steppin' dress. Yuh gotta have a hat."

'If you say so."

Hurrying to my room to get my hat, I passed Caprice in the hall, "Wow, Anna Lisa, where're you going, to a honky-tonk?"

I merely chuckled because I had no clue what a honky-tonk was.

Hudson held out his arm for me. I put my hand on the inside crease of his elbow then he put his right hand over mine.

He said softly, "I know it ain't polite to stare, but I'm gonna have a heck of a time keepin' my eyes off of yuh tonight. And it ain't polite to sniff yore skin, but man, yuh smell good."

Hugging his arm, I said, "You have my permission to stare and sniff."

He opened the passenger side of his truck for me and held my hand while I gathered the layers of my dress and settled in the cab.

He said, "No need to ride shotgun tonight, Annie. We ain't strangers. Slide on over next to me." I slid across the bench seat.

On the highway, he put one hand on the wheel and one on my leg. I saw an orange neon sign flashing erratically, *Studs & Sass Dance Hall – Best Honky-tonk in Town*. Hudson killed the engine and I could hear country music blaring through the wind wings. He opened his door and helped me down. Wearing boots with a dress was easier than evening shoes. I didn't have to worry about twisting an ankle.

At Studs & Sass, everyone wore hats and boots. People were on the dance floor, facing the same direction moving with matching steps. They turned counter clockwise a quarter turn and repeated the steps.

As we walked through the crowd, I noticed Hudson wasn't the only one staring. The people around the dance floor watched us. Their eyes followed us like portraits on a wall. Hudson felt my arm tighten. He whispered, "Don't worry, Honey. They ain't like them cusses at Rory's. The guys are checkin' yuh up and down wonderin' how I got so lucky."

He pulled his arm from my hand and placed it around my shoulders. I said quietly, "Does your arm around me tell them *I'm with you?*"

"You bet. It says, *back off, she's taken, and she's all mine.*"

Our eyes met and I placed my arm around him, "I better tell the cowgirls the same thing."

He smiled modestly, "Want somethin' to drink? A soda or water?" I told him I was fine.

The song ended and a new one started. Hudson took his hand from my shoulder and took my hand, "May I?"

"I'd love to."

He led me to the dance floor. I had observed the steps and it didn't take long to catch on. We danced to a couple of songs and the D.J. said he was slowing things down. I turned to Hudson and put my arms on his shoulders. He took one hand off and held it.

"Annie, yuh know two steppin'?"

"No. Hudson, tell me what to do."

"Put yore other hand on my shoulder. Take two steps quick-quick and two steps slow-slow. Keep that whatever yuh do. Follow my lead."

The slow music started. Instead of hanging on each other we danced across the floor. Hudson pushed me out and twirled me around. He must have notice that I didn't trip and wasn't dizzy so he sent me twirling again. He rolled me back into him. Our arms interlocked and we traveled forward. We did some type of move which felt like an octopus unraveling and we resumed the original hold.

He twirled me pushing this way, pulling that way. I was thankful for those ballet classes Mother dragged me too. Spotting was the only way to survive this whirlwind. I chose to spot on his eyes. Our eyes were locked and as soon as a turn took them away, I spun my head back to find those mountain blue eyes.

The D.J. rolled one song into another. The dance floor cleared but I didn't notice. I only noticed his eyes and felt the chiffon layers of my skirt, flying with each twirl, returning to wrap around my thighs, filling the air with Truthful Musk.

The music stopped, he pulled me to his chest, and whispered, "I thank God yure in my life."

We heard guys slapping their quads, whistling, and hooting, "Twirl that gal some more." I blushed profusely.

Hudson said, "Annie, I thought yuh ain't never been two steppin'. Where'd yuh learn to dance like that?"

"I followed your lead, like you told me."

"No filly can take that many spins. I thought after the first ones yuh'd be dizzier than a fly in a dust storm and tumble on yore keester."

"Ballet classes taught me how to spot," I said.

Hudson smiled, "So yure a ballerina too? What else don't I know about yuh? What secrets yuh hidin' from me?"

I smiled, "None. I promise."

He took my hand, "Time fer sparklin' water."

He led me through the crowd to a roughhewn wooden counter. A shrill country voice could be heard over the crowd, "Hey Hudson, where'd yuh find yore professional dance partner?"

Hudson smiled and said, "Howdy Dolly. Yuh got soda water?"

"Sure do and fer yuh lover boy, a Pepsi?" She grabbed his cheek and jiggled it. Hudson turned to me and we talked for a long time.

I excused myself to find the restroom and returned to find a stunning cowgirl and Hudson deep in conversation. She had beautiful blonde hair that hung in soft curls around a pretty face with light freckles. She chose a perfect tone of lip gloss to match her light hair and fair complexion. Her tiny flip nose could've served as a prototype for L.A.'s best cosmetic surgeons. A pang of jealousy shot through my body. Madison's story of Paxton charred its image in my mind. I took a deep breath, exhaled, and used a plethora of mental affirmations.

Walking behind Hudson, I placed my hands on his back. I pressed my thumbs into his shoulder muscles and pressed again just under his collar. I rested my hands on his shoulders. Without stopping his conversation with this babe, he took my hand in front of him and kissed the back of it. He turned my palm inward and held it to his lips. His lips were full and warm. He pressed his tongue against my ring finger and middle finger sending a shiver down my spine. All the while, he listened to her and nobody could tell what he was up to, except me.

The cowgirl paused chattering. Hudson pulled me around and said, "Annie, this here's Rella, Hoyle's baby sister. Rella, this is Annie."

I said, "It's nice to meet you, Rella."

She shrilled, "Yikes, yure a city gal."

"And you, no doubt, are a country girl," my tone smacked of sarcasm. Hudson excused himself leaving us alone.

Rella said, "Hudson's a good lookin' guy." She continued, "He could have any of these country gals. If he were to wink at one, she'd be all over him, takin' him home to meet her pa."

"Are you telling me he's a Casanova?" I asked.

"Naw, he ain't never showed no interest in gals."

"Are you implying he's gay?"

Rella shrieked, "Hell no!"

I said, "What are you trying to tell me, Rella?"

"I'm sayin' he don't need no city gal. Country gals got more respect fer themselves than spinnin' around on a dance floor flashing bright orange panties with *Love Pink* on their behinds. I felt sorry fer the dudes tryin' to figure out what day-glow orange has got to do with pink."

Turning red, I covered my mouth in shock. I had no idea my dress flared high enough to show my panties. I should've worn black.

Enjoying my embarrassment, Rella added, "Besides yore fancy panties, what does he see in yuh?"

I demanded, "I beg your pardon."

"Is yore pa rich or somethin'?"

"Rella, my father's financials are none of your business. What Hudson likes about me, is just me."

Hudson returned. The tension between Rella and me was apparent. Our tempers were hot and we glared at each other.

Hudson eloquently said, "We'll see yuh around Rella. I'll tell Hoyle we ran into yuh."

Hudson threw his arm around my shoulders and led me to the dance floor. We danced until last call. I made sure I didn't spin wildly again.

Back in his truck, I snuggled up to him. "It was a wonderful evening, Hudson. Thank you."

He put one hand on the wheel and another around my shoulders. "Yure somethin' special, Annie. It felt good showin' yuh off." He had no idea how much of me he showed off.

When we arrived back at the ranch, we sat enjoying the peace between us. Then he said, "Annie, fer me yure everything I want in life." I felt cherished and warm inside.

Hudson walked me to the girls' bunk house. I yearned for our first kiss. He tipped my hat back, kissed my forehead, and whispered, "Sweet dreams, Boot Scooter." He walked away.

It was 3:00 a.m. I had to be up at 7:00 a.m. for breakfast service. Since there was nothing to do in the dark, I took off my dress, boots, and hat, and pulled on pajamas. My roommates were asleep, so I quietly climbed onto my bunk. Thank goodness, no one pulled a prank on me. It was too late to deal with something like that. My eyes closed and I drifted to sleep.

CHAPTER TWENTY ONE

A CALL FROM MOTHER

Shelly shook me. The room was bright. The sun had been up for hours.

"Anna Lisa, get up. Trotter Blue's looking for you. He's asking us, *Yuh all sure she aint tradin' a day off with nobody?*"

Squinting at the light I asked, "What time is it?"

"It's after 10:00," she said.

I shimmied into jeans, whipped on a tee shirt, and sneakers. I didn't bother with socks. I brushed my teeth but skipped my hair. I darted to the dining hall. Trotter Blue called from his office, "Anna Lisa, get in here."

Madison said, "He might fire you."

"Good morning, sir. Please accept my apology for this tardiness."

He snorted, "Tardiness? Why darn near half a day passed and yure still imitatin' Sleepin' Beauty." He started his long tirade, "I gotta count on people. They gotta be reliable. That's the expectation of country folks."

"I understand, sir. This won't happen again," I turned to leave.

"Miss Clay, we ain't done here." I held my breath. Trotter Blue never called me by my formal name, "We got a bigger bone to pick. Honesty's important. Yuh tell me yure controllin' yore little white lies, but what about yore big fat black ones?"

I had no clue what he was talking about, "I beg your pardon, sir."

"I warned yuh. I said Hudson's like kin. I don't want him hurt. I hear yuh been livin' it up at the honky-tonk." My mind raced. I was bewildered. Was Trotter Blue upset because we went on a date?

He continued, "Puttin' on fancy duds, flirtin', and talkin' mushy mushy. Yuh got Hudson's hopes up. Thought he trapped himself a squaw. He was convinced yuh was a keeper - a gal with good breedin', and principles. He was callin' on yuh as regular as a goose goes barefoot and then yuh stomp on him. Why would a gal pull the wool over a fine gentleman like Hudson? Yuh tore a hole in his heart. He won't trust the female race again. Yuh should've left him alone. Lyin' and cheatin', Miss Clay, are big offences in these parts."

I was confused. I wondered what Trotter Blue heard about the night before. Was this Rella's revenge? Trotter Blue paused a moment and I took the opportunity to get clarity, "Sir, I went dancing with Hudson last night. We had a fabulous time. He was content when I last saw him. He expressed how important I am to him. I didn't dance with anyone else, and I didn't lie to him."

Trotter Blue's face turned red and his bushy gray hair started to shake, "Miss Clay, yure as shy from the truth as a goat is of feathers. I got many years on me and I'm wise. It ain't right to be smoochy with a feller and drag him along when yure engaged to another man."

"Another man? Engaged? What do you mean?" Under his barrage, it was impossible to remember manners.

"Yure engaged, Anna Lisa. We know it. Yuh messed things up worse than a pile of cow dung on carpet."

"I haven't messed up anything. I'm not engaged," I yelled.

"Yuh almost sound convincin' while yure covering yore story with a bright red Navajo blanket."

Gritting my teeth I said, "What gives you the idea I'm engaged?"

"Yore ma told me. Yure engaged to that college feller, Dr. Radcliffe's kid. Because of lyin' and betrayin' Hudson yure fired. Pack yore bags and skedaddle off my land."

"What?" I said shocked and motionless. The only thing moving was my pounding heart. Summer raced through my head. This meant going home. Dreadfully, I'd face Mother. Worse, I'd face Dad and his disappointment. He'd never let me out of the house again. I'd be a prisoner of that hoity estate. I stifled tears. This meant, leaving my friends who would still have fun working together, joking, and creating pranks. My biggest heart wrench was Hudson. How could I say good bye to the finest guy I knew? I hadn't told him I loved him yet. I still needed my first kiss. Visions of happiness blurred then drained away.

I got mad, and defensive, and raised my voice, "I was late once. That's all. One morning. You can't fire me. Hudson won't forgive you." Sounding like Hudson, I said, "He'll drop you faster than fleas on a flea-dipped dog. If you give me a chance, I won't be late again."

Trotter Blue pointed his finger at me.

"It's urbanites like yuh that scare us. Look at yuh, darin' to stand up and argue without flinchin'.""

"I won't flinch. I'll defend my honor and I'll fight for Hudson until I die."

Noticing my sincerity, he cocked his head sideways and looked at me. He looked deep into my eyes. I held his gaze. He studied me then Trotter Blue spoke calmly for the first time that morning, "I notice yuh ain't nervous like a long tailed cat under a rockin' chair. I'd almost believe yuh."

"I'm not engaged to Philippe or anyone else," I barked. "Call my father." I picked up the receiver shoving it into Trotter Blue's hand.

"Yore ma and I already had a chat," he said nonchalantly.

"Talk with Father, Mr. Blue, and you'll hear the truth." I dialed the number while Trotter Blue protested. I ignored him and pressed the speaker button, "Hello, Dad. Trotter Blue's with me. You're on speaker."

After their cordial salutations, Dad asked, "How's my little pumpkin? Why are you calling? Are you o.k?"

"No. Daddy, I'm not," I said tearfully.

Worried, he said, "Did you fall off a horse, break an arm, hit your head?"

I said sadly, "It's not like that. Mother called the ranch. Trotter Blue needs to talk with you."

Trotter Blue said, "Mansfield, yuh and me understand each other, right? Yuh know about bein' truthful."

Dad replied, "Of course. Did my child get caught in a lie?"

"Yure gonna have to answer that, sir. Yore wife, Velvet, called and said Anna Lisa's engaged to Philippe Radcliffe."

Stunned, Dad said, "What?"

"Yep, the doctor's comin' to visit with his son. Mrs. Clay wants me to give yore daughter down time so she and this boy can frolic and play at my ranch. I told her I ain't gonna do that because it shows no respect fer co-workers. Did this Radcliffe kid come courtin' and ask yuh fer Anna Lisa's hand?"

Dad replied, "Trotter, my wife has imagination. Annie's not engaged. In fact, she's never had a boyfriend." I plopped into the overstuffed chair.

Trotter Blue sighed, and said, "Mansfield, yuh gotta get control of yore mare. She's runnin' wild causin' damage to yore daughter's reputation and hurtin' others here at the ranch."

Dad said, "I'm sorry to hear that. I'll talk with Velvet." We said goodbye. Dad said he missed me. I hung up.

Trotter Blue stood staring at me. I stared back. "Annie, why would yore ma say she's plannin' to marry yuh off to this kid?"

I didn't know what to say. Explaining Mother's way of thinking was complicated. Although my mother's idiotic ideas were hard to comprehend, it was time to give Trotter Blue insight into my family.

"My mother wants me to marry money, power, and connections. The Radcliffe family fits her mold. They own a multi-billion dollar orthopedic company and they have powerful lobbyists in Washington D.C. They're connected to elite families in the United States, and around the world.

"Even though I've been raised to marry money, I've no interest in their son or their lifestyle. Mother networks parents of Ivy League sons relentlessly. She invites them to dinners that are stiff, boring, and pretentious."

Trotter Blue said, "I reserved a room fer the good doc and his son. They're comin' tonight."

"Ugh," I said, rolling my eyes.

Trotter Blue looked down and said, "Miss Lady Eyes, Hudson's feelin' hollower than a gutted steer. He's hurtin' somethin' horrible. He came to see me this morning. Yore ma called while he and I were conversin'. I took the call because it might've been a guest or an emergency. Hudson heard yuh got weddin' plans. Sweetie, yore ma's mighty convincin'. She could talk a cow out of her calf. Hudson plowed out of here madder than a conquistador's bull feelin' the picadors' jabs. I should've known yure not the two timin' type."

I put my face in my hands and cried. I knew Hudson's heart was tender. He told me I was *everything he wanted in life*. My mind wandered to the worst scenario, and through sobs, I asked, "Cowboys aren't prone to suicide are they, sir?"

Trotter Blue said, "Suicide? That's a sin. A cowboy wants to be up where there ain't no end of harps and free music. Little One, yore eyes look mighty sad."

"Am I still terminated, sir?"

He said kindly, "There's no way in Hades I'd fire yuh. I suggest yuh leave the breakfast mop-up to the other gals and find Hudson."

He added, "Send up a smoke signal if yuh got trouble explainin' the muddle. We'll talk man to man and sort it out. Hudson's lucky. I saw yuh love birds headin' to the truck last night. I hear yuh got the place in an uproar. They're talkin' about that good lookin' couple and the way his little damsel dances."

"Thank you, sir. I'm sorry I talked disrespectfully. I'm still working on that Code."

He smiled.

CHAPTER TWENTY TWO

GOLD IN THE CLEARING

I ran to the corrals. Skeebo was mucking stalls. "Skeebo, where's Hudson? Is he with the morning ride?"

Skeebo looked at me with disdain. He responded flatly, "Naw."

I snapped, "Where is he?"

Skeebo kept shoveling, "Yuh got no business here. He don't want nothin' to do with yuh. Nobody does. Yuh showed yore true metropolitan colors: two-timin', lyin', cheatin', user. I told yuh don't mess with my friend. Yuh gave me yore word. Look at yuh now, engaged to a rich boy."

Skeebo wouldn't have believed me, so I wasted no time in talk. I ran to the tack shed, grabbed a bridle, and headed for Mariah.

"Yuh ain't to ride Hudson's hoss no more," Skeebo said.

"Fine," I said turning to the nearest horse. Trixie was standing next to me. I flung the rains around Trixie's neck, shoved the bit in her mouth, flipped the bridle over her ears, and heaved myself up.

Skeebo screamed the entire time, "Yuh can't do that. That pony ain't green broke. Yure gonna kill yoreself."

"According to you, Skeebo, I deserve it. Now get out of my way."

I charged the gate. He had no choice but to throw it open. Trixie brushed against the post sending my sneaker flying. With Trixie running wild, I tried to control her direction. Thank goodness she didn't buck. I grabbed a patch of mane, just in case.

If Hudson was the romantic I thought he was, he would be at the clearing near the creek, the place he took me on our first ride. Trixie had exhausted herself by the time we got close. I dismounted and walked the remaining one hundred yards through the trees.

Hudson was sitting in the clearing tying a bull rope around his hand, examining it, and wrapping it again. He stood up, pulled the rope off, and threw it. He picked up a rock the size of a pomelo and shot putted it violently, "Huuh." It hit a pine on the far bank. He reached in his pocket and pulled out something gold. It glittered in the sun. He held it to his lips then let it fall to the ground. A tear rolled down his cheek and dripped off of his chin. He sat back down, picked a columbine, and twirled it.

I tethered Trixie to a branch. Phantom whinnied so Hudson looked up. "I believe that belongs in my hair."

"It did, but not no more. Those times are dead," he tossed it in the river and watched it float away. He got up and started toward Phantom.

"Hudson, wait. I need to talk with you," I said.

"Ain't nothin' to say. Save yore breath fer breathin'," he said brusquely as he smeared tears off his face.

I was choked up. I couldn't say anything. I looked at him in silence; not a peaceful silence like we shared before, but a dark, dense, menacing quiet.

He said, "Eight hours ago I had the best night of my life. I woke up, thought about yuh smilin', laughin', ridin', swimmin', the crazy things yuh did, even shoppin'. In an instant it's gone. Yuh strung me along. Had me believin' yuh were mine. I fell fer yuh hard. Nice actress job. Go back to Hollywood where you belong."

"Hudson there's nobody else," I said stifling tears.

"Yure full of hoss manure. Rory was right. I was yore *adventure with a cowboy*. Did you think I wouldn't find out about your stud? Why didn't yuh tell the truth, Anna Lisa?"

My full name cut like a jagged knife. "Hudson," my voice broke, "I'm not engaged."

"Hah, yure a lyin' fox. Trotter Blue told me about that Ivy League, spoiled brat yuh gonna marry. Go on. Scat. Save me the hurt."

I stayed there and said as calmly as possible, "I'm not marrying him. I'm not engaged."

Hudson said, "I've been sittin' here wonderin' why yuh lie? I would've appreciated knowin' the truth then, instead of findin' out now. If yuh told me in the beginnin', I might've competed to win yore heart. Instead, I woke up each mornin' thankin' God yure unattached and interested in me. What kind of fool am I?"

My tears started flowing, "I'm unattached and interested in you. This saga's my mother's doing. I never dated this guy. I swear I'm not engaged."

"Swearin's a strong word, Anna Lisa," he said with a snarled tone.

"Then I swear to God, Hudson." He flinched.

"Please, listen to me. My mother told Trotter Blue that because that's what she wants for me. That's not me. You know me."

Hudson said, "I thought I did."

I raised my voice, "I'm so disgusted with her. She has no idea what she's doing to us. I'm not engaged. I don't have a boyfriend. Please Hudson, believe me."

He stared at my eyes, "The good Lord knows I want to believe yuh but I can't. Yuh crushed me like a tin can." Hudson watched me cry and said, "Yore hair's wilder than a marmot's behind. Didn't yuh brush it this mornin'?"

"No. I overslept and rushed to work," I said.

"And, where's yore shoe?" he asked. I looked down and told him Trixie knocked it off against the gate post. He held still, "Yuh rode Trixie?" He looked in the direction I pointed. "Yuh could've been killed. Why didn't Skeebo stop yuh?"

I answered, "Skeebo hopes she'd kill me. Do you care?"

Ignoring my question, he said, "Anna Lisa, we got a lot of history but I can't be played with. Go on with yore life and I'll go on with mine. I'll say goodbye and wish yuh the best."

"No! You can't do that. I want you," I cried again. "How can I convince you? Can you believe me?" I sounded hysterical. "Please talk to Trotter Blue. Do this for us, for what we had."

He saw my hysteria and said, "I ain't expectin' miracles but I'll talk to him, so long as it stops yore rantin' and ravin'."

"Fine," I ran, untethered Trixie, mounted her, and took off galloping.

Hudson mounted Phantom and called, "Annie, whoa."

I heard Phantom catching up to me. I pushed Trixie faster. She was no match for Hudson on Phantom. He caught up with me and jumped onto her, grabbing the reins out of my hands. She started to buck.

He held me with his free arm, "What are yuh tryin' to do? Get us killed?"

I yelled, "Hudson, you wouldn't mind if she took me from the face of the Earth. In fact, you've already killed me. So what if Trixie does."

He got control of Trixie, slowed her to a stop, and dismounted. "Get off that pony and ride Phantom," he demanded.

I kicked Trixie and hollered, "Yeeha." Hudson stampeded next to me. He didn't dare jump onto Trixie again.

Hudson called, "Save yoreself. Turn that mare." We sped up the narrow trail, through the meadow, past the wranglers' bunk house, and guest quarters, to the main building.

Trotter Blue came running off the veranda holding his hat on his bushy hair. He bellowed, "What in blazin's goin' on? Yuh can't charge up here with those ponies. Annie, why're yuh on that wild filly?"

I swung off of Trixie. Through my sobs I gasped, "Tell him, sir. He refuses to believe me."

Trotter Blue said, "Annie, hand over Trixie's reins to Hudson. Hop on Phantom's back and see him to the barn. I'll have a word with Junior."

I overheard Trotter Blue say, "Hudson, this is as unexpected as gunplay in a Bible class. Yuh read the bulls but yuh got no clue how to read a woman. Son, yore lady's honesty is as prominent as a boil on a pug's nose." Hudson said nothing. Trotter Blue continued, "Hell, when it comes to women Hudson, yuh couldn't hit a bull's ass with a banjo. Don't yuh see she's a jewel? She'll make the finest blanket companion yuh ever …"

Phantom and I crested the hill. I couldn't hear how the conversation ended. Someone put my sneaker on the post. I retrieved it, put it on, and started down the trail on Phantom. He whinnied as Hudson entered the meadow leading Trixie. I directed Phantom further down the trail. He was a well-trained horse. He obeyed and didn't balk about being separated from Hudson or the herd.

I reached the dirt road and followed it to the clearing by the creek. Gold glittered in the grass. I dismounted Phantom and picked it up. It was a locket. The front was delicately etched with columbines. The back was engraved, *Annie, keep me in your heart.* Inside was a lock of Hudson's hair. I tenderly touched the blond curl. Tears welled in my eyes and I let them flow, not bothering to wipe them away. I put the long chain over my head and the locket reached my heart. I tucked it in my shirt, mounted Phantom, and walked back.

Hudson watched me approach the corral. He didn't say anything. I removed Phantom's bridle and put on his halter. I uncinched Phantom's saddle, and lifted it with the blanket and pad. It was heavier than expected. I lugged it to the tack shed. Hudson took it from me at the doorway.

"Thanks," I said.

I grabbed a brush and a horse treat. Phantom's big lips gently took the treat from my hand. The horse was sweaty. I started to brush him and Hudson's hand stopped me. I said, "I get it. I'll leave your horse to you." Hudson didn't look at me. "See you, Hudson."

"Yeah." It was obvious Hudson didn't believe what Trotter Blue told him.

I ran across the meadow and over the hill crying.

~ ~ ~

I arrived at the poolside, just in time to serve lunch. The waitresses cornered me. "What happened?" they said in unrehearsed unison.

I found an element of truth in the events and offered, "Trotter Blue has no tolerance for slacking off. He lectured me about being late. I apologized."

They eyed me with disbelief. Madison led the pack, "There has to be more to it, Anna Lisa. You were in his office a long time."

Pointing toward the guests, I said, "Madison, your table looks ready to order."

We served the guests. Some had planes to catch, so we were extra efficient. This was fine with me. There'd be fewer chances for grueling questions from the girls.

I took the wrangler's table. I was relieved to see Hudson, even though, he didn't look at me. He leaned back in his chair, put his boots on the table, and tipped his hat over his face.

Dash's cheek and Hoyle's eye were healed, yet they shunned me. Skeebo said, "Glad Trixie didn't kill yuh. We'd both be dead. Hudson would've scalped me alive. Boss Man's rightfully concerned about safety. Ain't toleratin' a hoss throwin' a rider, even if it's yore butt that's on it."

"Gee, thanks Skeebo," I replied.

Candy spoke, "I told Hudson to hook up with Hoyle's baby sister, Rella. She'd make him forget the misery yuh caused. Of course, he'd have to peel her off J.T. first. I told Hudson, competition will heal yore hurt mighty fast. Yuh know what Hudson says? *Rella ain't my type.* How do yuh like them apples? Here's a perfectly good country gal, yet she ain't his type, like cow spit from L.A. is? Hah!"

Candy thrust the pain deeper into my heart. She respected me before I became cow spit. Not only had I lost Hudson, I lost the respect of his peers. It was easier to be invisible again.

The other two didn't talk, Tiffany, because she was wrapped up in Tiffany and Lacey because she never respected me. Hudson didn't come to my defense.

CHAPTER TWENTY THREE

SPECIAL GUESTS

After lunch Trotter Blue called a team leader meeting. Meadow, Rebecca, Sam, Pip, Hudson, and I gathered in his tiny office. He told us about important guests arriving at the ranch. He wanted them well taken care of because they'd be a good referral source among the rich and famous. Trotter Blue explained, "I always wanted to spruce up this place. If I get folks like this comin' here, it's possible to turn this into a five-star resort. I want yuh to take extra care of these folks, in particular, the doc and his son."

These last words shocked me. I noticed Hudson stiffen.

"Becky, plan lots of country activities: rides, campfires, barrel racin' demonstrations. Yuh get my drift. Sam and I reviewed the menu. He's goin' all out on country fixins. Gonna take Anna Lisa's recommendation fer home-style pot roast." Hudson turned his eyes on me, but they weren't smiling. They were dull and somewhat swollen.

"Spirit Eyes, tell the waitresses to put on cowboy boots, hats, and snap button shirts, if they've got them. And, Sweet Thing, brush out that bushy, bushy hairdo yure donnin'. We ain't gonna have no Rastafarian locks."

Then he looked at Hudson while he said to me, "Yuh can put flowers in yore hair if yuh please, Lil Darlin'."

Trotter Blue turned back to Hudson and said, "Regarding the wranglers, tell them I want cowboy duds. Hudson, I want them in chaps. I don't care none if yuh ain't kneelin', shoddin', or trail blazin'. The guests ain't gonna know no better. I want these folks to get their country fill."

We departed and went our separate directions to get our teams ready. This was the most excitement the girls had in a long time. They speculated who this father and son might be. Each one out doing the other: a politician, a movie star, a Texas oil tycoon, a Saudi Arabian prince, a king. The list went on.

The waitresses and I headed to the edge of the parking lot. The wranglers arrived after us. Flabbergasted, we stared. The wrangler females were stunning. They were freshly showered and dressed in well pressed shirts and jeans. Their hair was styled in wavy locks and they wore blush, lip gloss, and mascara. Their hats were tastefully trimmed with gems and bits of silver. Earlier in the day, they were grimy, sweaty, and dusty cowgirls. By 4:00 p.m, they transformed into rodeo queens.

The men walked up after them. My eyes landed on Hudson. He wore his mountain blue shirt, pressed blue jeans that fit closely, his gold buckle, and chaps. As he walked past, I couldn't help stare. The straps of the chaps wrapped around his upper thighs accenting his handsome glutes.

Vans pulled up and Trotter Blue came to greet the guests. He asked me, "Which one's the good doc?"

Knowing Trotter Blue was a cowboy, I placed my eyes on Dr. Radcliffe and Philippe. Watching for my gaze, Trotter Blue stepped forward to introduce himself and welcomed Dr. Radcliffe and Philippe to the dude ranch.

Dr. Radcliffe and Philippe approached me. I could see the waitresses watching as Dr. Radcliffe reached out his arms and gave me a fatherly embrace. Philippe hugged me affectionately. He nestled his face in my hair. Hudson was watching. A thud pushed Philippe off me. Hudson pretended it was an accident, "Watch out fer that step." Hudson looked to see if his thud bothered me. I was relieved to escape Philippe's embrace.

Dr. Radcliffe said, "Anna Lisa, it's good to see you. Your father and mother send their love and Ruby sends her warm regards. They're curious about you." His voice had that air of L.A. posh I had forgotten.

I said, "Thanks." Dr. Radcliffe smiled and chuckled. I caught my error and said, "Thank you, Dr. Radcliffe. Please give Mrs. Radcliffe my regards, as well."

He continued, "Look at you. You have become a western girl. What happened to your jeans?"

I looked down at my one eyed jeans, "I got lassoed and fell down. It's a long story."

"Your mother would be appalled, but your father would be proud of you. You have healthy color in your cheeks and your eyes are bright and clear. Doesn't she look well Philippe?"

Before Philippe could answer, Hudson said, "She looks mighty fine." Hudson had been hovering around like a fly in the kitchen. He continued, "I'll be helpin' yuh with yore bags. Is that them?"

Dr. Radcliffe responded, "Yes. See to the bags, boy." I noticed Hudson tense up under the patronizing tone.

Hudson swung a black computer bag. Philippe commanded, "Don't touch that. I don't want it dropped. I'll carry it."

"Suit yoreself," Hudson said nonchalantly. He pitched the computer bag at Philippe.

It hit Philippe in the chest knocking air out of his lungs, "Ugh."

Hudson smirked then turned to the designer bags carrying three at once. He headed toward the guest quarters.

I said casually, "You'll need to get settled. I'll try to be your server at dinner. It will be in the dining hall."

I turned to walk away and I heard Dr. Radcliffe say under his breath to Philippe, "She's so cute. I think your mother and Velvet are right about this match."

CHAPTER TWENTY FOUR

SPIRIT OF BATTLE

The roller coaster of emotions combined with late hours the night before, left me exhausted. I pulled back the curtain and gazed into moonlit darkness. Clouds rolled in covering the moon. Still, I stared at nothing. Rain started and lightning flashed in the sky. Thunder roared shaking the bunk house. A metal pail on the floor caught the drops of our leaky roof. I cried. My heart hurt. I never knew love could be so excruciating. Sadly, there weren't pebbles tapping on my window. I cried myself to sleep.

As the sun rose, I jumped from bed making-up for my disastrous tardiness the day before. Brushing my teeth, I realized it was Monday, my day off. I braided my hair and went outside to pick columbines. I slipped the stems into my braid and headed for the dining hall for a freshly baked croissant, two carrots, and English Breakfast tea in a disposable cup.

Mulling over what Hudson and I usually did on our free day left me lonely. I absentmindedly walked to the horses. Too miserable to eat, I tossed the croissant into the trees.

At the meadow, wranglers saddled horses. Hudson worked with them. It was early, but the sun was strong. Hudson was sweaty and dusty. Dash elbowed him directing his eyes toward me. Hudson glanced up coolly, and returned to grooming the mare.

I caught up with him. "Hudson, have you changed your day off?" I asked while he picked a hoof.

"Maybe I should. Ain't gonna matter no more," he said roughly.

I asked, "Are you on this trail ride?"

"I gotta be. I'm lead wrangler and Trotter Blue was clear about his expectations." My disappointment showed. He paused and said, "Yuh can join in. Things aren't the same between you and me, but it won't trouble no one if yuh join the line. Yuh can ride and stare at yore beau."

I ignored his comment, "You've serious work to do and need to concentrate." I added forlornly, "Hudson, I miss you more than I miss riding."

I walked to the corrals. Hudson continued saddling. Mariah came to me and nuzzled her snout in my hand. I said, "You smell carrots, don't you girl?" My eyes welled with tears. I put my hands behind my back to avoid crying but it didn't help. A tear ran down my cheek. Hudson looked over. I looked into his eyes. His eyes softened, but he didn't attempt to comfort me. I dug my face into Mariah's neck to feel her warmth and wipe the tear. I gave her the carrot. She munched loudly. I gave the other one to Phantom.

I heard Skeebo say, "Hey Hud," directing his eyes across the meadow. I looked. Dr. Radcliffe and Philippe were walking toward us.

Hudson yelled, "Mornin'." Dr. Radcliffe and Philippe ignored him.

They greeted me, "Good morning, Anna Lisa. Did you rest well?"

I couldn't lie like I used to, so I said, "I tossed and turned. And you?"

Philippe answered, "Like the dead." I glanced at Hudson who mouthed behind Philippe's back, *I wish.*

Dr. Radcliffe started talking, "This is a good brain break for Philippe. Imagine doing something as mindless as riding a horse?" The wranglers paused from their work. "Yale is an intellectually challenging school. Doing something as trivial as riding, will be good for Philippe." Dr. Radcliffe was oblivious to the wranglers' body language. He stood next to me, "She's a lovely creature. Hey, ranch hand, may I ride this one?"

I looked at Hudson with a questioning look. He gestured toward me and commented, "Gotta ask her."

Dr. Radcliffe assured me he knew about horses having ridden dressage in New England, "Do you have an English saddle?"

"We have western saddles and bits," I said combing Mariah.

In the meantime, Hudson walked over, "Yale, yuh look like a sporty fella."

"Father was a sports medicine orthopedist before he started the company."

Hudson said, "That's handy." I looked at Hudson and wondered what he was up to.

Philippe continued arrogantly, "Knowing the benefits of sports, as father does, he encourages us to remain active."

Hudson repeated, "Active?"

"That means physical exercise. I play Cricket and Lacrosse."

Hudson said, "We got lots of crickets in the foothills. Do yuh run around squashing them, seein' who can kill the most?"

Philippe rolled his eyes, "It's a gentleman's sport with a bat and ball. It's from England."

Hudson offered, "Skeebo knows about baaga'adowe, what yuh folks call The-Cross."

With an exasperated huff, Philippe said, "It's called *lacrosse.*"

"Hey Skeebo, get over here and educate Yale about The-Cross." Skeebo stopped grooming and explained to Philippe it's the oldest sport of Native America.

I went to the tack house for Mariah's saddle. Hudson followed me. He said in a low voice, "Yore fiancé's ego is bloated as big as a kraut barrel." He continued with his affronts and questioned me about the insults my *fiancé* and *future father-in-law* shelled out.

I told him, "I noticed. They were rude with the luggage yesterday too. I know it's tough, but they're Trotter Blue's guests. Be polite and stop calling him my *fiancé.*"

Hudson looked at me, "I'll be polite alright to yore fiancé." I scowled at Hudson and he said, "Hey, my guys are workin' hard and anyone of them got more brains and common sense than the doc and Yale. See why we can't stand city folks?" Taking this disrespect personally, I glared at Hudson, grabbed Mariah's saddle, and stormed out of the tack room.

Mariah was ready. I lifted the heavy saddle onto her back while Dr. Radcliffe stood next to me merely watching. Mariah lowered her head and took the bit. I flipped her ears through the bridle and handed the reins to Dr. Radcliffe. He mounted her jamming the reins. Mariah backed up then he kicked her forward. Back and forth she moved while he gripped the reins tightly. She was unsettled and started to rear. Hudson caught what was happening. He hurried over, grabbed the reins, and pushed them toward her mane.

Hudson said, "Yuh gotta give the pony more rein."

Dr. Radcliffe responded, "Get out of my way. I know what I'm doing."

Hudson was fuming, "Settle down, sir. I'm lead wrangler and these hosses and your safety are my responsibility. Out here, I'm the boss and yuh gotta take my orders. She's not wearin' a split bit. It's a western curb. If yuh insist on over reinin' the hoss, I'll saddle up a tough mouthed old mare fer yuh. Mariah's sensitive. She neck reins. Yuh ain't gonna pull none. Put yore reins in one hand and hold them loose, or get off Annie's hoss."

I stared open mouthed at Hudson. He said, "Why's yore mouth hangin' open?"

I softly said, "You called Mariah *Annie's horse.*"

Hudson said curtly, "I misspoke."

Philippe stepped close to me, asking which horse he would ride. I told him Hudson would decide. Hudson watched as Philippe stroked my head and picked meadow flowers adding them to the Columbines in my braid. He touched my face, whispering in my ear, "Are you coming with us?" Then Philippe leaned to kiss my neck.

Squirming to get away, I looked for Hudson. The blood rose in Hudson's ruddy cheeks. I stammered, "N-no. This is time for you and your father to bond."

Philippe snatched my arms tugging me to his chest. He put his arms around me and in a suave voice said, "I'd rather bond with you, Anna Lisa Clay."

I slapped Philippe in the face and kicked him in the shin. Losing my balance, I fell to the ground. While Philippe stood rubbing his face, Hudson helped me up, took my hand, and led me into the tack shed. Brushing the dirt off my butt, he whispered, "Yuh o.k. Annie?" I nodded and he continued, "Ain't no way yure gonna wed that feller. He's as worthless as a pail of hot spit."

I burst into tears, "That's what I've been telling you."

Hudson opened his arms and I collapsed into his warm embrace. "I should've trusted yuh from the git-go." Holding me affectionately, he added, "Yure a gold buckle. Yuh never showed me nothin' but respect. How can I be so stupid to mistrust a gal who orders pot roast fer me?"

"Pot roast" I said with a sigh through my tears and runny nose. He pulled his bandana from his pocket and tenderly wiped my face.

He said, "Go ahead, blow yore pretty lil nose." I blew my nose. He took the bandana and stuffed it back in his pocket. "Annie, I've been behavin' like a wild ass mule. I'm not much good at this romance stuff. Forgive me."

He noticed the gold chain around my neck and said, "What yuh got here?" Pulling the chain until the locket came out of my shirt, he smiled, "Lil Raccoon, scoured the grass and found her locket. Yuh kept me next to yore heart the whole time. Yuh trusted I'd come back. Yuh learned to trust me, Annie. "

I breathed with relief and happy tears flowed. He held me against his dusty, sweaty chest. Then he looked at me and said, "Sorry to muck up yore shirt."

I was elated to have him back and cheerfully said, "I love your sweat and dirt. You can smear them on me anytime."

He laughed, "Whatever tickles yore fancy." He bent to grab another saddle and I licked a bead of sweat off the back of his neck. Hudson said, "Sweet Thing, does my sweat taste good?"

"You're delicious," I replied grabbing a blanket.

He reached for my neck, "I bet yuh taste like sugar."

I giggled, sliding out of his arms. He chased me as I ran from the tack house laughing so hard it hurt. The wranglers watched our cat and mouse game. They hooted and hollered *wahoo*, vicariously enjoying our reunion. Hudson wrapped me in his arms and lifted me off the ground twirling me in the meadow. He stepped in a gopher hole. We tumbled, still laughing in the grass.

From my horse, Dr. Radcliffe said, "Anna Lisa?"

I smiled, "Don't worry Dr. Radcliffe, I've good color in my cheeks. Remember?"

The wranglers shouted *yeeha*. Hudson lifted me gently from the ground, whispering in my ear, "Annie, I'd like to frolic with yuh all day and night, like a fly in a currant pie, but I think yore friend needs a hoss. I got work to do." He turned toward Candy. "Bring that buckskin."

She looked doubtful and asked, "Double Buck Bop?"

"That's the one. Yale's an athlete."

Only wranglers rode Double Buck Bop. Hudson tethered the buckskin far from the other horses. Philippe excitedly approached it, "Look Father, I'm getting a cowboy horse like in the movies."

Hudson said, "Ain't like playin' the Queen's baseball, but if yuh can handle Ojibway yuh can handle Double Buck Bop. Did Skeebo explain baaga'adowe good? Tell yuh it's played to make virile warriors and is dedicated to the spirit of battle. Back at yore school, yuh playin' it fer a spirit or Him?" Hudson said as he pointed to heaven.

Philippe replied, "I'm a physics major. All phenomena can be explained by scientific law. Spirits are for people who can't reason at higher levels and thus explain reality by imagining a creator or God figure."

Hudson called to Skeebo, "Hear that Skeebo? Yale don't believe in the spiritual world."

Skeebo replied, "Tell him to come to our bunk house. Bring Annie."

Philippe was rubbing Double Buck Bop's nose like he was cooing to a baby. Hudson cinched the buckskin firmly. It bit Philippe on the shoulder.

He cried out, "Owe. Why'd he do that?"

Hudson smiled, "It's pure physics. I cinch, he bites. It's one of those scientific laws. Higher bein's ain't usually standin' so close." I didn't know cowboys were passive aggressive, but that day Hudson was.

Philippe mounted Double Buck Bop and the gelding dropped his head and bucked him off before he fell into line. Lacey dismounted her Palomino, Pink Pearl. She ran over to Philippe to help him. I noticed their eyes met and rested there a second too long.

Lacey asked, "Are yuh o.k. Philippe?"

"I'll have a hematoma. No bones are fractured. Thanks."

Lacey held Double Buck Bop's bridle, "Here yuh go."

Philippe looked at her in disbelief, "I beg your pardon? You'd like me to mount this thing again?"

"Yuh ain't got no broken bones so get back in the saddle, Philippe," Lacey said sweetly. "I'll hold Bop's bridle while yuh mount."

He grabbed the reins and heaved himself up. This time he moved slower, like he was protecting an injury.

"There yuh go," Lacey said. "Don't' that feel bett…?" Before she got the *er* off her lips Double Buck Bop threw Philippe again. She helped him up once more.

Philippe got back on and tightened the reins, pulling in the slack. Double Buck Bop started to throw his head from side to side, and forward, and back. With every move, Philippe tightened until Double Buck Bop's poll slammed into Philippe's nose."

Hudson called, "Yale, what's that squirtin' from yore face?"

Indignantly and in pain he said, "My name is not Yale. My name is Philippe." Blood poured from his nose. Lacey charged over handing him her pink bandana.

She said, "Get off of that hoss and hold Pink Pearl." Lacey mounted Double Buck Bop, collected his head, and pressed her boots into his sides. She rode him in tight circles, serpentines, and circle eights switching leads until he focused. She headed for the weaving poles. Brooms, shovels and rakes were stuck in the ground in a straight line to imitate poles. She led the buckskin through them in a tight weave, not letting him knock any of the garden paraphernalia over. She pressed firmly with her legs and sped toward Philippe. She brought the horse to a stop by sitting hard in the saddle. "Here yuh go Philippe. He'll behave better now. He needed to get his head on straight. How's yore nose?"

Philippe stared at her in awe, "It stopped bleeding. Thank you." He mounted the horse and Double Buck Bop dropped his head preparing to buck.

Lacey called sharply, "Aaak." Double Buck Bop settled into an even stride.

Hudson led the trail ride. Dr. Radcliffe and Philippe were several horses back, near Lacey. Philippe had undergone enough physical suffering for one day.

What concerned me was Hudson's self-esteem which these two snobs trampled on. I went to the front of the line. Hudson was holding Phantom while the other wranglers checked the guests' cinches.

I motioned for him to lean down and whispered, "Remember they're ignorant. They say *ignorance is bliss*." I smiled and said coyly, "Unless the lead wrangler's involved. Then it's painful."

He laughed in his fabulous way, "Sure yuh ain't comin with me?"

"I'm certain. I've seen enough combat today. Lacrosse, or no lacrosse, I'm sure the spirit of battle is happy."

CHAPTER TWENTY FIVE

INVITATION

That evening Pip was scheduled to hold a campfire sing along for the guests. I joined the waitresses on the way to the fire ring. Dr. Radcliffe and Philippe were sitting in the top row. Even in dim firelight, Philippe looked bad. His nose was swollen. His eyes were black and blue and he brought a pillow to sit on. I took a seat next to him, "Philippe, you look awful."

He spoke in a nasal tone, "It's that bad?"

"Yes. Do you need ice?"

Dr. Radcliffe interrupted, "Philippe iced sufficiently this afternoon."

I addressed Dr. Radcliffe out of courtesy, "That's good. How did Mariah work for you, sir?"

With a lofty air he said, "Directing her was as difficult as maneuvering a yacht in the Cayman Islands during hurricane season."

A large, dusty, cowboy boot slammed down on the bench between Philippe and me. I looked up and saw Hudson towering over us. "Doc, that sounds like another filly I know," Hudson said squeezing my shoulder.

Shocked to see him at the guest campfire I said, "Hudson, what're you doing here?"

"Annie, that sounds like I'm as welcome as a wet dog at a parlor social. I was worryin' about yore friend."

He maneuvered between Philippe and me. His leg rested against mine, "Yale, what yuh gonna do about yore condition? What kind of medicine did the good doc give yuh?"

Philippe replied, "That's private health information. I'm in good hands."

Hudson contrived a smile, "The cowboys will be glad to hear it. Lacey'll be especially relieved." I noticed Philippe perked up at the sound of her name. Hudson continued, "She's a good rider, ain't she, Yale? And she was proud of yuh gettin' back in the saddle given the way old Buck was tossin', makin' yuh eat dirt."

Philippe answered with a dreamy tone in his voice, "Lacey's beautiful and great with horses."

Hudson replied, "Yuh took to her like a bear to a honey tree, huh? I'll tell her what yuh said. Pretty words make a woman happy." Hudson turned his head toward me and winked.

Not able to fit comfortably between us, Hudson leaned back, stretched, and put his arm around my waist. I was delighted with the warmth of his arm behind me and the campfire on my face. The firelight glowed against his skin. I had to resist my desire to rest my head on his chest.

Pip finished singing and Dr. Radcliffe and Philippe headed for their guest house. The two walked like a horse was still between their legs. Hudson called after them, "Yale, tomorrow yure invited to the wrangler's' campfire at the meadow. Remember to bring Annie. We'll test yore physics' hypothesis."

Philippe asked if Lacey would be there. Hudson replied, "I don't know how she-hens think, but I bet she ain't goin' nowhere if yure there."

Philippe sounded pleased in a nasal way, "Thanks for the invitation. Good night, Anna Lisa."

As they staggered away, I overheard Dr. Radcliffe and Philippe talking, "Why do they want you there son?"

Philippe replied, "The wrangler, Skeebo, told me a spirit possesses their bunk house. I promised to provide the scientific explanation."

Dr. Radcliffe said, "That's my boy. Set them straight. They're a bizarre bunch and Hudson's a highly unusual sort of fellow."

~ ~ ~

I turned to Hudson and asked, "What's with luring Philippe toward Lacey?"

"Ain't no better way to keep Little Lord Fauntleroy away from yuh than to get him focused on another gal. Can yuh sit with me awhile, Annie?"

Guests and workers departed. It was quiet except for a great horned owl calling to his mate. The mate across the ranch hooted a response. Hudson looked in my eyes.

Embers sparked and popped intermittently. It was a perfect setting for a first kiss. I waited. He said to me, "Yuh should see how yuh look in this light - a temptin' Siren teasin' old Odysseus."

Amazed, I smiled, "You like Homer?"

"He tells a good story, don't he? A man battles to get to his woman and she waits unwearyingly fer him to come back to her."

I rested against him, "No wonder you're a romantic."

Hudson said, "Thanks fer waitin', Annie, and fer trustin' I'd come to my senses. Seein' the way Yale manhandled yuh and sayin' those things is when all hell broke loose in my head."

Hudson's heart was mine again. He came back to me. Hudson was in my arms and all stress fell away.

The embers were almost gone. It was dark. We were alone. Still he didn't kiss me. His lips were chapped and a piece of skin hung off his bottom lip. I said, "Your lips are chapped."

He said, "So are yores." I raised my fingers to my lips to feel them.

He smiled, "Ain't yuh got no gypsy concoction fer chapped lips?"

I thought to myself, the best concoction would be a moist kiss. I chuckled silently and shook my head.

"I better get yuh to yore bunk house. It's gettin' late." We walked in silence.

"Good night, Hudson."

"Good night, Sweet Thing. Dream of me," his scratchy lips pressed against my skin. I put my fingers on my forehead trying to drill this kiss into memory.

CHAPTER TWENTY SIX

LACEY

The next day Philippe looked painfully horrid. Hoyle asked me, "Annie, why don't yuh make Yale-boy a yolk and herb treatment like yuh done fer us?"

Dash added, "Give him the fun-geek tea. That stuff worked fer me."

Madison didn't look over when the wranglers talked with me. She probably realized a battle between Hudson and Philippe was enough for this dude ranch.

I addressed the wranglers, "I don't think he would accept my remedies. Dr. Radcliffe and Philippe are engrossed in modern western medicine. They can't fathom traditional ways of healing. For Dr. Radcliffe, remedies have to come from major pharmaceutical companies, or it's hooey hooey."

Candy asked Dash, "Did she say *hooey hooey*?" He nodded.

I ignored them and kept talking, "He consults for pharmaceutical firms and robotics companies."

Skeebo almost gagged on his food, "What's he got a robot fer? Moppin' his floor and wipin' his a...?"

Hudson snapped, "Watch yore mouth, Skeebo. Ladies are present."

I grinned, "He uses them for surgery."

Skeebo retorted, "Ain't no robot operatin' on me. Gotta be the hands the good Lord gave a doctor."

Sam called. Their food was up.

It was hot after lunch. The girls and I decided to make it a pool day. We were splashing around and floating on rafts while Lacey walked up. She was dusty and grimy. Her hair hung in sweaty, damp chunks, quite different from the day Philippe arrived. She came to the edge of the pool.

Caprice yelled, "Sorry Miss Rodeo, no jeans in the pool." The other girls joined Caprice in laughter. I remained silent. Finding an isolated cowgirl made it easy for them to bombard her.

Lacey called to me, "Anna Lisa, can I talk with yuh?"

I replied, "Certainly, Lacey what's up?"

She leaned over, "In private?" I jumped off my raft, swam to the edge, and climbed out. We sat on the grass. She smelled like expensive lotion even though she was filthy. I waited for her to start, "Anna Lisa, is it true yuh ain't engaged to Philippe?"

I sighed, "Oh my goodness, Lacey, didn't Hudson explain?"

"Yeah, but I wanna be sure," she said with a drawl.

Thinking this conversation was unnecessary, I said, "Lacey, Hudson's honest." I snapped, "I get it. Since I'm a city girl, you didn't know if I lied to Hudson. Lacey, I'm not betrothed to anyone." I was perturbed by her assumption and wished I had laughed with the girls.

Lacey read my irritation, "Anna Lisa, yure different from city types. It takes gettin' used to."

Fed up, I said, "What do you want?"

She grinned sheepishly, "I think Philippe is mighty cute and I want to get to know him."

I said, "So you'd like me to get his cell phone number? Maybe his e-mail too?"

She looked pleased, "That'd be great. The problem is I ain't able to text him from here." I saw her thinking, "Get them fer me anyway. Tell me about the dude."

I explained he's an incredibly rich, only child. Dr. Radcliffe is preparing him to own the largest privately held company of its kind. "You would have to enjoy travelling throughout the world, wining and dining customers and their spouses. You'd have to like living with too much money."

Lacey was beaming the entire time. She said, "He's perfect. Papa will be happy."

I said stoically, "Your father wants you to marry a rich guy?"

"Naw. Papa's afraid of a boy marrin' me fer money?"

Stunned, I questioned, "You're from money, Lacey?"

"Papa owns most of Idaho. He sold off the skiin' areas to developers and movie stars. Says it's not good country fer us because yuh can't run cattle and hosses fer a good part of the year."

I asked, "Do you get regular facials? I mean, anyone who gets grimy and keeps a clear complexion has to get facials."

Lacey laughed, "Here I'm askin' yuh about the love of my life, and yuh wanna know about my skin care? Yure silly, Anna Lisa. I like yuh already."

At this, I exhaled. I was delighted to gain the respect of the last true wrangler. Lacey thought my cheerfulness was about her facial ritual, so she continued, "Mama and I get facials once a month. She sends fine potions from our department store so I can maintain my skin."

"Nice," I said, but my mind was thinking about Hudson's Lord Fauntleroy match making strategy and I wanted to get Lacey talking about Philippe. "Back to the *love of your life*, I have an idea. Philippe doesn't leave until Saturday. Why don't you and Philippe come dancing with Hudson and me Friday?"

"Yuh think he'd go with me?" she asked.

I replied, "I think he would. Do you want to ask him or do you want me to?"

She threw her dusty arms around me and hugged me. Her dust stuck to my wet skin. She said, "Yuh ask him fer me." She walked back toward the corrals with a spring in her stride. I jumped in the pool.

It was too much for Madison, "Anna Lisa, what was that about?"

I responded pleasantly, "Just girl stuff." I ducked under water.

CHAPTER TWENTY SEVEN

SKILLET

Philippe waited for me until the dinner shift ended. While we walked to the wranglers' bunk house, I told him the details of my talk with Lacey: cell phone, e-mail address, and dancing on Friday. His face lit up, "Really, she wants me to take her dancing? Wow. I don't know where to go." I told him it would be a double date with Hudson and me and the dance hall's not far.

At the bunk house, the campfire was ablaze. A violet blue wind rolled in and I heard Skeebo yell, "They're here." The wranglers welcomed us.

Philippe asked, "What causes the odd colored wind?"

Hudson said, "Physics Man, we need yuh to tell us. If it ain't no spirit, what is it? Got anything like this in yore laboratory beakers?" Philippe looked like Rodin's Thinker with an engorged nose.

The wind passed in and out of the bunk house. It dowsed the campfire. From the open door it flung a spittoon at me. I ducked. It missed. The tin missed Philippe too, but the chewing tobacco spit splatted across his face.

"Yale, yuh got chew spit on yore face," Hudson laughed. Philippe touched his face spreading the spit.

214

Tin plates and cups flew toward us. Philippe hid behind me to avoid the attack. I ducked, dodging the dishes. Philippe was hit by one and screamed. Turning to look at him, I didn't see what was heading toward me.

Hudson yelled, "Annie, look out." He tackled me. A cast iron skillet whooshed by us hitting Philippe on the head. He tumbled back, then didn't move.

Still covering me, Hudson yelled, "Hoyle get to Yale. See if he's dead. Start doin' that C.P. and R. stuff, breathe in his mouth, pump on his chest. Kick start him. He better not be dead."

Hoyle ran to Philippe. Shaking him, he yelled, "Yale, yuh hear me?" Hoyle called, "He's breathin'."

Lacey ran to his side. Philippe opened his eyes, looked at her, and asked, "What was that?"

"A skillet," she said. Philippe passed out again.

Hudson called, "We best deliver him to his pa. Annie, yure not stayin' here. Yure comin' with me. Hoyle, yure comin' too in case Yale tries to die on the way."

The wranglers draped Philippe over Phantom with his head dangling on one side and his legs hanging off the other.

Hudson didn't pay attention to Philippe. He looked at me and said, "Annie, yuh gotta forgive me. It was senseless puttin' yuh in harm's way because we want to prove to an insultin' cuss he ain't knowin' it all. Yuh could've been killed by the skillet. That violet blue's gettin' too aggressive with yuh."

Hudson saw me rub my hip, "Aw, My Love, did I hurt yuh? How yuh feel?" he gently demanded.

Previously, I'd have lied, but the Codes were a part of me now. I honestly said, "My shoulder throbs and my hip's sore." I saw the furrow on Hudson's brow and reassured him, "Don't worry, it'll pass. You saved me. It could've been me draped over your horse."

He brought Phantom to a stop and Philippe fell off. Hudson left him and said, "Hoyle, get over here. Annie's hurt."

I said, "Shouldn't you pick up Philippe?"

Hudson looked at Philippe's crumpled body and indifferently said, "Naw."

Hoyle approached me and I told them, "Philippe's in worse shape. We need to get him to his father."

Hudson said sternly, "Listen to me Little Lady, Phantom ain't takin' a step until I tell him." Hoyle pulled out a flashlight and checked my eyes for proper dilation. He took my pulse. Then he checked the tightness of my shoulder ligaments. He checked my hip range of motion. He asked, "What's yore name? Can yuh tell me where yuh are? Where've yuh been? What's this guy's name?" He pointed at Hudson.

I said, "Oh please. May we go now?"

Hoyle ignored me, turned to Hudson, and reported that I appeared to be fine, but I could expect more aches in the morning. Hudson and Hoyle grabbed Philippe by his limp arms and heaved him onto Phantom like a bag of mail. Hudson took the lead rope and we continued toward the guest quarters.

"This is why city people lie. I should've told you I was fine. Then we could've kept moving," I stated with a temper.

Hudson looked at me in disbelief, "Yuh wouldn't. How'd I know yure hurt? I expect yuh to tell the truth. This feller that's as limp as a neck-wrung rooster ain't of no importance to me. I got my priorities."

We reached the Radcliffe's cabin. I knocked and Dr. Radcliffe opened the door. Hudson and Hoyle carried Philippe. They laid him on the bed. Dr. Radcliffe grilled Hoyle about Philippe's injury. The doctor said, "I must start a line." He grabbed one of the designer suitcases pulling out his supplies, "Anna Lisa run to the dining hall and get ice."

Hudson said, "Annie, I'll get it."

Hudson came back with a bucket of ice. Dr. Radcliffe was still poking Philippe. Hoyle gathered the ice in a towel and knotted it so that it formed a dome. He placed it on Philippe's head.

Hoyle said, "Doctor, perhaps yuh'll let me give it a whirl."

Dr. Radcliffe looked down his nose at Hoyle, "What could you possibly know?"

Hudson immediately came to Hoyle's defense, "Doc, Hoyle's an Emergency Medical Tech. He starts lines all the time fer folks injured on these highways."

Dr. Radcliffe ignored Hudson and tried another time, missing the vein completely. Hoyle was already washing his hands.

"Fine, let's see what you can do," Dr. Radcliffe said with a doubtful sneer.

Hoyle palpated the back of Philippe's hand. He inserted the needle and released the catheter. Dr. Radcliffe handed him the heplock. He taped it in place. The line was started.

Hoyle stepped out of the way. Dr. Radcliffe took Philippe's vitals. We started to leave and he commanded, "No you don't. I'm going to stabilize my son and then we're talking with your boss."

Hudson said, "We'll be waitin' fer yuh outside, Doc."

Hudson offered the porch chair to me. Hoyle sat on the step and Hudson sat on the railing. Hudson said to Hoyle, "Yuh did good work in there." Hoyle tipped his head.

Dr. Radcliffe stepped onto the porch. I asked, "Is Philippe conscious?"

Dr. Radcliffe avoided my eyes and said severely, "No." He walked to Trotter Blue's office and we followed.

Trotter Blue's sleeping quarters were through a door behind his desk. Dr. Radcliffe knocked on the office door. Hudson stepped around Dr. Radcliffe, opened the door, and entered the office. He knocked on Trotter Blue's bedroom door.

A crusty old voice with apparently no dentures hollered, "Whose there?"

"It's me, sir," Hudson replied.

Trotter Blue yelled, "Hell, Hudson, it's the middle of the night. It better be mighty important like the ranch is ablaze, because I was sleepin' like a lizard on a hot rock."

Hudson and I looked at one another and he winked.

Trotter Blue pulled open the door and saw Dr. Radcliffe, Hoyle, and me. He was wearing fire engine red long johns and his hair was wild.

He closed the door quickly and called, "Hudson, why yuh ain't mentionin' there's a lady in yore presence?" In his room, he apparently put his teeth in because his speech became clearer. "Annie, I'm sorry. I wasn't intended to scare yuh." He came out in a plaid flannel robe with his tattered cowboy hat. Sticking out from beneath his robe were two spindly, white legs in cowboy boots. He said, "What's goin' on?"

Dr. Radcliffe talked first about how the wranglers *lured* Philippe to their campfire. Then they *pummeled* him until he was unconscious. He said, "I started an I.V. line and when I left, Philippe was stable but unconscious."

Trotter Blue asked, "Do yuh want an ambulance?"

Dr. Radcliffe said, "Definitely not. I'm a medical doctor. I want these three disciplined and relieved of their duties."

I couldn't believe what Dr. Radcliffe said. Anxiety rose in me. Hudson noticed and reached for my hand holding it gently.

Trotter Blue said, "Yuh want me to sack them?"

The doctor nodded.

Trotter addressed Hudson calmly, which soothed my terror slightly, "What happened to our friend Philippe, son?"

Hudson said, "Yale came to the campfire with Annie. He was gonna explain with' scientific expertise the violet blue wind. Yuh know how it's been lately, bargin' around like a moose in a wigwam."

Trotter Blue listened.

"The moment Annie and Yale arrived, it began tossin' plates and mugs. Yale hid behind Annie."

Trotter Blue interjected astounded, "He ain't standin' in front protectin' her?" He turned to Dr. Radcliffe, "Does this sound like yore son?"

Dr. Radcliffe said, "Philippe is risk averse and wise about protecting himself."

Trotter Blue said with disgust, "If yuh ask me, it ain't gentlemanly leavin' a lady in the aim of fire. Go on Hudson."

"Yale took a tin cup on the shoulder and started howlin'. Annie turned to look at his commotion when that hot spider come flyin' toward her head. I ran at her, knockin' her out of the way. Poor thing, in the tackle, I wrenched her shoulder and smashed her hip."

Trotter Blue asked, "Annie, yuh alright?"

"Hoyle checked me, sir, and says I'll be fine."

Trotter Blue said, "Glad to hear it. What happened to the fella cowerin' behind your dainty maiden?"

Hudson said, "The skillet took Yale head on."

Trotter Blue turned to Dr. Radcliffe, "There yuh have it, Doc."

Dr. Radcliffe raised his tone, "You're going to take the word of that unsound animal?"

Trotter Blue said forcefully, "First of all, Hudson ain't no animal. He's a man. Yuh heard how he risked his life to make sure his inamorata was safe. Dr. Radcliffe, he's certain about what happened."

"I cannot believe this," Dr. Radcliffe declared.

Trotter Blue said, "I suggest yuh wait fer yore son to come to and he'll tell yuh the same thing."

Dr. Radcliffe said, "You believe that country trash of a cowhand and his tramp who wants nothing other than to bed a cowboy?"

I gasped, clasping my hand over my mouth. Hoyle grabbed Hudson's fist before it flew at Dr. Radcliffe.

Trotter Blue said, "Hudson, let me handle this. Doctor, yuh may be my guest but yuh ain't got no right callin' good people trash and insultin' a fine, decent woman like Annie. How dare you attack her innocence? I ain't gonna tolerate yure assaults on Hudson's moral fiber. Yuh need to apologize to her and to the man who loves her."

Dr. Radcliffe said, "There's no way in hell I'd apologize to such repulsive individuals."

Hudson was fuming. His face was red and his muscles were tense. Trotter Blue spoke, "Hudson, take Annie away. This kind of talk ain't good fer ladies and it ain't doin' yuh no good. Hoyle, yuh head out too. I'll settle this with the doctor."

Hudson put his arm across my shoulders. We headed through the office door. "You can't leave Trotter Blue alone with that man. Go back," I pleaded.

Hudson was too mad to talk.

Hoyle said, "Trotter'll be fine, Anna Lisa. Remember he's a cowboy."

I responded, "But he's old and Dr. Radcliffe isn't a slight man."

Hudson spoke, "He ain't no man."

"Hudson, go back, please," I deplored.

He spoke softly, "Annie, I ain't gonna take away Trotter Blue's pride. He says he's gonna take care of things. How'd it look if I come in because I think he ain't capable? Besides, he's got a Smith n' Wesson in his drawer and a rifle under his bed. There ain't gonna be no trouble fer our Boss Man."

They walked me to my bunk house. Hoyle tactfully took off with the excuse of bringing Phantom to the corral.

I turned into Hudson and whispered, "I need you to stay with me."

"Anytime," he said as he sat down on the trunk of a sawed off tree. There was room for the two of us to sit side by side, but he placed me on his lap. Cradling me in his arms he said, "I feel bad yuh heard that foul mouth say those things."

I looked away, embarrassed and full of self-doubt.

"It bites, don't it, Princess?" he said as he gently pulled my chin toward him.

"Hudson, I've been through a lot but this hurts. Do I come across as a tramp?"

Hudson exhaled in disbelief and put his finger to my lips, "Annie, yure perceived as the purest, most untouchable woman on the ranch. No man dares lay a hand on yuh. It hurts because he's attackin' yore character. Pay no attention to that pompous, tyrannical M.D."

I wrapped my arms around his shoulders and hugged him to me, "I wonder how long it'll be before Ruby hears what a *slut* I've become?" Hudson winced.

"Are Ruby and yore ma friends?"

I nodded.

"Yuh worried about what yore ma will say? She ain't gonna come get yuh, will she?" he said increasing his hold on me.

I replied, "Ruby won't tell Mother. In these circles, if someone's child falls off the deep end, you don't mention it to the mother. Instead, you'll come up with a myriad of excuses why you can't get together with her, unless you can use her for a political maneuver or power gain."

Hudson said, "Sounds complicated. How do yuh keep it straight?"

I smiled, "It's urban culture. I worry about my dad. If Dr. Radcliffe talks to him, Dad'll be here the next day to take me home."

Hudson became quiet and didn't talk for a long time. He held me still and I rested on his chest. I listened to him breathing and pressed my ear against his heart, hearing the rhythmic beats. "What's yore pa think of Trotter Blue?" Not expecting him to talk, I jumped. "Sorry, Sweetheart."

I lifted my head and gazed at him, "Dad thinks Trotter Blue's a respectable man. On the phone, and when he dropped me off, they talked about honesty and trust."

Hudson lifted me to my feet, "I imagine Trotter Blue got rid of the jug head by now." He gave me a kiss on my forehead, "Sweet dreams, Annie. Never doubt yore virtue." He walked toward the dining hall and Trotter Blue's sleeping quarters.

CHAPTER TWENTY EIGHT

DEVIL DOC

I emotionally and physically ached the next morning. I didn't feel like confrontation and wondered if I should avoid the Radcliffes or hold my head up high and face them. I decided on the latter since I did nothing wrong. They sat in Grace's station.

"Grace, do you mind if I take that two top?"

"Thanks Anna Lisa, I'm swamped with the family reunion. They're picky. One wants her eggs poached hard, the other wants her eggs over easy. One wants extra butter on his muffin while his wife wants the muffin dry with butter on the side. Then there's the daughter who wants juice exactly half grapefruit and half orange. The son wants salsa on his hash browns. I brought the regular picadillo salsa and he threw a fit because he wants the habanera liquid type. It takes five sheets just to catch the order of ten people."

I complimented her, "Grace, if there's anyone who can handle difficult people politely, it's you. Let me know if you need backup." She smiled and sped to their table.

I headed toward the Radcliffe's table, "Good morning. How are you Philippe?"

Philippe looked at me and said, "What idea crosses your tiny mind, Anna Lisa?"

I ignored his insult and said, "I think you should keep icing and get well soon if we're going to the honky-tonk, Friday."

Philippe attempted a smile. Dr. Radcliffe curtly said, "Anna Lisa, you'll not partake in the Friday night romp. Your cowgirl days of frivolity and sin are coming to an abrupt end."

I consciously left out any words of respect like *sir* or *doctor*, "What do you mean?"

"Your father and I had a telephone conversation last night. He expressed disappointment in you. He's catching the first flight out of LAX today. He should arrive around four or five o'clock. You best have your bags packed."

I glared at him, putting my hands behind my back to force off tears, "What a monstrously evil thing to do. What you said about me was a lie. You're fabricating your own sick story to convince yourself that I'm not good enough for your son. You can't stand it that I don't want to marry Philippe. Face it, you can't deal with it. It's so far from your comprehension that the best you can do is attack me personally." Turning to Philippe I said, "Philippe, you may look like hell, but your father deserves to burn there."

I turned away leaving Philippe with a confused look on his contorted face. I overheard his self-absorbed comment, "Father, why'd you do that? I'm supposed to go dancing with Lacey, Friday. Anna Lisa and Hudson are showing me where to go."

Dr. Radcliffe said through gritted teeth, "Don't mention that brute's name and I'm not letting you date a lowbrow country girl."

I called, "Shelly, that deuce is yours this morning. In fact, it will be yours for lunch and dinner too."

I would've helped Grace, but my head was in turmoil. I couldn't deal with complicated orders. I picked up Shelly's two top with a sweet old couple, the Cartwrights. They were celebrating their fiftieth wedding anniversary. The Cartwrights looked as happy as they did when she was a fresh summer bride and he was a proud courting gentleman. They kept me busy with stories of their children and grandchildren.

I asked, "Mrs. Cartwright, what's the secret to your long, successful marriage?"

Flossey Cartwright replied, "Sweetie, you must marry the most honorable, trustworthy man you can find, like Duke here." She touched her husband's arm softly. "He has to adore you so thoroughly he'd lay down his life to save yours. Don't let anyone judge him. It doesn't matter what people say. Here's the key, you have to feed him well. For instance, you have to make the best mashed potatoes and pot roast." My eyes filled with tears at the sound of pot roast. The old guest grabbed my hands, "Aw Sweetie what's the matter?"

I replied through clouded eyes, "I found that man, but he's being taken from me by people who judge him."

Her voice was high pitched and crackled, "You must be willing to fight for him and discard any person who stands in your way. The only place you need to be is by his side." Trying to cheer me, she smiled, "That's if you want to eat fluffy mashed potatoes and delicious pot roast."

Her words of wisdom were uncannily close to the emotions I felt. That morning I had too much to process. I waited until the guests left before I headed to my meditation spot. I had to calm my racing mind and pacify my aching heart.

I sat on the boulder weeping until my eyes were dry. The last tears peppered the hot stone. The sun was intense, but I could see gray thunder clouds lying in wait. They were ready to roll in. It was going to rain again. It didn't matter. The weather changed in these mountains every two hours. I had grown used to the rhythm of the weather, the rhythm of the mountains, the rhythm of this lifestyle, and the rhythm of my heart. Tears welled in my eyes again. I took deep breaths as I walked through the woods on my familiar path, fearing this would be the last time. I noticed the pine cones, the roots sticking through the dirt, the columbines, and the aspen leaves fluttering in the breeze. I inhaled and filled my lungs with the sweet, pungent smell of pine. I took in the soothing green color of the trees. Mother Nature's balance established equilibrium. In my turmoil, I found peace. As I headed toward the poolside, I was composed and ready to serve lunch to my guests, with the exception of the fiendish doctor. I avoided the Radcliffes. They were now invisible to me.

Engrossed with my team, I enjoyed the company of the girls more than I had in the past. I laughed at Sam's jokes, even the bad ones. I noticed what Grace was wearing. I noticed Shelly's tan and bleaching hair. I noticed Madison's confident posture and Caprice's lanky body in dull clothing. I noticed details I took for granted.

A group of dusty cowboys crested the mountain. My heart stopped. I watched their relaxed gait. Dash and Hoyle were laughing and I saw Hoyle punch Hudson's upper arm. Rubbing his arm he jokingly punched back.

The wranglers sat at the eight top which was under the patio cover to avoid expected rain. I went to take the order. It seemed like I was moving in slow motion. Lacey smiled and said, "Howdy, Anna Lisa."

I could barely muster a small smile. Then Hudson's eyes met mine. His eyes were penetrating. At that moment, the storm broke loose. A bright flash of lightning lit the sky and illuminated his face. Seconds later, thunder roared. My eyes welled and silent tears rolled down my cheeks.

I turned toward Grace, shoving the order pad and pen in her hand. I ran through the rain. The cold rain drops fell on my face blending with tears. I heard a chair shove away from the table and boots running down the path behind me. Hudson caught me and whirled me into his chest. His big arms wrapped around my shoulders and held me still. I sobbed and heaved deep tearful gasps.

"What's wrong, Annie?"

Not able to talk, I shook my head.

"Yuh remember when we got caught in that nasty thunder storm? Yuh said it was romantic and I said it sounded like a violent courtship between buffaloes."

I knew he was trying to cheer me, but I couldn't smile. I gasped another sputtering breath.

His voice became softer, "What's got yuh rattled, Sweet Thing?"

Still holding me against him it took a few seconds to find my voice, "Dr. Radcliffe talked to Dad."

Hudson remained unaffected, "Yeah. So?"

I shrieked, "*So* is all you can say? You smile, and laugh, and punch Hoyle like it's not a big deal. I'm leaving today. Am I just another *gal* on your list?"

"Whoa, Annie." Hudson took a breath and embraced me tighter. He spoke quietly trying to calm my tone, "Yuh ain't goin' home today."

I replied in an emotional sob, "Hudson, you can't stop my dad. I'm his daughter. He'll be here in a few hours."

Hudson said in a steady voice, "He ain't comin fer yuh."

I was about to yell to get it through his thick head when he said, "Hear me out, Feverish Woman. Trotter Blue and I talked last night after Devil Doc used the phone. Trotter Blue called yore pa and explained what happened. He cleared it up. I was sittin' right there, Annie. Trotter Blue told me Mansfield said *this sounds more like my baby girl and he ain't surprised yure fallin' fer a cowboy*. Hudson winked at me and continued, "Then he said *give Annie a kiss, tell her I love her, and I miss her*."

I raised my head from Hudson's chest. I didn't need to ask *really*. I reached up, wrapped my arms over his shoulders, and buried my wet face in his hot grimy neck. "Thank you," I panted.

He was smiling, "It's my pleasure, Sweet Annie. Hey, yuh got my grime stuck on yore pretty face." He pulled out a red bandana, unfolded it, and gently wiped the dirt. The bandana smelled like him. I inhaled basking in his aroma and the thought of enjoying the rest of the summer at the ranch with him.

I headed through the rain to the door of my bunk house. He returned to his lunch. I took a hot shower to rinse the stress and sticky dust from me.

In the evening, I passed the Radcliffe's table. Dr. Radcliffe was cupping a goblet of cognac in his hand to warm it. I ignored him and said to Philippe, "We're still on for Friday night."

Philippe said, "You bet, Anna Lisa. I can't wait to see Lacey."

The doctor choked on his Courvoisier. Golden liquid gurgled down the rim of the goblet. There was gratification in hearing him hack. I smiled snickering out loud. My city feistiness was alive and well.

~ ~ ~

After dinner, Sam motioned to the back door. Hudson stood in the door jam. I went to him, "What's up?"

He replied, "Will yuh ride with me? Seems like yuh could use some plain old country fun away from Devil Doc."

"You're right. Give me a minute to wrap up." After clearing my guests' tables, I returned and met Hudson on the porch. He had Phantom tethered to the post, "Only one horse?"

"Yeah. That o.k?"

I nodded. He gave me a leg up onto Phantom's bare back. Mounting behind me he handed over the reins and said, "Take me someplace."

He slid his arms around my waist. I felt his touch and his body pressed against my back. Hudson put his mouth to my ear and licked it, "Yuh do taste like sugar."

I smiled and squeezed Phantom sprinting away from the trail that led to the wrangler's bunk house. We went down the dirt road toward the highway. "What's down the trail on the other side?"

With his warm breath on my ear, he said softly, "Take me there."

I carefully walked Phantom across the highway's black tar. The breeze picked up. I shivered. Hudson opened his jacket and wrapped me inside. The heat of his chest radiated, enveloping me in warmth. We walked Phantom up a trail and came to the edge of the tree line. In front of us was a large motionless lake. Reflection of stars sparkled on the water. It looked like a sequined black cloak under theater lights, "It's beautiful. Do you see the reflection of the Milky Way?"

He chuckled quietly.

"Hudson, you knew this was here. Why didn't you show it to me earlier?"

"Gotta keep surprisin' yuh," he said dismounting Phantom and helping me. Hudson took my hand and led me to the edge of the lake. Hidden between the rocks was a row boat. He pulled it to the water's edge. Holding his arm out for me, he said, "Climb in."

He pushed the boat into the water and leapt in without tipping it. Amazingly, he didn't get his boots wet. He sat across from me and took the oars. The reflection of stars danced from the swooshing of paddles and wake of the boat. We got to the middle of the sparkling lake. I looked at him, "You're fabulous, Hudson."

"Naw, I'm plain and simple." He put the oars down and moved next to me, "Annie, I think yuh were born in the wrong part of the Stars and Stripes. Yuh'd like a simple life."

I remarked, "Simple life? Like this sparkling wonder is simple? It's more intriguing and complex than anything man could make. Fabergé and Dior haven't captured beauty like this. I'm envious. This is your life and you have time to enjoy it. In the city, time's out of control, spinning too fast. My schedule runs me. Even my leisure time is on a schedule." I paused and put my hand on his thigh, "Listen Hudson, we don't hear a thing. It's peaceful and quiet. Back home, we try everything to find peace: massage, meditation, aroma therapy, yoga, tai chi, herbal tea, organic foods, hypnotherapy, the psychologist's couch, foot reflexology, detoxification teas, and seaweed wraps. Here, all you need to do is breath and listen to find peace."

"Annie, yuh gotta ask yoreself if yuh can live without those things. Would yuh be happy without packing your beautiful body in seaweed?"

I smiled into his eyes, "I've thought about leaving my city things. I wouldn't miss them. My life would be fuller and richer if I were to adopt this *simple life*.

"My friends wouldn't understand. I don't think they could stop running the rat race long enough to comprehend me."

He smiled and placed his hand over mine which was still on his thigh, "I'm glad. See what I mean? Yure born in the wrong part of the U.S. of A." We sat in the boat for a long time, quiet, and peaceful. It rocked gently. A barn owl screeched from a tree. Down the trail we heard the reply.

Hudson said, "Barn owls mate fer life."

I replied, "It must be love."

It would've been the perfect moment for our first kiss, except for the chance of capsizing. He didn't kiss me. He moved back onto his bench, grabbed the oars, and rowed to shore. Phantom whinnied. We rode quietly back to the dude ranch. Outside my bunk house, Hudson wished me sweet dreams and kissed my forehead.

CHAPTER TWENTY NINE

TIGHT FITTING JEANS

The next morning I saw Philippe. The swelling subsided but he still looked like he was in a brawl. Full of anticipation, he asked, "Annie, what should I wear tonight?"

Short of rolling my eyes, I replied, "Wear your jeans. There's a Tight Fitting Jeans Contest the third Friday of the month." I laughed, "Don't worry you won't win."

He replied, "But Lacey might." He grinned and left to catch the van for the gold town tour.

That evening Hudson came by the bunk house to get me and said, "Turn around. Yep."

"Yep, what?" I said.

He had a smile on his face and a naughty look in his eye, "Yuh'll win tonight."

I blushed. My cheeks felt hot, "Go away. I'm not tight fitting jeans material."

He crossed his arms and tilted his head, "Yuh don't know how beautiful yuh are, do yuh?" I clutched Hudson's hand and we went to meet Lacey and Philippe in the parking lot next to a silver Porsche.

Philippe said, "Hot car. Whose is it?"

Lacey replied, "It's mine."

Philippe said with surprise. "Really, it's yours?" I elbowed him. He quickly added, "It's nice."

She lowered the top as he stood watching. It rained earlier, so it would stay clear until the next day. The lot was muddy and full of puddles. Hudson held me while I jumped over them. He sloshed right through. He opened the door to his truck for me and held out his hand to help me climb in. I clicked my boot heels together to get the mud off. Not that I had to, the floor board was encrusted with decades of dirt. Hudson whispered, "Slide over to me."

I saw Lacey offer the keys to Philippe. He got in letting her open her own door. Hudson huffed quietly and said, "Look there. Makes Lacey open her own door. Ain't got no brains on how to treat a lady." We pulled out of the parking space and the Porsche fell in behind us. Hudson said, "Hold on, Annie."

He gunned the engine. The truck fishtailed with wheels slinging mud. It splatted on the windshield of Lacey's car and Philippe's hair. Lacey was fast. She ducked out of the way. Philippe flipped the bird - typical of urban road rage. I heard Lacey holler something unintelligible. Hudson grinned and looked at me. "You're as bad as Caprice," I chuckled.

He laughed, pleased with himself. Philippe turned on the windshield wipers smearing the mud across the glass. It was barely clear enough for him to see through the smudge.

That night we danced and danced. Lacey taught Philippe the steps. I was surprised he caught on quickly.

The slow dance came and Hudson twirled me across the dance floor. Philippe and Lacey stared at us along with the rest of the crowd. On the second slow dance, Philippe broke in to dance with me. Hudson reluctantly allowed it. Like a gentleman, Hudson didn't let Lacey stand alone. He held out his hand and took her to the dance floor.

Philippe said, "Anna Lisa, I thought you were insane when I learned about you and that cowboy. But, I can see you're happy with him. It's written on your face." He added, "He's wildly in love with you. I've never met a man willing to fight for a woman like this guy. Have you considered he might suffer from Borderline Personality Disorder?"

I glared at Philippe and pulled away. A flashback of Flossey Cartwright's wisdom crossed my mind, "Don't insult Hudson, Philippe." Hudson caught the rift between us and came over, taking my hand. He led me outside. I said, "Don't fret. I'm not going to duke things out with him in there."

"I know yuh ain't. Yuh got too much class. What's he sayin' to yuh?" Hudson asked.

I wished I could've lied and told Hudson it was nothing. In my state of anger, it was difficult in to come up with an honest statement that wouldn't hurt him. I said, "He thinks you're in love with me."

Hudson looked down, "That's what makes yuh mad enough to kick a hog barefooted?"

I replied, "Not that."

He exhaled in relief.

I explained, "Philippe said an ignorant insult and I'm done with dealing with the Radcliffes' lack of respect."

Hudson embraced me, "May I have this dance?" He took my hands and twirled me around on the porch in the open air. "Look up, Annie." The stars were bright. One shot across the sky. Hudson saw it. He grabbed me, pulling me into him and whispered in my ear, "Make yore wish." I silently made my wish.

"Make yours," I whispered.

A smile crossed his face, "Mines already come true."

The screen door of the dance hall flew open. Lacey yelled, "Yuh won the Couple's Contest. Better get yore squeezy buns in here to take yore prize." We hurried inside. Dolly handed Hudson a dinner certificate for two at Old Jack's Steak House. Rella won the Single Cowgirl Award. Philippe won the Single Cowboy Award. He walked up and the crowd hooted and hollered at this city boy in jeans, pink polo shirt, loafers, and argyle socks.

~ ~ ~

The next morning Grace shook me. I made her promise she wouldn't let me oversleep. "Thanks," I yawned and stretched. "I can't believe it's morning already."

"Did you have a good time?" she asked.

"I did. Hudson's a wonderful guy, Grace. But there's something that doesn't feel right. He only kisses me on the forehead. He hasn't attempted to kiss me on the lips, not even after our dates."

Grace replied, "Sounds like a true gentleman to me. But I'm old fashioned."

I considered, "Do you think he sees me merely as a friend?"

Grace said, "No way, I've seen how he watches you. Think of the gifts."

I got dressed, splashed cold water in my face, pulled my hair into a pony tail, and slipped on my boots. They were gorgeous boots, a bit scuffed by then, but fabulous.

Dr. Radcliffe and Philippe were leaving. Thank goodness. It was stressful with them there. I saw Lacey walk Philippe to the van. They were holding hands. He made her promise she would join his family over winter break at their ski chalet in Idaho. He kept asking, "Promise?"

"I gave yuh my word. What more do yuh want?" Lacey said. Philippe hadn't learned about a cowgirl's word. What happened next was a surprise. He reached out, put his arms around her and gave her a passionate kiss on the lips. Hudson looked at them as he loaded the Radcliffes' suitcases. He placed his eyes on me and I blushed. I hoped this display of affection would motivate Hudson.

Madison said, "Lacey'll be the next one to be fired. Trust me, Trotter Blue will call her to his office."

"I disagree, Madison," I said. "Trotter Blue follows the Code. It's o.k. for a girl to get a kiss from a guest. It's not o.k. for a male worker to stalk a female guest. Male ranch hands need to show respect toward women."

Madison barked, "Anna Lisa, you're saying this because your ranch hand hasn't kissed you."

I looked at Grace and raised my eyebrows. "Anna Lisa, how could you question me? I'm your friend. I wouldn't betray your trust. I didn't tell them."

Madison said, "Hah. It's true. Gorgeous probably has a girl on every ranch. He's playing you, Anna Lisa. Or is it, Annie?"

Grace got in Madison's face. She was standing tall like a drill sergeant and barked, "Shut up, Madison. Because your panties are in a wad, doesn't mean you can take away Anna Lisa's sense of worth." Grace had never raised her sweet, finch-like voice before that day.

CHAPTER THIRTY

DOLORES MATAFANTASMAS

There was less tension on the ranch once Dr. Radcliffe and Philippe were gone. It seemed things were back to normal.

Lacey was not sacked. In fact, she was invited to dine with Trotter Blue in the main hall. Their conversation was cheerfully intense. I overheard Trotter Blue say, "I know your papa. Buggy Honeycutt will take to Philippe. He might not like the kid's pa, but he'll be hospitable."

New guests with unfamiliar faces arrived. One guest, Dolores Matafantasmas came separately in a black Jaguar. She was tall and slender. She had long jet-black hair and skeletal fingers adorned with too many bulky silver rings with semiprecious gems.

Skeebo went to greet her. I knew it couldn't be his mother. Ms. Matafantasmas was too lanky and white skinned to have a robust, dun colored son like Skeebo. He enthusiastically carried her shiny Paton leather suitcase and hat box as he escorted her to her guest quarters.

Later that evening, I joined Grace, Shelly, and Caprice at the campfire. Madison was there. I made certain I sat furthest from her.

Chief Cheyevo was up from the city. This time he wore a black and red shirt with a Native American snake print. On his right hand he wore a turquoise stone embedded in worked silver. His coat was fringed. I wondered if it was deer hide.

VIOLET RIBBONS

As always, his stories were entertaining and intriguing. The previous time he told a delightful tale of seven maidens who escaped from a bear. After much ado, they became stars forming the constellation we call the Seven Sisters. As the full moon shone down on us that night, the Chief told a tale of the Purple Swan Maiden. "The legend says the maiden's mother decorated a deerskin dress with purple feathers and turquois beads. She painstakingly ground the purple centers of the summer columbines to make a dye. Then she dipped each feather into the radiant purple liquid. The squaw's mother wrapped fine leather lacing around each feather and strung these between two pines to dry in the breeze. She attached the dry feathers to her daughter's deer skin tunic adding turquois beads as an accent. Ancient tales claim this maiden was the loveliest squaw in the tribe. Some tales claim she was the loveliest in the West. The purple gown enhanced the richness of the plates of her dark hair. The turquois beads enhanced the glow of her fine complexion. One evening, she wandered farther than usual from home. A young warrior of a neighboring tribe was hunting for game birds by the lake. He was to bring the foul home for his mother to clean and cook in a stew of nettles and roots. His eyes fell upon the lovely maiden as she admired her stunning tunic in the reflection of the glass lake. Lost in her admiration she didn't notice the warrior until he snapped a branch under his moccasin. She turned around and spied him. Struck with fear, the maiden fled from the stranger. As she ran, a feather fell from her gown. The young man retrieved the feather and ran after her. He followed the purple light which glowed from her through the forest. She made it home, panting and gasping for air. Her father and mother questioned her about her apparent stress. She explained her encounter with the stranger. The maiden's father stepped outside and peered into the darkness. With his keen eyesight he spotted the tip of the warrior's bow sticking out from behind a bush where the lad hid. *Present yourself,* he commanded. The warrior could see from the man's highly decorated tunic that he held a high status in the tribe. Despite his fine attire, the father's head was a hideous mass of clotted blood. The warrior had no choice but to step into the fire light. Refraining from looking at the chief's head and shaking with fear and nausea, the warrior held out the feather. *I'm here to return this feather to your daughter, great sir.* The chief took the feather. *Thank you.* The chief looked quizzically at the young trembling man. *No warrior runs through the forest to return a single feather. What's your intention? Could it be you admire my daughter's loveliness? She is a fine maiden, the finest in our tribe.* The warrior nodded shyly in agreement. Stifling his queasy stomach he mustered the strength to ask the father for his daughter's hand in marriage. Before the Swan Maiden's father would grant this request, the warrior was to be put to a test. According to the warrior, if it meant the chance to betroth this fine squaw, no challenge would be too extreme. The young man was asked to retrieve the chief's scalp which a violent tribe held from a raid years prior. *Many men have tried to do so, none have returned.* Enthusiastic about this challenge and the opportunity to win the maiden's hand in marriage, the warrior set off through the forest. That night the warrior traveled many miles to the village of the violent thieves. At last, in the distance, he saw the old chief's scalp tethered to the top of a high pole. The warrior silently climbed a pine tree making certain he was out of the fire's glow. He perused the entire village from his look out. The members of the tribe built an enormous fire for their festival. They feasted and danced late into the night. The warrior remained hidden in the pine tree. Although he was exhausted from hunting, pursuing the maiden, and traveling, the warrior forced himself to stay awake. If his eye lids started to close, he focused on thoughts of the maiden, recalling her locks of dark hair, her glowing complexion, and the sweet scent of her as she ran through the woods. This kept his thoughts clear and he avoided nodding off to sleep. The tribe finally retired and all was still. He lowered himself down the tree and crept into camp. This time he was extra careful to avoid making a noise with his moccasins. Stealthful and quiet, he climbed the pole and untied the father's scalp. The warrior tucked it into his leather pouch, slid down the pole, and ran as fast as a puma to the maiden's father. The chief heard panting outside. He bravely stepped out and was surprised to see the warrior holding his scalp. *My son, come inside and drink water. My appreciation is deeper than the hawk is of his keen eyesight. It is grander than the appreciation the turtle has of his protective shell and the eagle of his sharp talons. You have risked your life for the hand of my daughter. There is no love stronger than that of risking one's life for another. At dawn we will prepare the wedding feast. Now eat and sleep for in two days you will be wed.* The maiden's mother served the warrior a generous portion of venison broth with root vegetables. Then she prepared a warm bed of furs near the fire for the exhausted man."

Chief Cheveyo rose silently, leaving us mesmerized by his superb storytelling. I sat and stared into the campfire, contemplating the power of love, and admiring Hudson for risking his life for me. Madison caught my melancholy mood.

She jibed, "Anna Lisa lost in thought. What a ridiculous romantic you are. Do you think the buff cowboy would do something as daring for your hand in marriage?" I ignored her and she skirted off.

As I lifted my eyes from the flames they fell on the face of the intriguing Dolores Matafantasmas. Her white skin barely masked the bony features of her face. She had a distinguished nose that formed into a point. Her lips were a mix of deep burgundy and crimson. She stood gracefully as she conversed with Hudson and Skeebo.

They walked toward me. Skeebo said, "Hang around, Anna Lisa after the guests leave. We need to talk." The guests departed and Skeebo said, "Anna Lisa, this here is Dolores Matafantasmas. She's a, how might yuh say…"

I said, "Skeebo, I know. Dolores' name says it all."

Dolores looked at me and a pursed smile came across her gaunt face, "You speak Spanish."

"I'm fond of romance languages," I said.

Skeebo asked Hudson, "Why's Anna Lisa talkin' about *romantic language?*"

Hudson said, "Skeebo it ain't *romantic* language it's *romance* language."

"Romance, romantic. Whatever. I ain't followin'."

Hudson whispered, "Shut up, Skeebo. Let the ladies talk. Annie's smart. She knows Dolores is a ghost killer."

Skeebo looked confused, "Huh? How'd she know?"

Dolores said, "We're set. Please allow me to inspect the location first. It would be wise for you to join us in half an hour."

Hudson said, "I'll escort Annie down."

They left for the wrangler's bunk house. Hudson and I waited in front of the smoldering embers. It was a chilly night. He saw me shiver, took off his coat, and draped it around my shoulders. He pulled me against his chest, "Are yuh scared, Annie?"

"Not if Ms. Matafantasmas knows what she's doing. How'd you find her?"

"Skeebo's been lookin' fer one fer a couple of years. He went to a palm reader in the city. That gypsy knows Dolores and gave Skeebo her number. The palm reader said since Skeebo got that wallop on his noggin he's been sensitive to the spiritual world."

After a half hour, Hudson and I headed to the bunk house. The forest wasn't ominous with Hudson holding my hand. We entered and Dolores said, "Annie, sit on this quilt. I understand it's where Hudson sleeps."

I sat down and a violet blue wind circled me. It spun faster, and faster, whipping my hair, and pulling my skin. I couldn't make out the faces of the wranglers around me. It was blinding. It was so strong I couldn't scream. Hudson placed his hand on my shoulder. He saw my fear and demanded, "Put a stop to it, Dolores."

Dolores chanted. The violet blue wind subsided and Hudson pulled me from his bunk. He enfolded me protectively in his arms and said, "Yuh gotta teach us that chant. How'd it go?"

Dolores Matafantasmas said, "I don't know. Each spirit draws out a different command. I don't remember the words."

Skeebo said, "What do yuh think we're dealin' with? Is it gone?"

Dolores spoke in her melancholy voice, "It's unfortunately not gone. It has returned to its burial place. This is an angry spirit. Violet and blue are cold colors. Unlike spirits of yellow and gold, which are happy visitors. Cold colored spirits are mean and vicious. We know it's female. She's determined. She rests in the ground under Hudson's bunk and wants something Hudson possesses or has power over. Hudson, do you have belongings, perhaps, an heirloom from years past? Something you have control over?"

"Got my pa's Blue Lightnin'," Hudson offered.

Dolores looked confused, "Come again?"

I said, "It's a pistol."

"No, that wouldn't be it. Spirits cannot shoot. They can kill, but not by the hand of a gun."

A shiver ran down my spine. Hudson noticed and tightened his hold on me. He asked, "When Annie's here it comes out madder than a peeled rattler. Why's that?"

Dash added, "And the noise is worse than the time my old sow got her teat caught in the gate."

Dolores quietly said, "Skeebo was right to research Native American culture. This bunk house is on a hill overlooking a meadow. Most of the tribes in North America had burial grounds on this type of geographical layout. I believe the spirit is that of a Native American woman. Unfortunately, until we find out what she wants, we'll have no solution."

Hudson was upset, "Yuh meanin' to say if I ain't able to figure out what I should give this thing, Annie's got as much chance as a rabbit in a hound's mouth?"

Dolores solemnly said, "I am afraid so, Hudson. Keep Annie as safe as you can."

CHAPTER THIRTY ONE

BITE THE DIRT

At the end of the week Dolores Matafantasmas departed. Under Hudson's command I was to stay away from the bunk house and meadow.

On the days and nights we went riding, Hudson brought Mariah to me, groomed, and saddled. I was yearning to groom her and wouldn't mind if she stole carrots from my back pocket.

There was an after-lunch trail ride for guests and I decided to join them. Hudson didn't like the idea because it meant lining up in the meadow. I explained to Hudson nothing happened since Dolores left so perhaps the chant was effective.

"Annie, I ain't takin' no risks with yuh. I don't want yuh comin'. I promise I'll take yuh on a long ride tomorrow."

"Please, Hudson. I miss grooming Mariah. The guests will be there. If the spirit isn't gone yet, she probably won't come out. She's never revealed herself in front of guests. Please," I begged.

"All right. Make a loop around the dice house and when yuh mount if somethin' ain't feelin' right, grab the night latch."

I looked at him with confusion, "This is a day ride, isn't it? What in the world is that night thingy for?"

"That *night thingy* is what might save yore life," Hudson replied. "See the heavy strap near the nubbin, stick yore hand through it and yuh'll stay on. It ain't called a *night thingy*. Annie, it's called *night latch*. The cowboy who takes night watch on a cattle run might come upon somethin' as unexpected as a rattler in a bed roll, and his hoss'll spook. If he ain't got a night latch he'll bite the dust and break a bone. His hinges, bolts, and nuts will all get loosened."

I brought Mariah extra carrots and an apple. She enjoyed my grooming and closed her eyes as I brushed her. We saddled the horses. Hudson matched the guests with the appropriate horse. He took the lead followed by Bev, six guests, and me. Dash brought up the rear.

It was a beautiful afternoon. White clouds dotted the blue sky. We went down the twisting trail to the dirt road. I was stress-free and decided to dangle my boots out of the stirrups. As I relaxed in my seat, Mariah collected further, dropping her head low.

Where the brook crossed under the road, a violet blue wind kicked up water. Mariah crow hopped, lifting all four hooves off the ground. It was unexpected and I was unprepared. There wasn't time to grab the night latch. I fell off and hit the ground hard. The air was knocked out of my lungs and I was in pain. Dash called, "Rider down."

Hudson said, "Which hoss?"

Dash replied, "Mariah. Anna Lisa bit the dirt."

Hudson told Bev to hold the line and turned Phantom charging toward me. He knelt beside me and ordered Dash to go for Hoyle.

"Where're yuh hurt, Annie?" Hudson asked. I hadn't caught my breath yet so I couldn't answer. "Hold on, Annie. Dash's gettin' Hoyle."

A few horses ahead of me, a guest said, "I'm a doctor. May I help?"

Hudson replied forcefully, "What in name's sake yuh doin' lollygaggin' on yure pony. Get down here and help Annie."

The doctor asked me to squeeze his fingers. He told Hudson to take off my boots slowly and carefully without pulling on me. The doctor tickled my feet and asked if I could feel his fingers. I nodded. He let out a sigh of relief.

Hoyle arrived and also crouched over me. The doctor continued his exam. He looked in my eyes. Hoyle was prepared, he handed the doctor his flashlight.

"Trace my finger. Good. It looks like she'll be fine. She'll be sore. The best thing for her is a long soak in a hot bath."

"I don't have a bathtub," I said.

"Not a problem, Annie. We got one," Hudson said tenderly.

Hoyle said, "Hudson that thing ain't been cleaned in twenty years. Yuh can't put her in there. She'll grow fungus and a whole cavity of crawlin' homesteaders."

"Don't listen to him, Annie. I'll get it clean and bright like a new mirror." He turned to Hoyle, "Hoyle yuh think what the doc says holds water? After Yale's pa, I'm losin' faith in the Hippocratic Oath."

Hoyle said, "This one's as straight as a wagon tongue."

Hudson gently lifted my upper body, "Rider up." He lifted me to my feet. "Get on yore hoss, Miss Annie and don't try to reach the clouds again."

The doctor said, "She isn't going to ride."

Hudson said, "Yuh bet she is. Get on, Annie."

The doctor fumed and said, "What are you crazies doing?"

Dash said, "Docs are full of insults, ain't they?"

Hudson said, "Doc she's getting' on her hoss like she's got to. We're mighty crazy, but we take care of our own real good."

I mounted Mariah and for a moment I thought perhaps the doctor was right because I was dizzy. Hudson mounted behind me. He held me with one arm and turned Mariah back toward the ranch. Phantom trailed behind. We took the long route to avoid the meadow and wranglers' bunk house.

Hudson said, "I'm mighty proud of yuh gettin' back on yore hoss. Why ain't city folk understandin' if yuh don't get back in the saddle yuh'll grow a fear that'll make the hair of a buffalo robe stand up?"

I wanted to laugh at this analogy, but couldn't. I said meekly, "Hudson, I'm too sore to talk. Let's listen to Mariah's breathing."

"Anything yuh want, My Love."

~ ~ ~

Hudson helped me dismount at my bunk house, "Gotta get that wash tub scrubbed. Sit yoreself down. I'll be back real soon." He headed to the kitchen to get bleach.

An hour later, Hudson came for me and we rode double. "I got yore hot soak ready."

The bathtub was sparkling clean. A dozen votive candles from the dining hall flickered around the tub. The aroma of lavender filled the bathroom.

"Hudson, you remembered. Where did you find lavender bubble bath?"

"I made it. Sam says his Herbes de Provence got lavender. We mixed them with dish soap. I'll leave yuh to it, Annie. Better jump in before the heat escapes," Hudson said as he closed the door gently.

I got undressed and slipped into the aromatic bubbles. The doctor was right, a hot bath felt great on my muscles. I relaxed watching the candlelight dance across the simple bathroom. Hudson had stacked two towels on a rough wooden stool near the bathtub. They were the fluffy white Turkish towels reserved for guests. They appeared inviting after months of crusty ones. A hook on the back of the wooden door held a lush white terry guest robe with *Trotter Blue Dude Ranch* embroidered in sapphire.

I closed my eyes and sank under the water. I surfaced. The candles were out. The violet blue spirit whipped around the small bathroom. She forced my head under the water. I struggled to surface gasping for air before she submerged me again. I sloshed my arms and legs around trying to escape.

I heard Hudson call, 'Annie, yuh O.K?" He hollered, "Lacey, Candy get in there and pull her out." They tugged on my arms and pulled me out dropping me on the floor. The violet blue spirit left through the glass window pane.

Hudson called, "Is Annie breathin'? Cover her with the robe. I'm comin' in." Hudson held a finger under my nostrils, "It's mighty slight, but there's air." He lifted me from the floor, carried me to his bunk, and placed me gently on his pillow. Tears ran from my closed eyes. I turned my face away from them so they wouldn't see me cry.

Hudson saw me heave, "I'm glad yure breathin', Annie. I'm so dumb I couldn't track a fat squaw in a snow drift. What was I thinkin' bringin' yuh down here? Why yuh cryin' Sweetie? Yure safe now."

"I'm sad. I hate this spirit. You plan wonderful things for me, a campfire, shaping my hat, a bubble bath by candle light, and in the end, they suck."

Hudson didn't comment. I was right and he knew it. Then he said, "Let's get yuh back before that pleasure buster acts up. I'm tryin' my hardest to think of what it wants."

I replied, "I know you are."

Hudson helped me onto Mariah. He climbed on behind and held me tightly with one hand. In the other, he held a wad of my dirty clothes.

We arrived at the girls' bunk house as Madison, Caprice, and Shelly headed toward it. Hudson helped me dismount. He kissed my forehead and wished me sweet dreams.

Inside the girls cornered me, and Madison scolded, "Anna Lisa, you've out done yourself. Riding with Hudson wearing nothing but a bath robe? What do you think you're doing? Testing to see how far you need to go before Trotter Blue throws you out? Next you'll be Lady Godiva riding naked through the woods."

Shelly added, "That will make her cowboy kiss her."

Fortunately, the doctor knocked and poked his head in. "Excuse me ladies, I need to check on Annie." He turned to me, "How'd that hot soak feel? Did it help your aching muscles? You took quite a spill. Let me check your dilation one more time." He took out a little flashlight and shined it in my eyes. "Good," he said. "Sleep well. Don't be surprised if tomorrow you feel like taking another hot bath."

There was no way that would happen, at least not until Hudson figured out what that violet blue demon wanted.

CHAPTER THIRTY TWO

CAMPIN' TONIGHT

The next day, Hudson and I went for a leisurely ride. He wanted to make sure I didn't develop a fear of horses. He held me in his arms and said, "Yure campin' tonight."

"I'd love to Hudson, but tomorrow's Tuesday. It's not my day off."

"Can't yuh trade with no one?" he asked.

I said softly. "I've been strict with the waitresses regarding shift switching practices."

He looked disappointed, "Annie, a boss gotta to be fair, firm, and friendly. Otherwise, yuh get caught in yure own loop."

Hudson was right again. I had so much to learn from him.

At the evening shift, I asked Shelly to trade with me. "Anna Lisa, you've got to be kidding. Did you forget I needed to trade with you so I could hang out with Scotty? No way. You burned your bridges with me."

Trotter Blue's office door flung open and he called, "Spirit Eyes, get yure tail in here lickety split. Team Captain, yuh've had all summer to train them gals. Yuh gotta delegate if yuh plan to be successful. They'll work mighty fine with yuh gone."

That didn't sound like job security.

"Anna Lisa, I got a lead ranch hand that's as good as yuh can find. That boy's worried about yuh stayin' here unattended. He wants yuh safe while he's gone. Only way to do this is to take yuh along. Yuh won't be slackin' off. The wranglers will put yore behind to work. Yuh'll pass around the reloading outfit. Don't forget the spoons. Yure servin' whistle berries and rodeo steaks. In the mornin' yuh'll rise early and brew the belly wash. Yuh'll do yore share, fair and square."

"Really?"

Insulted, he raised his brow and tone, "Yuh questionin' my word?"

"I'm sorry, sir. I can't wait to camp out. Thank you, sir," I could've hugged him but I held my composure. Trotter Blue smiled.

I stepped cheerfully out of his office and said, "Shelly, you're in charge tonight and tomorrow morning. Take care of things." She gaped. I marched past her out the dining hall into the fresh evening air.

Hudson was waiting off of the veranda. He was sitting on Phantom holding Mariah's lead rope. She was saddled with a rolled sleeping bag in tie strings. Hudson must have noticed my eyes travel to it. "Got yure velvet couch right here. We're gonna have a rip-roaring time, Annie. Rider up," he smiled.

"How'd you know I'd come with you?" I asked.

"Annie, a cowboy's gotta know his worth and put it to work. I ain't askin' Trotter Blue or nobody fer nothin'. When I need somethin', they take me seriously."

"You need me at camp tonight?" I asked as I mounted Mariah.

He laughed, "Yuh bet I do. Yure workin'." He hollered, "Yeeha," and we were off.

I asked, "Hudson, what's a *Reloading Outfit* and *Whistle Berries*? I assume *Rodeo Steaks* are Rib Eye or New York steaks."

"Annie, sometimes I think yuh live in a cave. Yuh ain't heard of Rodeo Steaks? Really?"

"You're not questioning my word are you?" I laughed at my cocky reply.

Smiling, he told me you can't eat fancy steaks at the rodeo. They're hot dogs. Whistle Berries are beans and the Reloading Outfit is a compilation of utensils, plates, and napkins. It was getting easier to follow the grammar and dialect of Hudson, but Trotter Blue still challenged me.

We cantered to catch up with the others. Dash and Candy drove the truck with coolers of food and drinks. We rode along the river. The mountains began to glow in orange and gold as the sun lowered in the western sky. I looked back at Hudson. His skin was aglow in the dusk. His blue eyes shone like lapis gems. They were satisfied eyes. I was content.

At the campsite we unloaded the truck. If I grabbed something heavy, like a cooler, Hudson moved in and took it from me. He was a gentleman. I was left lifting biscuit baskets, knives, forks, and spoons. Hudson and Dash stacked wood in a stone ring. Hudson handed matches to me. I struck one and lit the fire.

Wranglers arrived shortly after with guests riding among them. The guests dismounted and sat on logs encircling the campfire. The wranglers unsaddled the horses and led them to a wooden corral where they munched on their evening meal of Bermuda and Alfalfa.

Hoyle said the dinner prayer, inviting guests to bow their heads. After *Amen,* we plated the food and served the guests informally. They ate and chatted among themselves. We offered adults additional drinks. Some were getting loopy on beer and whiskey. High altitude and alcohol was a risky combination. Since no one was driving, the wranglers kept the guests' Red Solo cups filled.

A lady with coiffed hair stopped me while I was passing a bottle of whiskey. "Where'd you get that Juicy Couture tee shirt?" she said pointing at the logo on my chest.

"This thing?" I asked.

"Yes, that *thing.* You wouldn't know, but it's an exclusive brand. It's expensive. Did you get lucky at a thrift store, or did a guest accidentally leave it, and you snagged it?"

"No ma'am," I laughed. "I bought it on Rodeo Drive."

In disbelief, the lady let out, "Hah." She saw I didn't change my demeanor and asked cautiously, "Where're you from?"

"Bel Air," I answered.

"What on earth are you doing here? Did you run away from home? Do your parents know where you are?"

I nodded.

The polished lady continued, "You should be spending your summer at the country club, dining poolside, and pampering yourself in the spa. How can you tolerate working like this?"

"I chose to come here. I love it," I said.

"But you're a privileged child," the lady retorted.

"There's no privilege like the beauty of these mountains, ma'am. Fresh air filled with the scent of pine beats aroma therapy out of a spa bottle. Think of the beautiful river, the Columbines, the meadow grasses. Listen to the raptors squawk on their hunt. Look at the sky tonight. You've never seen so many stars. They're more fascinating than city lights. Have you stopped to hear the aspens rustling in the breeze? It's the softest sound - like angels whispering." I said melancholically, "Angels whispering among snorts and whinnies of horses." In a serious tone I added, "I have food in my tummy and a roof over my head. What more could I want?"

Pointing at the wranglers who were sitting on logs, eating dinner, she said, "How can you stand working with lowbrow, motley, dirty red necks like them?"

"I beg your pardon?" I said forcefully. "For your information, these are the most honorable people you'll meet. They're honest, hardworking, kind, and the guys are respectful of women. They'd give the shirts off their backs if you needed it, even a Juicy Couture. They love our country and they're God fearing. As for dirt, they clean up well."

I noticed the wranglers had stopped eating and were staring at me. I looked for Hudson. I found his face in the group. He was smiling. I caught his eyes. He winked. I took a breath, held my head up high, and turned to join the wranglers.

As I passed the lady, her husband grabbed my butt, pinching it swiftly. I swung around and kicked him in the shin. He stood up and lunged for me. In his drunken stupor he missed and fell. I ran toward the wranglers. The husband picked up an empty beer bottle and flung it hitting my head. I fell to the ground.

In my delirium I saw Hudson jump over me and run toward the drunken husband. There was commotion. I heard the drunk slur, "Briiiiingggg it on youuu big tough guyyyy. Thattt hotty was a ggood hhhhandful."

Lacey yelled, "Hold Hudson." I looked up even though my head throbbed. Hudson's fist was clenched and it took Dash, Skeebo, and Hoyle to hold him.

Skeebo said, "Whoa, Hudson. Easy now. Annie needs yuh." Hudson looked over and saw me toddling on my knees. He ran to me and eased me to the ground.

Candy instructed Dash and Skeebo to take the drunkard back to the ranch. She told Hoyle to tend to me. Hoyle grabbed ice from the cooler. He plunged it into a plastic bag and told Hudson to hold it to the egg forming on my head. Hoyle tested my ability to follow his finger circling in front of my eyes. He told Hudson, "Annie'll be o.k. Make sure she doesn't puke and don't let her sleep fer an hour."

Hudson looked up at the sky. I followed his gaze. There was nothing to see except emerging stars. "Was that a prayer?" I whispered.

"Yeah," Hudson sat on the ground near one of the logs. He held me close. I closed my eyes to rest. "Annie, don't sleep. Annie?" I opened my eyes. "Don't sleep. Promise me." I leaned against his chest. He held the ice pack steady. The sting of the cold was tolerable. I drifted to sleep.

The sun was rising through the trees casting long shadows and I woke up confused. A soft leather saddle bag was under my head. My sleeping bag was draped over me. Under me was another bag. This one smelled of Hudson and horse. Candy was awake nearby.

"Candy, what happened?" I asked in a panic.

"That plumped up lady sippin' on belly wash gave yuh a go around. Her drunken husband grabbed yore derrière. Yuh managed to spin around and whack the feller with the toe of yore boot. He started hollerin'. Then, he chucked his beer at yuh and it hit square on yore noggin. Hudson was on him faster than a roadrunner on a rattler. Our guys pulled Hudson back and took the guest..."

"Candy, I remember that. My head still hurts. Why am I on Hudson's sleeping bag?"

"Oh, that," Candy said.

"What *that?* Tell me now," I barked.

"Easy Annie. Nothin' happened. It was hard to stuff yuh into a bag. So we put one under yuh and one over yuh."

"If I'm on Hudson's bag, where'd he sleep?" I demanded.

Candy calmingly said, "He didn't sleep. Yuh see that tree by yure head? He sat against it all night doin' night watch. Each time yuh moaned, he'd wipe yure tears and shush yuh softly. I learned somethin' about Hudson. He's a tender Range Man."

Hudson walked over with two cups of coffee, "Mornin', Beautiful."

I smiled.

He gave a cup to me and handed a cup to Candy, "Thanks fer taken' over the mornin' watch. How'd she do?"

Candy replied, "As good as yuh can expect with the blow she took."

Hudson rubbed his red eyes. Candy was right. He hadn't slept. I shouldn't have doubted him. These guys weren't like fraternity brothers who slip something in a girl's drink to take advantage of her.

We packed up camp and rode back. Hudson insisted I ride with him on Phantom. We trailed Mariah. The morning was beautiful and I was content I had participated in a camp out, even though it was brutal.

CHAPTER THIRTY THREE

OLD FAITHFUL

The weeks passed quickly. August afternoons were warm, sometimes hot. Guests left and new ones arrived. We served meals, swam, and I rode with Hudson. He kept me away from the wranglers' bunk house and meadow.

I dreaded the passing of summer. The employees had a strange mix of melancholy and anticipation about heading home. For me, there was no sense of anticipation. I wished summer would last year round and Hudson and I could spend countless hours together.

My thoughts were interrupted once the last van of giggling guests arrived. Most of them were cheerful. There was an exception. A father and son stood out. They had sullen faces, low energy, and morbid attitudes.

Hammond Thing and his son Malpance barely greeted us as we introduced ourselves and directed them to their guest quarters. I assumed they had an argument that soured their mood.

The day passed too quickly for me. The waitresses and I decided to attend the last guest campfire. It was a triple whammy: Pip leading camp songs, S'mores, and storytelling by Chief Cheyevo.

The chief sat before the fire. He began, "Today I am going to tell you a tragic story of Purple Swan and how she became ostracized by her people.

"Purple Swan was the loveliest maiden in her tribe. She was born to a great leader who was a proud and just man. He was renowned throughout the land as a fair and fearless leader. His daughter, Purple Swan was wed to a young warrior from a friendly, neighboring tribe. The young warrior adored Purple Swan. She bore him a son and the couple couldn't have been happier. Purple Swan was well aware of her beauty for it was spoken of throughout her youth. One day a handsome man, with rich dark skin and flowing long hair came to Purple Swan's village. His name was Bear and he was in search of a wife. His eyes fell upon Purple Swan. She felt his gaze and turned to see him. She was in awe of his beauty and he of hers. Purple Swan's husband and son were away on a hunt so Bear and Purple Swan began to talk. They became more attracted to each other as the long afternoon passed. At nightfall, Purple Swan told Bear to head out for her husband and son would be home soon. She told him of the cave up the hill behind the village. She assured him he would be comfortable there. Bear decided to sleep in the cave nearby so in the morning he might catch another glimpse of her beauty. In the morning the warrior and son left to hunt once more. Bear watched them leave and descended to see Purple Swan. He decided this was the woman he wanted. They plotted to run away together. Purple Swan packed roots, herbs, and dried venison in a leather pouch. They agreed to meet at the cave to avoid suspicion from tribe members. Bear headed out first and waited for the beautiful woman. Purple Swan joined him later and they were off. The warrior and his son returned. Villagers told them of the handsome visitor. The two had not been seen all afternoon. The warrior and son chose to track them and bring Purple Swan home. For days Bear lead Purple Swan through the forest. Purple Swan arrived at Bear's home and settled in quickly. She prepared a warm, delicious meal that was satisfying after their long travels. They relaxed in front of the fire. The warrior was an exceptional tracker. Suddenly, he and the son burst into the home. The minute the warrior saw his lovely wife in the arms of Bear he became enraged and lost control. The warrior and son attacked the couple and killed them. They took the dead body of Purple Swan back to the village and buried her without proper honor which would usually be bestowed on the daughter of a great chief and the wife of a stately warrior."

Chief Cheyevo rose and departed for his guest quarters. He stayed the night since the last campfire of the season ended late.

Awake in my bed, thoughts of Purple Swan, relationships, and trust crossed my mind. I waited for Hudson to arrive at my window. It was late. I looked at the crest of the hill. There wasn't a sign of him. Out of the corner of my eye, I saw him walking toward me from the main building. His gait wasn't as energetic and splendid as it usually was. His head hung low and he walked slowly. I thought he had end of summer blues.

"Hello, Annie. Sleep well," he said kissing my forehead and turning to leave.

"Hudson, wait. I haven't asked how your day was."

"Don't," he said.

I gently said, "I won't. I can see it was bad. You were crying."

I kissed my pinky and touched the outside corners of his eyes, "Your tears smudged the grime on your face." I reached to hug him and was glad he didn't resist. He buried his grimy face in my neck and heaved a deep breath. It was the type of heave a guy takes in order to avoid crying in front of a girl. I softly said, "Hudson, talking isn't only for adventures. It's also for helping someone carry a heavy load."

He slowly said, "Today was bad. Yuh know that rotten kid, Malpance?" I nodded. "All guests obey my rules. I say yuh gotta cross the highway at a walk, no matter if there's a truck barrelin' down the road, stay calm, and walk. The trucks see us and stop because it's a straight away. I tell guests a paved road is like an ice arena fer shod hosses and they can't ice skate. That Malpance Thing fiend ain't obeyin' nothin'. Before we crossed, I rode over to him and made it clear that he ain't crossin' unless he listens up. Know what he does, Annie? He kicks Old Faithful and sets her to gallopin'. Sure enough, she goes down."

"Did Malpance get hurt?" I asked in shock.

Hudson replied, "I wish he had. It was Old Faithful. She busted a leg. There's no hope fer a hoss with a broken leg. Poor thing tried to hobble with no luck. Leg snapped right in two. Old Faithful looked at me with them beautiful eyes." Hudson tried to stifle his tears, "I had to put her down. Took my six shooter and shot her in the head." Hudson's tears flowed.

I grabbed his shoulders and pulled him to me. We cried together.

There was nothing I could say and nothing he needed to hear. I held him, quiet, and still. He said painstakingly, "We brought her to the meadow to pay our respects. Animal Control's comin' fer her carcass tomorrow. Sleep, Annie."

"You too. I'll light a blessing candle for the Lord to receive Old Faithful gently home."

Hudson looked at me, "She'd like that. I'll tell the wranglers."

~ ~ ~

The next morning I didn't see Hammond or Malpance. I wouldn't have been surprised if Trotter Blue sent them home. Chief Cheyevo sat at my table. This was good for two reasons. One, it got my mind off Old Faithful. Two, I had questions regarding his story the night before. "Good morning, Chief," I said.

"Good morning. Is it Anna Lisa?" he asked.

I nodded, "How'd you know my name?"

"Skeebo talks with me and your name comes up now and again."

I said, "May I ask a question regarding the story you told about Purple Swan?"

Chief Cheyevo nodded.

"Last night you mentioned Purple Swan wasn't buried with the honor due a chief's daughter and warrior's wife. Why did the warrior bother bringing her body back to the tribe?"

The chief said, "That's a good question. There are a couple of elements to consider. The warrior presented the body. This upheld his honor. In other words, he did not give up on finding his wife. He showed the virtue of persistence.

"He told the elders a recounting of events. Her behavior wasn't worthy of a proper burial. Purple Swan was an Ute. According to Ute tradition, honorable burials require individuals be buried with one or more horses. The quantity depends on their status. Since Purple Swan wasn't buried with a horse, her spirit had no way of traveling to the world of the Great Spirit. Her spirit remains trapped on Earth."

I froze.

"Anna Lisa, are you o.k? Does this make sense? Anna Lisa?" the Chief asked.

I slowly replied, "Yes. I'm sorry. I have to leave. There's something I've got to do. Please, excuse me." I turned to Madison, "See to Chief Cheyevo and divvy up my tables."

I ran out of the dining hall. My feet couldn't travel fast enough. I had to get to Old Faithful before Animal Control did. I charged into the wrangler's bunk house.

Dash said, "Gee, Anna Lisa, yuh ain't got no way of makin' graceful entrances."

"Dash where's Hudson? It's important. Tell me," I said panting.

"Whoa. Easy girl. Boss is in the meadow next to Old Faithful."

I ran to Hudson. He'd cut off the tail and wrapped the top with leather lacing. He was braiding Old Faithful's mane.

"Ahem," I coughed. Hudson didn't look at me. I put my hands on his shoulders, "Hudson, I hate to interrupt."

"Then don't," he said.

I sternly said, "I wouldn't if it wasn't important."

He said, "Annie, don't bother yoreself with wrangler stuff."

"This isn't wrangler stuff. It's our stuff. You have to listen to me," I said.

"Not now," Hudson replied.

"Yes now," I barked.

"Seriously, Woman. Stop yore caterwauling. This ain't no time fer jawing," Hudson snapped.

I retorted, "Call off Animal Control."

Hudson bit back, "If they ain't comin' today, things'll get nasty. Turkey buzzards'll rip the body apart. Flies'll eat whatever they want, and ants'll go up her nostrils eatin' her brain. Yuh want that?"

"Yes. I do," I screamed.

"Yure off yore rocker, Woman." He shook his head, "Yuh ain't got a clue what yure sayin'."

"Listen to me," I demanded. "Bury Old Faithful here."

"Annie, yure plumb crazy," he said exacerbated.

"She wants a horse from you."

He finally looked up, "Who wants a hoss? This one's dead."

I said, "Hudson, it came together this morning. Utes need a horse."

"Annie, yuh ain't makin' no sense," Hudson said brusquely.

"I talked with Chief Cheyevo. He's been telling tales of an Ute maiden, Purple Swan, who was dishonorably buried because of the way she cheated on her husband.

"Anyway, it is a long story. According to Ute legend, Ute's must be buried with a horse in order to travel to the world of the Great Spirit. If not, they're trapped on Earth. Don't you see? The violet blue spirit is Purple Swan. Ms. Matafantasmas said this is the perfect setting for a burial ground. This is what she wants from you. You control the horses."

Hudson said, "Tell me then, why she's mad at yuh? Annie, this better not be yore big Hollywood imagination speakin'."

"She hates me because the Cheyenne and Utes were rivals. Remember what Skeebo said about my name? Please, please, bury Old Faithful with Purple Swan under the bunk house. She'll travel to the spirit world and be free from her entrapment. We'll be free too."

Hudson sat still. He eventually spoke and asked, "Did yuh run it past Skeebo?"

"I don't need to. Chief Cheyevo made it clear. Don't you trust me?" I piped.

"Of course I do. Yuh're smart. I gotta set the wranglers to work. We gotta dig a big hole by the wall where I sleep. Yuh done good, Annie." We walked in silence to the bunk house.

The wranglers listened in earnest as I told the story of Purple Swan and her burial.

Skeebo said, "Anna Lisa, we've questioned why Hudson did some heavy courtin' over yuh. Turns out he saw yore true grit. Yuh uncovered a mystery Trotter Blue and I scratched our heads over fer years."

Hudson and I left the wranglers, bridled Phantom, and rode to tell Trotter Blue about my theory.

Trotter Blue said, "Makes sense. Leave it to lovely Anna Lisa to untangle this rat's nest. I've been plumb stumped fer two years. Hudson, yuh got a gal as cunning as a she-wolf with pups. Yuh know a filly like this is worth her weight in gold. That's enough verbal lather from this old cowboy. Yawl got diggin' to do. It's gonna be a mighty big hole. I'll be down in time to give the mare our respects."

Hudson passed Old Faithful's laced tail to Trotter Blue. The old man held it in his weathered hands like he was holding a strand of pearls. He took it to a butcher hook in the corner of his office where two other tails hung. Then he waved his arms shooing us out while he said he would call Animal Control. I haven't a clue what Trotter Blue said to convince them not to pick up the horse carcass.

We took turns digging the grave. The violet blue wind kicked up and for the first time it wasn't sharp and attacking. We came across long bones and a severed skull revealing a blow from a tomahawk. It confirmed our theory.

By evening, the grave was deep. Before sunset, the wranglers hitched a couple of horses to Old Faithful and pulled her across the meadow. We pushed and heaved Old Faithful into her final resting spot.

Trotter Blue came down with a leather covered Bible. Thumb prints had worn the leather thin in places. The pages were yellowed and the ink faded. He said a few words, "Earth to earth, ashes to ashes, dust to dust. May the road rise up to meet you. May the wind be always at your back. May the sun shine warm upon your head; the rains fall soft upon your fields, and may God hold you in the palm of His hand."

He placed the first handful of dirt on the grave. The wranglers tossed handfuls too. I scattered columbines. After the symbols of finality were complete, we continued to bury the horse remains.

As the last shovel of dirt was mounded on the grave, a roaring violet blue light galloped across the sky. The wind gusted, "Ku'-vwa! Tog'oiak."

Skeebo said, "That means *thank you*." He called to the night's sky, "Ride serenely to the Great Spirit. May yuh and Old Faithful find God's peace."

Hudson added, "And let Sweet Annie be."

CHAPTER THIRTY FOUR

HERE IS MY PROMISE

Nothing could be done to slow time. Summer was coming to a close and Dad left Los Angeles heading for the ranch. Hudson and I sat in the aspen clearing where we went on our first ride. It seemed years ago since we shared that afternoon. I felt our waning time with all my senses. The lush green grass had dried turning into dry brittle shoots that scratched my skin. The columbines were gone from sight. The brook gurgled less spiritedly and the smell of warm summer air was gone.

"Dad will be here tomorrow," I said breaking the silence.

A pang of pain crossed his face. He said, "Yure drivin' back to yore reality and this ranch and me will be a passin' memory. In three days yuh'll be at yore estate. That's time enough to put things in perspective. Yuh'll text yore friends, meet up with the Ivy League dudes, go to debutant balls, and shop on Rodeo Drive.

His cowboy pronunciation interrupted the seriousness of his ranting, "Hudson it's pronounced Ro'day'o Drive."

"Yuh sure about that, because it's spelled *R-o-d-e-o*?"

I nodded.

"Sweet Annie, whether yure shoppin' Ro'day'o Drive or Rodeo Drive, yure gonna forget me. Yuh'll erase my simple life from yore memory.

"Yuh ain't gonna remember this redneck who stood on the back of a hoss, steamed yore hat, drew a lavender bubble bath, took yuh to a honky-tonk, visited yuh every evenin', kissed yore pretty, soft forehead, wished yuh sweet dreams, and most of all, bestowed his heart upon yuh."

I smiled, "We made memories, so how dare you say I'll forget you? Trust me, I won't. As soon as I drive out the driveway, I'll start daydreaming about the next time we meet." He started to say something and I raised my hand saying, "Don't talk. I won't listen to it. You're wrong. I don't want what we have to end tomorrow. I want it for evermore."

"It's a castle in the sky, Annie. There ain't no foundation."

"You're not serious," I pulled away.

"Annie," he put his arms around me and pulled me to his chest. "I ain't never felt like this. Yore goodbye's killin' me. I'll be lonely without yuh."

Resting in his arms, I asked, "Where are you going?"

Hudson said, "There's that P.B.R. I got my eyes set on."

"What about school?" I asked.

"I passed the high school exit exam early. I might go to college once I settle down. Right now, I'm pleased to be a cowboy. Maybe I'll head down to New Mexico or Coastal Texas to do some day cowboyin'. It's good money, $175.00 to $200.00 a day. I'll save up until I can afford a piece of land to build yore castle on."

I smiled. There was nothing more to say. We rode back to the guest ranch in silence.

At my bunk house, waitresses were exchanging phone numbers and e-mail addresses. I grabbed my notebook and wrote down the contacts:

Grace kindness@earthlink.com,

Caprice capricious@yahoo.com,

Madison brainy_one@aol.com,

Shelly sweetpompoms@hotmail.com.

Hudson stood in the doorway watching the hubbub of girl chatter, promises to call, write, and visit. I turned to him, "Do you have an e-mail address Hudson?"

"Sure do, Annie. It's htevermore@hotmail.com."

"Evermore. Is that your last name?"

He nodded.

I walked outside with him, "I fell for you and didn't know your last name. *Anna Lisa Lona Evermore* or *Annie Evermore* -sounds good doesn't it?"

He smiled, "Sounds better than the peep of a chick."

"What's T for?" I asked.

"That's fer Ty."

I said, "*Mrs. Hudson Ty Evermore*. What do you think?"

He laughed, "Annie, now that I got rid of that Radcliffe name, any way yuh use mine sounds good to me." He hugged me like he wanted to fuse me to him. Then he kissed my forehead and wished me sweet dreams.

~ ~ ~

I heard pebbles tap against my window. It was still dark. Pulling back the curtain I saw Hudson on Phantom, holding Mariah's lead rope.

"Morning, Annie."

I said in a hushed voice, "Hudson, what time is it?"

"Somewhere past midnight and before sunrise. Come on, Sweet Thing, we gotta make the most of each minute. Yuh packed?"

"Yes. I couldn't sleep so I organized my bag. Today's goodbye kept racing through my head. Wait for me."

"Always," he said.

I slipped on my one eyed jeans, snap button shirt, socks, and boots. Grabbing my hat, I ran into the bathroom, brushed my teeth, and braided my hair.

Outside, I said, "Hudson, this is a surprise."

"Ain't I told yuh, I got lots of them? Mount yure pony before the sun rises."

We rode down the dirt road. He turned taking the path to my meditation spot. We dismounted and climbed the boulder. He sat down and motioned for me to sit with him. He wrapped his arms around my torso.

It was quiet except for the sound of the breeze in the pine trees. The mountains changed into the coral-colored aspen glow. I looked into Hudson's face. His blue eyes sparkled in contrast to his warm tan glow. "You're gorgeous, Hudson."

He smiled and I melted into his arms.

The sun crested the mountain and he said, "Let's go, Annie."

We mounted the horses and trotted back to the dirt drive. Then we galloped to the main building.

"Grab us some fixin's. Here's my war bag," he said tossing a leather bag, while he held Mariah's reins.

I grabbed muffins, apples, grapes, yogurts, and two spoons. Sam had cooked sausages and bacon so I rolled some of each in tin foil. I grabbed carrots for the horses. Looking in the cabinets, I found a thermos. I rinsed it and filled it with coffee, or *belly wash*, as Hudson called it. I laughed to myself. I would miss his quirky words.

We tied the bag and thermos onto the saddles and headed past the wrangler's bunk house. Purple Swan was at peace and I didn't have to fear for my life. The meadow was aglow, not with violet blue, but with a warm golden hue.

Hudson looked over and said, "The ceasefire feels good, don't it?"

"It feels wonderful, but I wish *goodbye* wasn't looming over us."

He said, "Shhh, Annie. Enjoy what we got." Then Hudson yelled, "Yeeha," and we charged across the meadow, down the trail toward the dirt road. We rode hard to the swimming hole. The horses were sweaty and panting. We let them drink and graze. Hudson spread a woven Ute blanket on the grass. Unpacking our breakfast, he said, "Glad yuh brought piggies and belly wash."

I laughed.

"Why yuh laughin'?" Hudson asked.

"The way you talk," I said.

"There somethin' wrong with it?" he queried.

"No. I love it," I said.

He looked serious and said, "Know what I love?"

"What do you love besides pot roast and apple pie?" I joked.

"I love the way yuh sound sophisticated and…" he hesitated, looking into my eyes, "I love yuh, Annie."

I waited motionless for a kiss. I thought *I love you* was followed with a kiss. Instead of kissing me, he undid my braid and spread my hair around my shoulders. I was baffled.

We ate and rested in the morning sun, relaxed, and silent. Hudson stretched, "We better head back. I don't want yore pa shootin' me fer keepin' yuh. He's gotta be chompin' at the bit."

On the ride back it rained so we tucked under a pine to wait it out. He looked at me intensely and held me tight. The horses were antsy and stomped the dirt. As soon as the rain stopped, we mounted them. I said, "I'll race you."

Hudson smirked, "Yuh got a summer of ridin' in yore pocket and yuh think yuh can challenge me. Don't get callouses from pattin' yore own back, Darlin'. Yeeha."

We charged down the dirt road, up the trail, across the meadow, and over the hill. The horses galloped hard with hooves rumbling. We hollered and hooted.

Hudson yelled, "Yeow. Phantom's sweatin' like a hog butcher."

I was in the lead and hollered, "Wahoo. Hudson, get that paunchy cayuse up here." I almost plowed into Dad and Trotter Blue. Dad had a surprised, yet pleased look on his face. Trotter Blue was smiling from ear to ear.

Trotter Blue said, "There's yore daughter, Mansfield." Trotter continued, "Those two get along like two pups in a basket."

"Wow, you're here," I said dismounting. "Dad, you look so…put together."

He replied, "And you look so . . . grimy." He pulled me into a hug not worrying about me mucking up his Brioni suit. The hug was familiar and wonderful.

I called to Hudson, "This is Mansfield Clay. Father this is Hudson Ty Evermore."

Hudson swiftly dismounted and shook Dad's hand. "It's a pleasure to meet yuh sir. Yore daughter's become quite a cowgirl."

I stood still, then, slowly turned toward Hudson, *Cowgirl?* I admired Hudson's honorable character all summer. I tried to replicate it and practice the Ten Codes. *Cowgirl* didn't mean I could ride. It meant I fit into a set of praiseworthy qualities.

Dad said, "Cowgirl Annie, let's get your bags and get you home."

Hudson said, "I'll take care of that, sir."

The two of them walked toward the girls' bunk house.

Trotter Blue said, "Yuh comin' back next year, Spirit Eyes?"

I replied, "Yes, sir. Thank you."

He held out an envelope, "What's this, sir?"

He laughed, "That's yore moola." I forgot this awesome experience came with a paycheck.

Hudson placed the suitcase on the edge of the parking lot.

He turned to my dad and said, "Excuse me, sir. May I talk with yore daughter a minute? I got a gift fer her."

Dad nodded in agreement and walked to the veranda to join Trotter Blue at a rickety table.

Hudson led me to Phantom. He untied a leather pouch and walked me among the pines. From the pouch he pulled out a leather necklace with the carving of a horse.

"Hudson, this is what you were whittling, it's Mariah. She's beautiful."

He reached back in the pouch and pulled out another figure, "And this one?"

"That's Phantom. Look he's beefier," I said with delight.

Hudson slipped the second horse on the leather lacing, "They belong together. Turn around." He tied the leather lacing around my neck.

"Thank you," I said admiring the figures.

He watched me and leaned against a tree, "Annie, promise me yuh won't forget me."

I replied, "Here's my promise." I pressed my lips against his. He returned my kiss and his arms wrapped around me folding me in a warm, sensual embrace. His lips were chapped. They were warm. It was the best sensation.

As the kiss ended Hudson hollered at the top of his lungs, "Wahoo." He turned to me and said, "Annie, I've been waitin' fer that all summer." With his warm breathe on my ear he whispered, "Promise me again, Little' Darlin'."

I leaned against him placing my hands on each side of his face. We kissed. It was a long, passionate kiss. He ran his fingers through my hair. Then he placed one hand on my neck and one on the curve of my lower back. I felt each sensation. In his desire, he kissed my neck and I let my head lean to reveal my skin. His lips traversed to my ear, nibbling it. He found my mouth again. My lips were waiting and I opened my mouth to taste his breath.

Our passion was unleashed and we couldn't stop kissing. We would have continued had we not been interrupted by, "Ahem."

"Sorry, Mr. Clay. I'll see Annie to yore vehicle," Hudson said in his deep voice as he placed a hand on my suitcase and a hand in mine. "Which one's yore's, sir?"

Pointing to a sky blue convertible Mustang with white leather interior, Dad said, "That one."

"Dad, that's not your car," I said.

"You're right, Annie. It's not mine. It's yours."

I couldn't help squealing. What a day, first kiss, first car.

Hudson said, "Nice wild hoss, Annie. Did yuh read the license plate?"

10Codes I said, "Dad, how'd you know?"

"The day I met Trotter Blue I knew you'd learn a thing or two at the ranch. I heard from Dr. Radcliffe you fell for the cowboys. Trotter Blue assured me it was one, respectful cowboy. If you captured a cowboy's attention and he was true, you'd learn the way he thinks, feels, lives, and apparently loves," Dad winked.

"But how do you, a city-slicker, know about the Ten Codes?"

"That, Annie, is a long story, perfect for our ride home. It's time you learn about your great grandfather Hooper Clay, and his true love Lona."

Dad handed me the keys. Hudson opened my door. I moved in slowly, looking into Hudson's blue eyes whispering, "I'll see you next year. Dream of me."

Hudson whispered, "Yuh'll be the leadin' lady of all my dreams, Miss Annie Lona."

I turned the key, backed up, and headed down the dirt driveway. Hudson mounted Phantom and galloped down the drive passing us. He stopped and waited. He tipped his hat. I pulled up next to him, put the car in park, set the hand break, and clambered onto the top of the driver's door in my boots. I reached up and said, "I love you, Cowboy." We kissed. It didn't matter that I was balancing on the door or that my dad was sitting in the passenger seat. All I felt was the tenderness of his kiss and warm tears running down my cheeks.

Made in the USA
Lexington, KY
14 November 2019